Author Note

After the Norman Conquest of England in 1066 there was a period of rebellion that lasted until 1069. This resulted in William's retribution, known as the Harrying of the North. Men escaped across the borders into Scotland or Wales, returning to fight their oppressors and carry out raids. Additionally, many of the barons appointed by William saw the uncertain times as an opportunity to increase their own land and status.

Dispossessed Saxons who refused to submit to their oppressors took refuge in the forests of England. They became known as '*silvatici*' or 'wildmen'. Among the most well-known were Hereward the Wake and Eadric the Wild, both of whom eventually reached peace with their new rulers and were pardoned. It is these men and others like them who are my basis for Aelric.

This story takes place in Cheshire. Hamestan is the name given in the Domesday Book to the Hundred that covers the area where I now live. Readers wishing to investigate the locations that inspired me should search for Alderley Edge, Mow Cop, Lud's Church and The Roaches. Thanks go to my husband and children for accompanying me on frequent muddy walks.

As always, each of my books has a song. This time it was 'It's All Coming Back to Me Now'. The best version, in my opinion, is by Pandora's Box.

THE SAXON OUTLAW'S REVENGE

Elisabeth Hobbes

Published in Great Britain 2016
by Mills & Boon, an imprint of HarperCollins*Publishers*
1 London Bridge Street, London, SE1 9GF

ISBN: 978-0-263-91741-3

Our policy is to use papers that are natural, renewable and recyclable products and made from wood grown in sustainable forests. The logging and manufacturing processes conform to the legal environmental regulations of the country of origin.

Printed and bound in Spain
by CPI, Barcelona

Elisabeth Hobbes grew up in York, where she spent most of her teenage years wandering around the city looking for a handsome Roman or Viking to sweep her off her feet. Elisabeth's hobbies include skiing, Arabic dance and fencing—none of which has made it into a story yet. When she isn't writing she spends her time reading, and is a pro at cooking while holding a book! Elisabeth lives in Cheshire with her husband, two children and three cats with ridiculous names.

Books by Elisabeth Hobbes

Mills & Boon Historical Romance

Falling for Her Captor
A Wager for the Widow
The Blacksmith's Wife
The Saxon Outlaw's Revenge

Visit the Author Profile page at millsandboon.co.uk.

To Laura and Tim,
for endless speculation about what was in the box

Chapter One

Cheshire—1068

They hanged the rebels in the market square. Rain hung in the air. Heavy drizzle that characterised this part of England: thicker than mist and turning the world grey and damp.

A cheerless day for a brutal act.

Constance Arnaud wished she could leave this cold, unwelcoming country and return to Normandy where the sun was visible some days even in October. She wiggled her twisted foot to rid herself of the dull ache that ran from her toes to knee and pulled her fur-trimmed cloak tighter. She tipped the hood forward. The folds of heavy wool would not block out the sounds, but she would not have to watch the men die.

The old thegn stood between two guards, his fine tunic torn and filthy with blood and grime.

He wore fetters but was bowed down by more than the weight of the chains that held him.

'Brunwulf, formerly Thegn of Hamestan, for conspiring to incite revolt, your remaining land and title is forfeit. As tenant-in-chief for my liege and King, it is my duty and right to pass this sentence on you.'

From the dais Baron Robert de Coudray's voice rang clear across the square. A muttering of anger rippled around the crowd, dying away quickly as the soldiers raised their weapons.

Constance wondered how many of the serfs and villeins that huddled behind makeshift railings understood what her brother-in-law had said. She had lived in England for eighteen months, but a year after moving from Winchester to Cheshire the accent still seemed thick and impenetrable to her ears.

'Your life and the lives of those who raised swords against your King are also forfeit,' Robert continued.

Brunwulf raised his head at this and stared at Robert. His eyes were bruised and almost forced shut with the swelling, but the hatred in them was clear. He spat a reply, the name and sentiment familiar to Constance.

'The Bastard of Normandy is no King of mine.'

Another murmur, this time of approval, sped round the gathered people and a few cries of agreement rose up. Constance shifted nervously. People must have come from half of Cheshire to witness today's executions and, though these were farmers and craftsmen, serfs and women, there were a lot more of them than there were soldiers in the baron's retinue.

Robert's cheeks reddened as he bellowed his reply. 'The crown has been William's for two years. We rule England now. If you had submitted you could have retained control of your lands as our vassals, but you refused to see sense. Now you will pay the penalty.'

A cruel light shone in the baron's eyes. 'You will be the last to die. You will watch the deaths of your countrymen and sons first though, so you understand how utterly you have failed. Let this be a warning to any who think to oppose us.'

Robert jerked a thumb and a dozen bound men were brought forward from the heavily guarded cart and pushed to their knees alongside the thegn. They bore the same signs of rough treatment as Brunwulf and like him wore clothes that once spoke of quality. These were not serfs or slaves, but thegns and housecarls themselves.

Three at a time the condemned men were dragged up the steps to the scaffold in the centre of the square and nooses tightened around their necks. As the first three executions were carried out wails of sorrow broke out among the crowd.

The voices of wives and mothers, sisters or lovers. The soldiers standing in front of the huddled, grieving women crossed their pikes to hold them back in case the women rushed forward in attack. Constance could not help the sigh that escaped her.

Sitting between Constance and the baron, Robert's wife turned pale.

'Don't pity them,' Jeanne de Coudray whispered harshly. 'What compassion would they have spared us? Would they have cared if we had starved?'

Constance reached for her sister's hand and squeezed tightly. The answering flutter was so slight it tore at Constance's heart. Jeanne was six years older than Constance, but would have passed for double that. Fifteen months of marriage to Lord de Coudray had destroyed any softness Jeanne had once possessed and beaten the bloom from her cheeks. Seeing her sister change into this wraith reminded Constance how fortunate it was that though she was prettier than Jeanne, her twisted foot had prevented Robert choosing her as his bride when the sisters were offered.

Constance stared back at the faces that blurred into a mass of pale eyes and shades of blond hair, so different to her own dark eyes and hair. She knew they hated her and all her countrymen. The women would have doubtless rejoiced at their grief and spat on her pity, but Constance remembered the sorrow that had numbed her following the death of her father at the Battle of Senlac. Her heart still broke for them. She wiped a hand across her eyes and looked at the ground, pulling the hood further forward so she did not have to think about the bodies twisting in the biting wind.

'Open your eyes and watch how those who would threaten your King die, girl,' Robert commanded in an undertone. 'Don't shame me before these Saxon savages or I'll whip the skin from your back.'

Constance raised her head obediently and forced herself to watch as man after man was lifted high alive and cut down a corpse. Some resisted as the knots were pulled tight, one or two looked on the verge of weeping; others walked with dignity to their deaths. Without exception all spat towards the dais where Robert's household sat, fixing any Norman who met their eye with a loathing that made Constance shiver with fear.

Their deaths were not quick or easy, but if the uprising had not been prevented and they had joined with those in other counties, how slow and degrading would her death at their hands have been? She'd heard the tales of what had happened elsewhere, of children speared in their beds and women shared between the rebels until they begged for death. Even a twist-footed cripple like Constance would not be spared the degradation. Jeanne was right, it was relief she should feel, not pity.

Finally only three men remained alive. Their ages spanned a decade at least, but the reddish tint in their straw-blond hair and beards marked them as Brunwulf's sons. The youngest, a man in his middle twenties, could barely walk. His leg was bound to a splint and he clenched his teeth with pain as he was half-carried up the steps. As they were pushed forward to the waiting nooses Brunwulf finally groaned aloud with despair and to Constance it seemed he shrank in stature before her eyes. The eldest called something to his father, his words rapid and in a dialect so thick Constance could not make out a single word. Brunwulf's lips twisted into a grimace. He nodded and his sons raised their heads to stare at the baron defiantly. As one man they leapt off the ladders, causing their necks to break with the violence of their swing.

Without warning a roar of rage erupted from the back of the crowd. Robert leapt to his feet. People began muttering and jostling as a figure pushed through them. Someone screamed in alarm. Brunwulf swore.

Robert barked orders rapidly and soldiers plunged in among the gathered watchers to find the source, roughly knocking people aside.

Cries of indignation and alarm filled the air until eventually two soldiers returned dragging a struggling figure dressed in a dark blue cloak. The soldiers marched to the dais and threw their captive to the ground in front of Robert. One dropped a short sword alongside him. The other ripped the cloak from him and threw it aside, revealing a scrawny figure dressed in a worn tunic and hose with leg bindings where a sheathed dagger was stuffed. He pulled the dagger loose and threw it alongside the sword.

As the prisoner raised his face to glare at his captors Constance got her first clear look at his face. The sight caused her stomach to knot and vomit to rise in her throat. She gave an involuntary start forward in her seat.

Jeanne touched her arm gently and looked at her questioningly.

'Are you in pain?'

Constance shook her head and gave a half-smile, hoping her sister could not read the shock in her expression. She sat back, her mind whirling and filled with memories of occasions she had put behind her. Unconsciously she raised a hand to her lips, then realised what she had done, lowered it quickly and looked at the boy on the ground.

Aelric. Brunwulf's youngest son.

To call him a boy was unjust. He was young and couldn't yet be described as a full-grown man, but he was older than Constance by a year or two. He did not resemble his father at all. His tangled hair was reddish-blond and flopped across angular cheeks that were barely graced with a downy beard. Whereas Brunwulf was burly, Aelric had long limbs that he had not grown to fit completely.

As long as she had lived in Hamestan he had been there as Lord De Coudray's ward, though everyone knew *ward* was another word for *prisoner*, lodged within the manor grounds as a guarantee of his father's obedience. And now his father had broken that peace in the worst way possible and the boy would suffer. He had vanished from Hamestan after the uprising had been quashed and Constance had hoped he would have been long gone.

One of the soldiers twisted an arm up behind the boy's back to what looked like breaking point. He seized hold of him by the hair and wrenched his head back, causing the boy to let out a string of expletives, only some of which Constance knew.

'Why are you here?' Robert demanded. 'I thought you had fled to save your neck.'

'I came to save my father,' the boy shouted. He winced and gave a gasp of pain through gritted teeth as the soldier twisted his arm higher.

'You're too late for that,' Robert said coldly.

'Then I will avenge his death and those of my brothers,' Aelric snarled.

Constance glanced at the men swinging from the ropes and their father waiting in chains. Brunwulf stood, shoulders tense and expression stricken. Robert left the dais and walked to where the boy knelt in the mud. When he reached Aelric he leaned over, putting his face close to the boy's.

'And how do you propose to do that, Aelric, son of Brunwulf?' Robert asked. His voice had taken on the cold, mocking tone that Constance had come to dread.

Aelric's blue eyes bored into Robert, staring down the man twenty years his senior.

'By killing you.'

Robert was silent. The crowd hushed in frozen expectation. Constance gripped Jeanne's hand, waiting for Robert's response. For him to strike the boy or run him through. Instead he did something unexpected, yet far crueller.

He laughed.

Aelric's face reddened.

Robert waved a dismissive hand and turned away.

'Hang him with his father.'

The soldiers seized hold of Aelric, who cried out and struggled as they dragged him towards his father. Constance's stomach twisted as if someone had taken a stick and wound it through her guts, coiling it tight.

'Please don't!'

The words left her mouth before she could stop herself. She realised she had pushed herself to her feet.

'What do you think you're doing, girl?' Robert rounded on Constance, his face knotted with fury far greater than he had shown to the condemned men or the boy. The blood in her veins turned to ice, but she could feel her face flushing. The eyes of everyone in the square were on her.

'Set him free,' Constance said.

'Why should I do that?' Robert demanded incredulously.

'He's so young,' she said softly.

'Should I wait until he's older? I'm sure we can find a gaol for him until he's managed to grow hair on his chest,' Robert scoffed.

Aelric looked up and his eyes met Constance's. The sick feeling returned.

'He helped me once,' Constance said, aware of the heat rising to her cheeks. 'When my horse lost a shoe last winter.'

It had been a cold January day. Her horse slipped in the mud as she rode along the gritstone ridge. The half-familiar boy working in the fields under guard had left his position to take hold of the bridle. Speaking calm, unfamiliar words—to the animal or her she wasn't sure—he'd held the animal still while she remounted. She'd thanked him, nervously trying out the Saxon tongue. He'd grinned at her attempt, but kindly, before returning to his companions. They had looked at her with the contempt she'd come to expect, but he glanced back and nodded before walking away.

She told her brother-in-law only part of that. Not that they had met again. Times met and deeds done that she must not think of for fear Robert would read the emotions on her face.

'And because of that I should pardon his attempt to murder me today?' Robert asked.

Vomit rose again in Constance's throat. She had been nauseous for days with the anxiety of what today would bring. What attempt had it been really? Aelric could never have succeeded. Robert had been in no danger and he knew it.

'Not my boy,' Brunwulf begged.

'Your boy was safe while you obeyed me,' Robert mused. 'Why should he live now?'

'He took no part in the uprising. I saw to it he knew nothing of what we planned.'

Murmurs of agreement fluttered across the square. Brunwulf dropped to his knees in supplication.

'If you spare him, I will swear loyalty to your King here and now. You can tell William you secured my allegiance before my death.'

Robert was going to refuse. Constance could tell from the set of his jaw. The thought of Aelric's death was unbearable to her. Shaking Jeanne's hand from her arm, she dropped to her knees, ignoring the stiffness in her ankle.

'You've shown them you can be fierce. Now show them you can be merciful,' she pleaded. 'There has been so much death today.'

The murmurs grew louder and angrier. Robert's face was scarlet with fury.

'Very well,' he snapped. 'He lives.'

Aelric was hauled to the foot of the gallows. The bodies were cut down and Brunwulf was dragged forward. Though his chains weighed him down he climbed the ladder unaided and stared straight ahead as the noose was passed over his head. He gave his oath of loyalty as he had promised. He cast a look at his son that spoke of so much affection that tears welled in Constance's eyes. Then he went, face serene, to his death.

Many watching wept, Constance among them. Aelric remained dry eyed.

'And now to deal with you. I said you'd live. I made no other promises,' Robert said to Aelric. He turned to the guards. 'Secure him to the scaffold. Ten lashes.'

Aelric was bound, hands high, to the frame where his father's body hung. Constance turned to Jeanne in horror, but her sister's eyes were blank.

'Be silent,' Jeanne hissed, 'unless you want Robert to suspect the boy means more than you claim.'

The tunic was cut away, leaving Aelric's back exposed. As the first blow struck his scream of pain tore through the marketplace. He was ready for the second and made no sound, but by the sixth his cries with each blow came as weak, throaty sobs. Constance bunched her fists, digging her nails into her palms. Only later would she notice the half-moons of blood she had raised to the surface. When the tenth stroke was done Robert strolled to where his captive sagged.

'I have no need to keep you here any longer. Tomorrow you'll be sent to Chester where Earl Gerbod can find a use for you in the fields or salt works.'

Robert drew a dagger, grabbed hold of Aelric's left ear, twisting his head back.

'I'll leave you something to remember me by.'

He drew the tip from Aelric's collar to below the ear then turned the blade and smoothly sliced the lobe away. The boy gave a shriek and, as this last cruelty finally broke him, slumped against the scaffold frame in a faint.

'You shamed me in public! For that alone I should beat you until you scream!'

Robert's rage was incandescent. Constance looked to her sister but Jeanne sat, head bowed over her embroidery, and said nothing. She would get no support there.

'The boy did not deserve death.'

'Never mind that. What were you doing befriending Saxon filth?' Robert turned to his wife. 'Madam, is your sister a wanton?'

'No, my lord,' Jeanne answered meekly. 'Her behaviour is as shocking to me as it is to you.'

Constance's scalp prickled. If Robert knew the truth about what had passed between her and Aelric his wrath would be too great to withstand. Robert seized hold of Constance by the arm and dragged her roughly to her bed, flinging her on to the straw mattress.

'You are almost seventeen. It's time you were married. In the morning I'm sending you to a convent until I can find a husband who can tame you.'

He stormed out, leaving Constance holding her face and trembling with anger.

She lay on the truckle until it was dark, waiting until the voices in the Great Hall were at their most raucous. She gathered what she needed and wrapped cloth around the end of her walking stick, though it was unlikely to make any noise on the rush floor. She crept from the room and passed through the Great Hall. Robert and his retinue were around the fire pit, listening to the bard singing, and did not notice her leave.

She made her way to the marketplace. There was no light other than from the sliver of moon and the square was empty, everyone having returned home before the curfew. Although a soldier patrolled the boundary of the square, no one stood guard over the figure still bound by the wrists to the gallows. Presumably Robert believed no one would dare approach him after the afternoon's display of authority.

The iron scent of blood hit her as she neared Aelric, turning her stomach. He was leaning the full weight of his body against the frame. He groaned and turned his head at the sound of Constance's stick tapping.

'Constance!'

His voice was a hoarse whisper of surprise. His hair flopped across his face. Constance smoothed it back, unable to tear her eyes from the bloody scab that was his mutilated ear.

She held a flask of wine to his lips and he drank greedily.

'You'll get into trouble,' Aelric said.

'I won't be missed.' Constance hoped it would be true.

She tipped water on to the cloths she'd brought and began to clean the crusted blood from his back. He stiffened his shoulders and gave a sharp intake of breath. She blushed as her fingers traced the contours of his shoulder blades and muscles. She was glad of the darkness.

'Does it hurt a lot?' she asked.

'I can endure the pain,' Aelric said bitterly. 'You should have let them hang me.'

'You don't mean that!'

He twisted his head and gazed at her, his brow knotted. 'At least I'd have died with honour. You've condemned me to live and die a slave knowing I failed to avenge my family.'

She'd come hoping to ease his suffering, but his tone was harsher than she'd ever heard. His words cut into her deeper than the rope that had split his back open. She couldn't have watched him die, but how could she let him live the life he described?

'You don't have to,' she whispered. She looked around cautiously and drew out her dagger, one of a pair that had been the legacy from her father. The blue stone in the hilt caught the light. Aelric's eyes fell on it.

'Make it swift,' he said, his lips twisting downwards.

'I'm not going to kill you!' she exclaimed in shock. 'I'm not a savage! What do you take me for?'

'A Norman,' he said bitterly, ignoring the implied insult.

'Your friend,' Constance said, biting back the

hurt his words caused. 'I came to free you. You can run away.'

Aelric's eyes flickered. 'It's revenge I want. Where is the honour in running?'

Constance stepped back and threw her cloth to the ground in irritation. 'Nowhere, probably. But why throw away your freedom for the sake of pride?'

'Pride is all I have left,' Aelric growled. 'And vengeance.'

Constance picked up her stick and turned to walk away.

'Wait!' Aelric's voice was urgent.

'Why? I would free you because you aren't a killer, not so you could become one. I'm not risking myself for that!'

'You would put yourself in danger to help me? Why? Because I brought back your horse?' Aelric asked. 'Is that the only thing you will remember me for?'

'You know it isn't,' Constance said quietly. She refused to let the memories out.

'I don't want you to come to harm,' Aelric said, holding her gaze.

Constance felt again the sharp pain from Robert's slaps, thought of Jeanne crying in the night and dead-eyed by day. If someone were to kill Robert she would not grieve, but Aelric would never succeed.

'I'm being sent to a convent tomorrow, I'll be safe. If I cut you down you have to swear to leave tonight and not to try to harm Robert.'

Aelric tugged at the bonds on his wrists. 'If it will make you happy I won't attempt to kill him.'

'Swear,' Constance said. 'On something that matters.'

He looked furious, but she held his gaze until he sighed.

'I swear by my honour, and on the name and soul of my father, Brunwulf, that I will not raise arms against Robert.'

She nodded, satisfied. Keeping her eyes from Aelric's, she quickly cut the ropes binding him. Aelric sagged to the ground, massaging his wrists. Constance helped him to stand, warmth spreading along her fingers from his hands that were so cold.

'Now I am in your debt,' he said. He lifted her hand to his lips, then put his hand to her cheek, drew her close and planted a soft kiss on her forehead. Constance raised her head and brushed her lips against the edge of his mouth. She felt his lips twist into a smile.

'I won't forget what you've done for me,' Aelric whispered.

The enormity of what she had done crashed over Constance. She did not want to think what Robert might do when he discovered the boy had disappeared in the night.

'Take me with you,' she asked impulsively.

'You don't mean that,' Aelric said. 'I don't know where I'll go, but it won't be suitable for a girl used to the life you lead.'

'I don't care how hard it might be,' Constance whispered.

'I do,' Aelric said firmly.

'Please,' she begged. 'I have nothing to keep me here. We could be together.'

Her eyes filled with tears. She gazed into Aelric's eyes and put a hand on his arm. He closed his hand over it.

'I'll wait by the old cowshed at the fork in the Bollin until dawn,' he said. He gave a slight smile. 'You know where I mean.'

Constance blushed and looked away, knowing very well where Aelric meant.

'Take this,' she said. She handed him the dagger. His hand tightened over hers then he slipped away.

She watched until he became a shadow and disappeared from view, then picked up her stick and returned to the house. She wouldn't need much. She didn't have much to take anyway.

She made it back as far as the bedchamber and had pulled the dagger's twin and her spare kirtle from the chest when a hand seized her hair roughly from behind. Robert hauled her to her feet.

'Where have you been?'

'Nowhere,' Constance whimpered.

'Liar! You were seen leaving the house,' Robert bellowed. 'Tell me the truth or I'll beat it out of you.'

Robert slapped her without warning, the palm of his hand setting her cheek ablaze.

'Nowhere,' she repeated. If she told him now then Aelric would never escape.

Another slap. This time backhanded and with force that left her reeling. Robert unbuckled his belt.

'I've tolerated your waywardness for too long,' he said.

Constance tried to duck past him, but he pulled at the neck of her gown and swung her around. She landed heavily across the table face first, the stab of pain in her belly making her retch. Robert brought the leather strap down upon her, buckle end swinging free. Lights burst in Constance's head as it caught her the bare flesh of her shoulder and she screamed.

She knew then she would never meet Aelric.

Aelric watched the dawn rise.

Constance wouldn't come, but there was a spark of hope within him that refused to die. He caressed the dagger that she had given him. It was well made and the stone set into the end would fetch a good price alone: enough to see his belly full for a month or two at least.

When the sun was a half-circle behind the hills he pushed himself to his feet. He wrapped the sacking around his shoulders, biting down the pain in his back where the rough cloth grazed every cut. He stared back towards Hamestan, hoping to see the familiar dark-haired, slender figure making her way towards him, but the road was deserted.

Reluctantly he turned away, trying not to care. While they lived under the same roof he had entertained daydreams of marrying her, Norman or not, but what well-bred noblewoman would really swap a life of comfort for one of uncertainty and exile. It was for the best. He could move faster alone.

Casting a final look over his shoulder he walked away, knowing it would be a long time before he saw these hills again.

Chapter Two

Worcestershire—1075

Constance folded the parchment over and ran her finger across the two halves of the thick seal. She dug her thumbnail into the wax until the edges chipped.

'Do you know what this letter says?' she asked her guest.

Hugh D'Avranches, Palatine Earl of Chester, reached across to the low table and refilled their goblets. The jug nestled among the remains of the late meal they had shared. It had been pleasant before Hugh had produced the parchment.

'I can hazard a guess,' he replied, handing Constance her wine. 'When your brother-in-law asked me to carry this message I asked if he would like me to bring your reply back to Cheshire. He said there would be none as he was certain you would obey his instructions and begin your travel preparations immediately.'

Constance suppressed a shudder.

'He would have me travel in December! He expects me to return to live in Hamestan.'

She flung the hateful letter to the floor beside her and began pacing around the chamber, her stick striking loudly on the stone floor. When she had left Hamestan seven years ago she had intended never to go back.

'Who is he to command me to do anything!' she exclaimed. 'And why now? You should have refused to bring this to me.'

Hugh folded his arms; a calm, thickset, tawny-haired man who was more jowly every time Constance saw him, despite not yet being thirty. He regarded Constance with an expression of mild reproach, then beckoned her to sit down. It was impossible to stay angry with him for long so she returned to the settle by the hearth and eased herself on to the cushions, stretching her leg on to a low stool.

'Robert de Coudray is one of my tenants-in-chief. It would have been churlish for me to refuse to bear his letter as I was travelling past Bredon on my way to Gloucester. Besides—' Hugh smiled and took Constance's hand '—I would not pass up the opportunity to visit you. I have seen you so rarely this past three years. My new responsibilities keep me busy.'

Such familiarity was unbecoming, even if she was a widow. If anyone were to find them in such a position she was risking scandal, but Constance was beyond caring. One way or another she would be gone before long.

'I'm glad to see you, Hugh. I have so few friends. I don't want to quarrel with you when you're here for such a short time.'

Hugh placed the letter on the table alongside the wine jug.

'You could intervene and make Robert change his mind,' Constance suggested hopefully.

Hugh pursed his lips. 'Not without causing bad blood and I need the loyalty of all my vassals at this time. As much as you hate it, now you are a widow, your brother-in-law is your legal guardian. If Robert commands you to live within the protection of his household that is his right.'

The notion of Robert de Coudray offering any sort of protection would be laughable. Except it wasn't funny. Not when she wondered who would offer protection from Robert himself. She rubbed her ear, feeling a faint scar beneath her fingertips left by Robert's belt buckle.

'I don't want any man's protection,' she said. She stared into the fire, watching the flames rising from the logs and entwining sinuously, like lovers dancing.

'You cannot stay in Bredon,' Hugh said.

'My late husband's nephew has inherited the land and title. He has agreed that I may live here until twelve months have passed. After that I intend to return to take holy orders at the convent at Brockley.'

'Constance, you're far too young to shut yourself off from the world in such a way,' Hugh exclaimed.

Constance took a long drink of wine. She didn't feel young. Dark shadows under her eyes and a permanent worry crease on her forehead was evidence enough of that. The ever-present stiffness in her leg merely accentuated it.

'I am twenty-three. Many women commit themselves to life in the cloisters from a much younger age and, as you say, I have to live somewhere.'

'Why Brockley?' Hugh asked. 'Why not somewhere closer to here?'

Constance clasped her hands around her arms and shivered.

'The sisters cared for me when I arrived there from Hamestan. I would have stayed then if I'd been permitted, but once Robert brokered my marriage I was brought here.'

'You never speak of that time,' Hugh mused.

Constance lifted her chin and fixed him with a fierce glare, her stomach lurching violently. None but the nuns knew what she had learned about herself when she had arrived there and she intended to keep it that way.

'No,' she said curtly. 'I don't.'

After an unusually tactful length of time Hugh broke the silence by throwing another log on to the fire.

'Tell me…why did you question the timing of this letter?' he asked.

'Piteur—' Constance winced slightly as she always did when mentioning her deceased husband '—has been dead for nine months. Lord de Coudray has made no attempt to communicate with me until now.'

'Perhaps he has finally realised the necessity of deciding your future,' Hugh pointed out. 'If you had borne an heir matters would have been different.'

That was the problem. Five years of marriage had produced no child who had lived. Hugh, like all men, would think only of the lineage that must be carried on and her failure to provide the required child. The grief for her daughter, dead after only four days in the world, was still raw after three years. It seemed unlikely ever to diminish. The pain, helplessness and indignity that had accompanied her other failed pregnancies, before and afterwards, still clawed at her in nightmares.

She thought back to the first baby. The one she had not even suspected she was carrying and tears burned her eyes. Tears of sorrow, and hatred for the man who had unknowingly caused its death.

Hugh took her hand gently.

'King William dislikes widows living alone. You know you will have to marry again,' he said. 'I know your husband granted you a legacy when he died.'

Piteur's legacy had been earned many times over in ways Constance did not wish to contemplate ever again. She would crush every jewel and melt every ring if she could.

'I'm sure I could find a dozen husbands who would look past my deformity—' she indicated her crooked foot '—and spend it for me, but I have had enough of marriage,' Constance said bitterly. 'I'm done with men using me for their own ends.'

'If I had been in England when your brother-in-law was searching for a husband, I would have put myself forward.'

Constance's eyes widened in surprise. She was fond of Hugh, but it had never crossed her mind his feelings ran that deep.

'I'm flattered,' Constance said sincerely, 'but you are married now so that is not a possibility.'

Hugh stretched out his stocky legs towards

the fire. 'That is true, but I would gladly become your patron and protector if you would become my mistress.'

She should be shocked. She should dismiss him immediately from the room, but she didn't.

'You don't mean that,' she said gravely.

'Sometimes I do,' he answered. 'Especially when the night is cold and the wine is sweet and I think how soft your lips are.'

Hugh's eyes slid to the corner of the room where Constance's bed stood and a suggestive smile played around his lips.

'It's late and my horse is tired. It would be cruel to make him travel further tonight,' he said roguishly. He reached for Constance's hand again and began to run his fingers up and down her arm. 'Come to bed with me. If you're determined to cloister yourself away you should have some memories to look back on fondly. Perhaps you will change your mind.'

She was almost tempted, just to see what it would be like. Hugh was kind and reputed to treat his mistresses well. Not all men could be as brutal and demeaning as Piteur and his companions had been. She'd loved a boy once before, in her youth, and that had been sweet and exciting. It was the memory of Aelric that tipped the scales against Hugh.

'I don't think that would be wise,' Constance

said, withdrawing her hand. 'I'm done with men and men are done with me. You are welcome to my hospitality in every other respect though. Speak to my steward and he will find you a bed. Come and say farewell before you leave in the morning,' she instructed.

Hugh accepted her refusal with a good-natured bow. Constance stood and held out her arm and together they walked to the door.

Hugh stopped in the doorframe.

'I know you don't like to speak of your time in Hamestan, or the circumstances under which you left, but I am asking you to consider returning to Cheshire. It might be to both our advantages.'

Constance looked at him suspiciously.

'I haven't been entirely honest. The timing of Lord de Coudray's letter troubles me, too,' Hugh admitted. 'Rumours are beginning to emerge that in certain parts of the country there is talk of dissent.'

'From the Saxons?'

Images Constance had buried for years flashed through her mind. Bodies swinging from the gallows on a foggy day. A pair of blue eyes still defiant despite unendurable pain. Her heart throbbed unexpectedly, surprising her. She had believed it had petrified beyond beating with such intensity.

Hugh's lips tightened. 'Not only them. None have dared to rebel since William's harrying. The earls in Mercia are becoming restless and William fears Cheshire may follow.'

'Why should this involve me?' Constance asked.

'Your brother-in-law's name has been mentioned indirectly and it would be helpful for me to have a connection close to his household. So much of my time is taken up dealing with the Welsh borderlands.'

'I don't want to return there,' Constance said quietly. 'I can't forget what he did, or forgive him. What advantage is there for me?'

'Do this for me and I will make sure you are safe,' Hugh said. 'If you will not become my mistress I cannot prevent you being required to marry, but if Robert were disgraced, or condemned for treason, he would have no influence in the matter.'

'What will happen to Robert if I find any indication he is involved in conspiracy?' Constance asked.

Hugh's eyes were steely.

'If he is involved in any treachery, he will be brought to justice.'

Constance turned her head so Hugh could not see the emotions assailing her. He was her friend, but first and foremost he would protect his lands and King. His protection might be the only hope she had. Moreover, aiding him would be a fitting revenge on Robert.

For the first year since leaving Hamestan her hatred for Robert had seared her from within. When she was given to Piteur, her husband replaced him as the object of her loathing, as a black shadow obliterates the grey rock. Now the emotions that had diminished came back in a rush.

'I'll think on it,' she promised.

Hugh's face broke into a smile. He kissed her briefly on the cheek and left. Constance summoned her serving girl and sat before the fire as the maid combed and plaited her chestnut hair until it shone. She re-read the letter until she could recite it word for word. It was curt to the point of rudeness, but she expected nothing less from Robert. There was no word either of or from her sister, but as Jeanne was not a skilled writer this was to be expected as well.

Constance climbed into bed and drew the furs up high. In the fading firelight she stared around the small chamber that had been her sanctuary since her wedding. Piteur had seldom entered it. He had kept his quarters in the adjoining room, summoning Constance when he required her presence. She shivered with instinctive revulsion. When he died she had burned his mattress and coverlet, ignoring the protestations and gossip of his servants and tenants who excused her behaviour as the actions of a grieving young widow.

This house was not hers and despite her words

to Hugh, she had no real inclination to stay here. She fell asleep, wondering about the previous owners before Piteur had been rewarded the land. Perhaps they had been hanged like the old thegn of Hamestan. She realised she couldn't remember his name. She would never forget that of his son, however. How could she after what they had done together? He was probably long dead, believing she had chosen to stay behind. It made her unaccountably sad.

Blue eyes and a wide grin flitted through her dreams that night, for the first time in years. Blood and screaming followed. She woke before dawn drenched with sweat and trembling and sat wrapped in blankets, hugging her knees until light.

When the morning came her decision was made. She joined Hugh in the snowy courtyard as his horse was saddled and he prepared to depart.

'I'll do what you ask, but it isn't enough that you will stop Robert deciding my marriage. I want you to swear that if I find the proof you need to convict him you will help me reach the convent.'

Hugh put his hand over his heart. 'You have my word. I'd found an order myself if it would keep you happy.'

Constance nodded in satisfaction. 'When you return to Cheshire tell Lord de Coudray I will come when my year here is up. I will stay with him for a year. No longer.'

Hugh's forehead creased. 'That will be early March. That's no time for travelling.'

Constance shrugged. 'I doubt he'd wait longer and this country is miserable whatever the time of year.'

'Then let me send an escort to you,' Hugh said. 'The countryside is swarming with wild men.'

'If my brother-in-law wishes me to return, he can stretch to the expense of an escort himself,' Constance said. 'Besides, I can travel inconspicuously.'

Hugh smiled. 'I look forward to hearing of any information you discover. Remember, I want him to be dealt with openly as a warning. I need proof.'

He swung his large frame into the saddle and galloped away. Constance watched him go, wondering what secrets Robert was keeping. She owed him no loyalty and if she could uncover anything that could do him ill she would not weep over that!

Cheshire

The man who called himself Caddoc crouched in the undergrowth. His thighs and back ached from holding the stance so long, but when his target came within his sight it would be worth the discomfort. Sleet dripped down his neck and he pulled his leather hood closer to his cloak.

A flash of brown between the trees caught his attention. She was closer now. Another few paces and he would have clear aim. He drew a silent breath and pulled back his bowstring. There was a crack behind him as a foot stepped on a twig and the bushes moved. The doe stiffened, and then was gone.

Caddoc swore and turned to see a redheaded man, twenty years or so his senior. He eased his bowstring back.

'Thank you, Ulf. I didn't want to eat tonight.'

Ulf grinned, showing a collection of broken teeth. 'Lucky it was me and not one of the Earl's men or you'd have lost your eyes as well as your ear.'

Caddoc scowled. He scratched his thick tangle of beard.

'It's unlikely they'd come so deep into the forest this late in the day. Let's hope someone else had better luck.'

He stood, twisting life back into his aching limbs. He stowed his bow and arrows and checked for the dagger he always wore at his waist, then the two men made their way through the dense forest to the camp they shared with a handful of other men.

Anyone watching would think their path was

haphazard unless they happened to notice the small notches and marks cut into certain trees. A single slab of moss-covered rock concealed a narrow gap through which they could pass single file. A boy of fourteen stood guard at the furthest end, brandishing a scythe.

'It's us, Wulf.'

The boy lowered his weapon as Caddoc and Ulf pushed back their hoods and raised their hands in greeting as they passed. They scrambled over rocks upwards until they reached a flat ridge overlooking the edge of the forest. Beyond that the ground fell away giving a view over the plain and the hills beyond.

Home was the remains of a derelict watchtower built then abandoned by some bygone people Caddoc neither knew nor cared the name of. Wood had been added to an upper level and it had been covered with skins and bracken, creating a structure that was sufficiently weatherproof and well concealed. A scattering of small shelters huddled alongside. This camp would do for another month or two, until spring came, but after that they would have to move on. To stay anywhere too long risked someone revealing the location, accidentally or otherwise.

Caddoc went inside, called a general greeting, removed his wet cloak and settled himself cross-legged on a pallet by the fire. Old Gerrod sitting to his left passed him a wineskin and he tossed the ale down his throat.

'No luck hunting. I almost had a doe, but Ulf surprised her.'

'Osgood and Wulf brought back a couple of bucks. They're almost ready for the pot,' Gerrod said. He jerked his thumb to the corner where his wife, a thin woman named Elga, was hacking a rabbit into pieces.

As they ate the men talked. Caddoc closed his eyes as he lay back on his straw-filled mattress and let the voices wash over him. The pottage was good and his feet were nearly dry. He was almost approaching contentment.

'Do we get a song tonight?' Ulf asked him.

Caddoc shook his head, tempting though it was to unwrap his *crwth* and lose himself in the song. 'My fingers are still too cold to play tonight.'

'I heard in Acton this morning that Fat Hugh of Chester has sired another bastard on one of his mistresses,' Ulf said.

'Another mouth to steal the bread from ours!' Gerrod spat a rabbit bone into the fire. He waited for the murmured agreement to die away. 'That's no news. I have better. The Pig of Hamestan is awaiting the arrival of something important… and valuable.'

Caddoc's jaw tensed at the name. He kept his eyes closed, but listened closely.

'De Coudray? That isn't news,' Ulf said. 'Rollo, his reeve, has been bragging for weeks in every alehouse he enters that he's being sent to bring something.'

'What do you think it might be, Father?' Wulf asked greedily, coming to sit by Gerrod. 'Gold?'

'Doubt it. Isn't he rich enough already?' Gerrod growled.

'He has to spend it on something, though,' Ulf pointed out.

'I heard he plans to buy a new bride,' Osgood said.

'I heard in the market it's a bride he's having brought,' cackled Wulf.

'That can't be right,' Ulf scoffed. 'His wife has only been in the ground three weeks.'

'It's what I heard,' Wulf said belligerently. 'It's what I'd do if I had money.'

There was a roar of laughter, led by Gerrod. At fourteen Wulf's every concern was of filling his belly or wetting his staff. Caddoc didn't laugh. At that age iced fire had filled his veins, flooring him in the presence of any girl. One in particular had turned his insides into something resembling a squashed beetle with a single smile.

'Perhaps his wife's death wasn't as natural as they say,' Osgood suggested. 'Perhaps he helped her on her way.'

'Why would he do that?' Ulf asked.

'Why wouldn't he?' Caddoc muttered under his breath. The whey-faced woman who had sat beside de Coudray on the dais had seemed half a corpse even seven years ago. He stared into the fire, not seeing flames but bodies twisting in nooses. He'd played no part in the discussion so far and a hush descended on the room.

'You sound like you know of him?' Gerrod asked.

He pointed to the missing lobe of his left ear and the scar leading beneath his collar. 'De Coudray did this.'

'You said you were from over the border,' Osgood said accusingly.

Caddoc grimaced, annoyed at his slip. He'd journeyed far in the years since his exile, but his feet had always brought him back to Cheshire, before the anger and pain led him off again once more. Like most of the wild men he had been intentionally vague about his origins, but the mention of the hated name had caused his blood to run hot through his veins.

'I ran to Wales when I was exiled,' he said.

He looked around, wondering who they had all been. Carls? Serfs? He knew Osgood could write a few of his letters and Gerrod's fingers had been taken for poaching when he was younger than Caddoc was now. Ulf had served Brunwulf; he was the only man who had known the boy Aelric before he became the man Caddoc, but loyalty to his former thegn kept him silent.

It no longer mattered when they all had reason to hate their persecutors.

'Of all the Normans I've encountered he's the cruellest.' Caddoc spat. He felt again the lash against his back. 'He executed my family and he'd have hanged me, too.'

'Why didn't he?' Gerrod asked.

Caddoc broke off and stared into the flames, seeing a pale face, angular in a manner that made him think of a vixen. He drew his eyes back from the past.

'He didn't need to. He'd already destroyed me when he took everyone and everything I loved. I'd kill him if I could, but he's beyond my reach.'

And he had sworn not to. He remembered the vow he had made years before. That had been easy to keep, at least, with no opportunity to get close to de Coudray.

'Gerrod, are you sure what you've said is true?'

'Yes. I heard from one of the monks at Malpas he's having something important sent from down south in a week or two. He needs lodging for the escort for a night.'

'If your rumours are right it's important and valuable,' Caddoc said, 'I want it.'

He felt all eyes turn on him. The blood pounded in his veins. For years the dream of vengeance had consumed him and it was too much to hope the means were finally within his grasp. De Coudray could be having anything brought to him. Caddoc sat forward abruptly and gestured around the bare room.

'For seven years I've lived like this and I've had enough. We live in this hovel while the men who stole our homes get richer by the year.'

'Rich, were you? Before you ran?' Osgood asked, crossing his arms. 'Some of us have always lived like this.'

Another slip. Careful, he warned himself.

'Whatever we were, this is no way I want to live. The Normans took our lands and our lives. We steal a pitiful amount from their tenants and woods, but it's time we took more. Who cares what the Pig has got himself? I don't want him to have it.'

'And if it is a bride?' Wulf asked, determined not to let go of his idea.

Caddoc grinned. He fingered the dagger at his waist.

'Then we'll steal her, too.'

Chapter Three

Constance hated travelling. The weather made matters worse. Despite having no eagerness to be in Robert's company she would wish away the journey to Hamestan in exchange for a soft mattress and no more early rising to be on the road in fog that dampened every layer of clothing. The long hours in the saddle made her leg ache and the company that had been inflicted on her made each day seem twice as long. She would have preferred to ride faster but Rollo, the escort Robert de Coudray had sent, had insisted on travelling at a stately pace since they had entered the Cheshire forest.

She let her mind wander; counting the shafts of sunlight that peeked through the trees, casting shadows across the narrow road. Her companions were equally silent. After almost two weeks in each other's company they had reached the stage where light conversation was neither necessary nor welcome. Constance wondered which of them would be reporting her conduct back to Robert. Rollo, probably, though it could equally be the guards in black who rode with Constance's strongbox and possessions strapped to their panniers, or the grey-cowled monk who never strayed far from her side.

'Can we rest for a while?' she asked.

'Not until we're through the forest. This country is crawling with rogues who would slit your throat as soon as fart,' Rollo grunted. His eyes roved up and down Constance's body, lingering on her knee-length tunic that revealed hose-clad calves. 'Or more if they see through your disguise.'

Constance scowled, not prepared to have the same argument again. Her choice of clothing had already raised eyebrows, but she insisted nevertheless. Skirts were too cumbersome for long rides and her thick winter cloak and hood would attract much less attention from any thieves waiting in the woods than the finery of a well-dressed lady. With her hair tightly coiled at her neck and concealed under a woollen cowl she looked more like an unassuming page than a woman.

'If you're right we should move faster, especially if we want to reach the inn before sunset,' she said. Rollo hacked up spittle and slapped his horse's rear, increasing from a walk to a trot. Constance resisted the urge to break into a gallop and leave him behind, knowing it would lead to even more disapproval.

'Are there really men living wild here?' she asked the monk.

He nodded solemnly. 'Everywhere.'

'Murderers, thieves and exiles. They had to crawl somewhere when our lords took their lands,' Rollo added. 'We'll be at the bridge soon, then we can breathe easier.'

Constance eyed the deep forest nervously, half-expecting to see a figure lying in wait behind every tree. She fingered the dagger at her waist for reassurance and increased the pace a little.

The rough road followed the path of a stream that widened until the river was in full flow with snow melt. She searched for signs of familiarity in the rising hills, but there were none. Of course she had been in no condition to observe the scenery last time she had travelled this path. Insensible with pain in her back and head, bleeding and bruised, she had been borne on a litter to the convent in Brockley. Vomit rose in her throat at the memory and she almost turned the mare's head to flee until she remembered her promise to Hugh. Continuing to Hamestan was the only way to secure her future and serve retribution on Robert.

As they neared the crossing Rollo swore. A cart had lost a wheel, spilling its load of logs across the bridge while the ragged hooded driver tried unsuccessfully to right it using a thick log as a lever. Rollo dismounted and began to bellow at the old man, presumably believing that would clear the obstruction.

'We should help him clear the path,' Constance said. 'That will be quicker.' And kinder, she did not say aloud.

She climbed down, pulling her stick from the pannier at her saddle, and began to walk forward. The monk dismounted and walked towards the bridge, leaving only the two guards mounted.

It was then the ambush occurred.

The cart driver swung upright with the log he was holding, catching Rollo under the chin. He went down like a felled tree. As Rollo hit the ground another man clambered from beneath the bridge, short sword in one hand and a heavy cudgel in the other. He was long limbed and lean, dressed in a rough brown tunic with a leather jerkin on top of that. A hood was pulled low, casting a shadow over his face.

'Now!' he cried.

The monk dropped to his knees in front of Constance.

'Run, child,' he said urgently, before he began to pray loudly.

Knowing she would get no true aid from him, Constance turned around in time to see a further three men also armed with swords and wooden staffs bursting from amid the trees. They hurled themselves at the mounted guards who kicked out, trying to beat their attackers off while they struggled to draw their swords. The cart driver who had felled Rollo had turned his attention to the monk. He was not as old or frail as Constance had first imagined. The monk offered no resistance when the man began roping his hands behind his back and only increased the volume of his prayers.

The air filled with cries of anger and exertion. The guards were pulled from their mounts, but had succeeded in drawing their weapons and began to return the blows they were dealt.

Stomach knotting, Constance staggered back against her horse. Running was futile. She was too slow and where would she go anyway? She crouched on the ground, trying to make herself as unobtrusive as possible against the mare's legs.

The man from beneath the bridge had been kneeling beside Rollo. Seemingly satisfied that the bodyguard was no threat, he cleared the ground in a handful of strides. The guards would be no match when the odds were four against two.

But four against three...

As the hooded man passed her, Constance hurled her stick at his legs. It caught him a blow on the ankles and he tripped forward. He threw his arms out, recovering his footing almost instantly, and whipped his head round to see who had obstructed him. His hood slipped back and Constance caught a glimpse of his face, or at least the hair that flopped down to his neck and the wild, shaggy beard that covered his jaw. His blue eyes were strikingly bright amid the blond tangle and now they narrowed with fury as they regarded Constance.

'There's another over here!' he shouted.

Cursing her own stupidity Constance pushed herself to her feet. The assailants had been so intent on capturing the guards they had overlooked her presence so to draw attention to it had been the height of foolishness. Now she was most probably going to die alongside the guards. She lurched sideways as her weaker leg sent her off balance, but threw herself in the direction of the woods. She aimed herself blindly at the thick undergrowth, her only hope being to find somewhere to hide. Before she had gone five paces a pair of hands seized her from behind.

'No, you don't, lad!'

The man she had tripped wrapped his arms tight around Constance's waist, pinning her arms to her side. She threw her head back, trying to wrestle free, but his grip was unbreakable. His arms locked around her with a strength she had never before encountered and she felt herself lifted off the ground as easily as a child. She kicked and bucked wildly, but her resistance made no difference and she was carried back to the road.

Her captor threw her to her knees and cuffed her round the ear with the back of his hand. The blow wasn't very hard, clearly intended as a warning rather than to cause injury, but nevertheless it set her head spinning. Once she had been hardened against such treatment, but now the violence came as a shock. She bit back tears. No man would weep at such a blow.

'Stay still and you might live, boy,' he growled, his accent curling oddly in Constance's ears. Whoever he was his accent did not sound like the men of Cheshire.

The man trained his sword on Constance's breast, hardly casting a glance at her face. Despite her terror Constance let out a long breath of relief. Her disguise had not been discovered. She tilted her head to try to see what was happening behind her. Her blood chilled. One guard lay dead, the other bravely stood his ground against three men, but even as she watched he was knocked to the ground and pinned on his belly by a foot in the back. The cart driver hauled the monk to kneel beside Constance as the nearest brigand began to hack at the straps holding the pannier containing Constance's strongbox to the saddle.

'Get the box quickly, Ulf,' Constance's captor

said, speaking with an authority that confirmed what she had suspected—he was the leader. 'I want to be gone before anyone else appears.'

He reached down and seized hold of her by the neck of her cloak, leaning his face into hers. Constance braced herself for discovery of her deception, but a roar of rage made them both start. At the river's edge Rollo had clambered to his feet and was staggering towards Constance, blood smearing his lips and chin. She sobbed with relief, her terror abating slightly, but her optimism was short lived as her supposed saviour lumbered past them, knocking Constance aside as though she had not existed. He aimed instead for the two men who were freeing the small, iron-hinged box from its leather bindings.

Constance's mouth fell open in shock and disbelief. The bodyguard was supposed to protect her above all else. Rollo drew his weapon as he ran. Constance's captor let go of her cloak, closing the distance between himself and Rollo with a bellow of warning, but he was too late. With a cry Rollo thrust his sword straight between the shoulder blades of the nearest man, who buckled at the knees, falling forward. With a speed that stopped the breath in Constance's throat the hooded man twisted round. He had his weapon raised by the time he completed the turn but before he could reach Rollo the cart driver had pushed the monk aside and planted his own weapon deep in Rollo's back, twisting viciously.

With a grunt Rollo fell forward, landing almost on top of his victim. The cart driver fell to his knees beside the bodies and gave a keening sob of anguish.

'Wulf! My son!'

He pushed Rollo's corpse to the side and rolled the limp body on to its back and cradled it protectively. The hooded man dropped to his knees alongside and put his arm around the older man's shoulders. He gently pushed the dead man's hood back and the victim's head lolled to one side.

He was only a boy. Constance sagged back on to her heels, a burst of compassion punching her in the stomach at the sight of the father's grief. Her head felt far too light and she feared she might faint, but through her terror it struck her that she was unobserved once more. The two deaths had granted her a reprieve that she would surely not get again. She began slowly to edge towards her horse, never expecting to make it, and surreptitiously releasing her dagger from its sheath as a precaution.

There was a cry, then hands on her shoulder. She twisted around and swiped sideways with the dagger at whoever was behind her. It barely penetrated the leather jerkin of the hooded man and didn't strike flesh. He seized her wrist, tightening his fingers and digging the nails in until the pain forced her to let go of the weapon with a shrill cry. He kicked it away and pushed her to the ground.

'I told you not to move. It wouldn't take much for Gerrod to spear you like a pig ready for the spit and right now I wouldn't stop him.'

'Why not let him?' Constance said. Her throat tightened with terror. Somehow she had had the presence of mind to deepen her voice. 'You're going to kill us anyway, aren't you?'

Did she mean it? Every sense screamed no, she wanted to live, whatever it took.

'You don't have to die if you're sensible,' the man said. 'We want what's in here, not your lives.' He gestured to Constance's strongbox.

'That's mine!' she exclaimed angrily.

The man laughed without humour.

'Is it worth more than your life, lad?'

Constance sat back on her knees, her leg burning with pain. She bowed her head.

'You've got ballock stones to keep trying, I'll give you that,' the hooded man said, a touch of admiration creeping into his voice. He snapped his fingers and pointed to Constance. 'Osgood, search him.'

A short, broad man stalked towards her.

'Put your hands up,' he instructed.

She lifted them a little.

'No. Behind your head.'

Constance did as she was instructed, aware of how the action caused her breasts to lift and jut forward. Osgood's hands fumbled at her waist.

'Nothing else, Caddoc.'

He began moving higher up her body. She recoiled in horror as he brushed against the swell of her breasts, then closed his hands over them. He gave a cry of shock and let go as though he had been stung.

'He's a woman!'

Constance brought her fist round and smacked Osgood hard across the nose. He cried in pain. As his hands came up protectively she spun away, rising to her feet only to be seized by the neck from behind. She glared up into the blue eyes of the hooded man, Caddoc. He pulled her close to him so their faces were almost touching and examined her intently.

'Who are you?' he demanded. He lowered his hood, tilting his head to one side and narrowing his eyes.

Constance's heart missed a beat as the gesture sent her spinning back through time.

'I know you!'

'I don't think so,' he said curtly. His gaze moved to Constance's dagger that was frustratingly just out of her reach. His jaw set. He pulled Constance's cowl off to reveal the coil of hair she had concealed so carefully.

'Tell me who you are,' he repeated. He looked back at her and brushed a hand through his hair, pushing it back from his face. A deep white scar ran the length of his neck and his left ear was missing the lobe, coming to an abrupt stop at the cartilage.

Constance's heart stopped and she blurted out the name without thinking.

'Aelric!'

His face twisted with shock.

A searing hot flush raced across Constance's throat and chest, turning to a chill that left her trembling violently from head to foot. Nausea overwhelmed her, tightening her throat and twisting her belly.

'Help me, Aelric.'

Her voice sounded distant and dreamlike in her ears and her legs began to shake. She felt herself slipping away from the world, floating to the ground. Felt his arms seize her before she hit the track. The last sight she saw was his eyes; wide, disbelieving and filling her vision, before blackness consumed her.

The man who called himself Caddoc looked down into the ashen face of the woman he held in his arms. He had caught her instinctively when she began to fall, though after the many attempts she had made to run or fight he could not discount that this was yet another escape attempt.

He blew on her cheeks. She gave no indication she felt his breath. Her head lolled to the side like a recently slaughtered lamb and when Caddoc pulled back one eyelid with a fingertip he saw her pupil had rolled back. This was a true faint and the comparison he had drawn turned his stomach. He lowered her gently to the ground, stepping back carefully.

'She called you Aelric,' Osgood said, his voice thick and muffled from clutching his swollen nose. 'Why did she call you that?'

Caddoc felt his stomach clench. The name was not one he had heard spoken aloud for over seven years. One he had buried deep inside himself. There was no one other than Ulf from his present that would know it and few people from his past were alive to identify him.

'I asked who she was,' he said indifferently. 'Perhaps the name is hers.'

He didn't expect the men to believe his feeble excuse and sure enough Osgood grimaced. Ulf looked up scornfully from where he knelt binding the hands of the remaining guard.

'Aelric?' Osgood scoffed. 'That's not a woman's name. It's not even a Norman name for that matter and she's definitely that.'

Caddoc bent to pick up the dagger he had wrested from her hand.

A woman.

Guilt coursed through him as he recalled how he had twisted her arm until she yelped. Worse, he had dragged her from the woods and given her a blow to the head. He hadn't known she was a woman, though, and she'd fought back fiercely enough. She'd even begun the assault on him by throwing the stick under his feet.

A woman who knew his name.

He stared at the unconscious woman, hoping to see some sign of familiarity, but her face was smeared with dirt and her brown hair was dishevelled. Her lips were full and enticingly pink and long lashes framed each closed eye. He crouched on his heels beside her, wondering how he could possibly have mistaken the high cheekbones and delicate features for those of a boy.

Her dagger lay in the grass. Caddoc reached for it and turned it over in his hands. For the second time a blow struck him between the shoulder blades, knocking the breath from him. His hand twitched to his belt and closed around the familiar handle of the dagger that Constance Arnaud had given him on the night she had set him free. The dagger he held bore the same design and engraved initials. The stone in the hilt was the twin of his, only red instead of blue.

The forest and clearing vanished and he was lost in the past, staring at the woman before him. It could be her. The hair was the right colour and years had passed for her as much as for him. For months he had gone to sleep and woken with that face in his mind and name on his lips until he had forced himself to forget the girl from Hamestan.

His mind began travelling down a long untrodden path, waking senses that had slept for years. He caught himself, ashamed that he should be thinking of such things at a time like this.

She had begged him to help her. He bunched his fists. Once he would have protected Constance Arnaud unthinkingly, but she had made her choice when she did not follow him.

'Wulf was right,' Ulf muttered, breaking his reverie. 'It was a bride the Pig was bringing.'

Caddoc flinched and looked at Gerrod who was still cradling his son's body, oblivious to everything that was happening around him. Wulf's name was too raw to be spoken without grief drowning him.

The boy had been wrong, though. If this truly was Constance Arnaud she could not possibly be a bride for de Coudray. He couldn't tell the men that without revealing he knew her identity. He'd worked hard to be accepted in the group and if he revealed himself as a friend to Normans he'd put that in jeopardy.

'Do you think the baron's bride would travel in such a manner? This could be anyone,' he said. 'Probably the knight's whore.'

Constance—until it was confirmed otherwise he could not help thinking of her as that—was beginning to stir. A hint of pink was returning to her cheeks, giving them an alluring blush. Caddoc pushed himself to his feet.

'This changes things,' Osgood said. '*She* changes things.'

'It changes nothing,' Caddoc answered. He frowned at the enormity of the lie. The plan had been simple. They had come for the contents of the box, yet here he stood with two dead bodies, his companion beside himself with grief, and a woman he had never imagined seeing again. The cur that now lay dead had ignored the lady's plight in preference for saving the strongbox. Whatever it contained must be important to de Coudray if the bodyguard was willing to risk the life of his charge to protect it.

'We take the box and anything else with us as we planned. Tie the prisoners together. Hurry, there's no guarantee the road will be empty for long.'

'Let's just kill them and be done with it,' Gerrod snarled.

'No!' Caddoc said sharply. 'I wanted no killing in the first place and I don't want any more now.'

'What about her?' Osgood asked. 'What do we do with this Norman bitch?' He glared at Constance, still cradling his nose between his hands in a manner that promised trouble.

Caddoc pursed his lips. He was happy to leave the men to take their chances, but leaving a woman undefended in the forest to whatever might befall her was wrong. Besides, a sister could be as useful an instrument to use against de Coudray as a bride.

'She might be useful. We'll take her, too.'

Chapter Four

Caddoc.

That was his name now. He had worn it so long that his old one sounded false in his ears and he laid claim to no other. When Constance awoke he would impress that on her. By whatever means it took. He placed Constance's dagger in his belt alongside the sheath containing his own.

As he expected, his declaration they would be taking her was met with mixed reactions. Ulf began protesting about the dangers of letting an enemy into the camp, Gerrod tore himself from his son's body and began growling for revenge. Only Osgood showed any approval. He finally let go of his swollen nose and moved his hands to their more usual position between his legs.

'If that was her man he has no more use for her.' He grinned, glancing at the corpse of the bodyguard. 'She can warm our beds instead. Do you think Norman dugs taste as sweet as English when you suckle them? They feel similar enough beneath the fingers.'

Caddoc moved to stand in front of Constance, blocking Osgood's view.

'She'll not be used for that,' he said sharply.

'Not by us, you mean.' Osgood's expression darkened. 'I saw the way you looked at her. You want her yourself.'

Caddoc looked behind him to where Constance lay, his eyes roving from her feet to head. The tunic she wore was a man's, cut to the knee and revealing legs that were shapely inside hose that were bound at the calves with cords. The foot sticking out at an awkward ankle was the final confirmation he needed that this was Constance Arnaud. Her cloak spread beneath her and the heavy tunic hinted at a figure that was obviously not male, cinching in by means of a belt at a narrow waist and rising over the swell of her breasts.

Caddoc's guts twisted with desire. She'd grown from a slender girl into a full woman in the years since he'd last seen her. Or touched her.

Of course he wanted her. Who wouldn't?

He tore his gaze away.

'She'll not be used by any of us. No one touches her.' He mustered a crooked smirk that he bestowed on Osgood. 'Though I'm sure the sight of her will give us all the means to sweeten our nights.'

He strode to the monk and guard who knelt by the horses, hands bound behind them.

'Who knew you were travelling with a woman?' he asked quietly. 'Did either of you?'

Both men nodded.

Caddoc delivered a swift kick to the knee of the guard who cried out in pain.

'And neither of you cared to protect her when we attacked?'

'We were told to protect the contents of the box,' the guard muttered.

'By Lord de Coudray?' Caddoc asked.

'By the lady,' the guard answered, 'and she insisted on dressing like that despite Rollo telling her it was unfitting.'

Caddoc raised his eyebrows. So the box was important to Constance, too. She had said it was her property. Jewels probably in that case. Constance could try buying her freedom with a bangle or two. She gave a sigh that drew his attention back to her. Her eyes were closed, but she was moving her head from side to side. Her skin was slick with a sheen of sweat, causing tendrils of hair to stick to her cheeks.

'Get some water from the river,' he instructed.

Ulf pulled the leather cap from his head and filled it. He returned and poured it over Constance's head. Before Caddoc could protest that wasn't what he had meant Constance's eyes opened and her body convulsed.

With a cry of shock she pushed herself to a seated position, scrabbling back on her heels. Her hand whipped to her waist, feeling the empty sheath where her dagger belonged. She stared frantically around her, then she paled at the sight of the four men standing over her.

Caddoc pushed forward and knelt astride her. She opened her mouth to speak and he clamped one hand across it, pressing down firmly, the other behind her head, buried deep into her thick coil of hair to stop her twisting away. Constance's brown eyes widened and Caddoc watched as the emotion in them changed from confusion to terror.

'My name is Caddoc,' he said. He lowered his voice low so only she could hear. 'You don't know me. If you want your throat to stay unslit, you will give no indication that we have ever met, much less were friends. Do you understand?'

Her lips moved beneath his palm, her breath warm, and the movement making his skin tingle. It sent a shiver up the length of his arm. Constance gave a slight nod.

'I'm going to let go of you now,' Caddoc said, loud enough for the men to hear. 'If you try to run as you did before, you won't get three paces without a sword through your leg. Nod if you agree to be sensible.'

Another nod, but now her eyes blazed contempt. Caddoc removed his hands and stepped away. Constance climbed unsteadily to her feet. She brushed her hands down her body and legs to straighten her tunic, then froze. Her eyes travelled round her audience and she pulled her cloak around her body protectively, reaching up to lift her cowl over her head.

'We know you're a woman,' Osgood reminded her. She dropped her hands to her sides.

'Who are you?' Gerrod growled, stalking across to tower over her.

Caddoc watched as the short, slender woman faced the giant bear of a man. He expected her to cower, but instead she straightened her back, raised her chin and looked him in the eye. In a voice that betrayed none of the fear he imagined she was feeling she answered, 'I am Constance Arnaud. I am travelling to Hamestan to the house of Robert de Coudray. When he finds out what you have done he will have your heads.'

She included Caddoc in the look of hatred she flashed around. He doubted any of them heard her threat because at the name of de Coudray they began shouting over her. He cursed his lack of foresight. He had warned her not to speak his name, but had placed no injunction on her not to reveal her own.

Gerrod seized her by the arms and began dragging her across the path until he had backed her against the trunk of a tree.

'Give me a sword,' he roared. 'I'll send her back to the Pig a piece at a time.'

Constance's face drained of colour.

The guard started to struggle to his feet, only to be kicked in the chest by Ulf. Osgood picked up his staff and advanced on the monk.

'Enough!' Caddoc roared.

Gerrod spat an oath. He pulled the rope from his waist and began to bind Constance to the tree, overpowering her struggles with ease as he passed the rope around her waist and chest, pinning her arms to her side.

'I said get me a sword.' Gerrod turned to Constance and snarled, 'My son died today. Your blood can join his.'

'Please, no,' Constance begged. 'I have harmed no one!'

Her lips trembled and Caddoc realised her self-possession was ice thin. She turned her wide brown eyes on her captor.

'Please, have compassion.'

'There is no place for compassion in the world you people have created,' Gerrod snarled.

Constance winced.

Caddoc pressed his fingertips to his temples. He looked to where Wulf lay, his face serene in death. He was younger than Caddoc had been the year of the conquest. He would never reach the age when Caddoc had been whipped and mutilated by this woman's brother-in-law. He brushed his finger over his lobeless ear. How could he deny Gerrod the revenge he sought when every day the same yearning for vengeance had consumed him for years?

'Then you?' Constance said. Her face was white and her eyes wide with terror. Caddoc's heart thundered with an intensity that was painful. Perhaps she read it on his face because her expression changed, courage flowing into her face.

'Will you intervene for me? Caddoc.'

A spear of lightning coursed through Caddoc at the inflection with which she spoke his name. Was she threatening him? It sent an unexpected thrill through him. He came closer, masking the admiration he felt. He put a hand on Gerrod's shoulder.

'Let me speak to her,' he asked. 'I want to know what she thinks she has to bargain with.'

Gerrod moved back to Wulf's body like a sleepwalker and began cradling it once more. Caddoc crossed his arms, planted his legs apart and faced

Constance a pace away from her. She looked away first and his lips twitched into a triumphant smile.

'These are the men I live with. I owe them my loyalty. Why should I save you?' he asked.

'Because I saved your life,' she reminded him quietly. She raised her head and met his gaze. 'I won't insult you by asking for compassion. I can see you don't possess that, but you owe me a debt. A life for a life. Yours for mine.'

No compassion? It wounded him deeper than he expected, but what room did he have in a life such as his for a thing such as that?

Caddoc ground his teeth. She clearly did not intend to invoke the closeness they had once shared, though she could not have forgotten it. Perhaps it meant so little to her she did not think it worth recalling. He pictured Constance's body swinging on the scaffold in Hamestan marketplace. Saw the look of anguish on de Coudray's face as he beheld the corpse of his sister-in-law. The Pig's cries rang like song in Caddoc's imagination. Bile filled his throat. He swallowed it down, shutting his eyes in denial of what he had wanted to do. He opened his eyes to find Constance still staring at him.

'Very well. If they will accept my intervention, my debt is repaid, but that is all I can do for you. Your courage is admirable, but if you insist in provoking trouble I will not protect you further.'

He turned his back on her so he did not have to read the expression on her face.

'There's no point in acting rashly. If she is a friend of de Coudray, she may be more use to us alive than dead,' he said. 'It's getting dark and I want to be gone. If things change we can reconsider how we use her, but no one else is dying now.'

Gerrod raised his head. He peered through red-rimmed eyes at Caddoc, then past him at Constance.

'I'm sorry for your loss,' she whispered.

Caddoc tensed, waiting for Gerrod to explode. Was the woman determined to die after all? He had always believed her intervention in his execution had been motivated by her feelings for him, but now he wondered if she was simply incapable of keeping quiet when she should know better.

Gerrod sagged like a sack losing its contents.

'Take her alive if you will,' he said to Caddoc, and sighed. 'But anything that happens will be on your head. Let's be gone from here.'

The men sorted matters quickly. The remaining guard was stripped of his boots, cloak and mail and left blindfold with his hands bound behind him to the bridge.

'Tell whoever finds you that Caddoc the Fierce sends his regards,' Caddoc growled.

The cart blocking the bridge was righted and

Wulf's body, wrapped in his father's cloak, was gently placed in the back alongside the strongbox and panniers. The two other corpses were left beside the path. The monk pleaded and was allowed to speak his prayer over them. Gerrod did not protest when he glanced towards Wulf and allowed the monk to repeat his prayer before securing him alongside the guard.

Through it all Constance had said nothing, but when Caddoc loosened the rope binding her he noticed the tracks in the dirt on her cheeks. They could have been from the water Ulf had thrown on her, but she saw him looking and violently wiped a sleeve across her face.

'You'll travel in the cart at first, but soon we'll be walking,' he told her.

'I'll need my stick,' she answered, pointing to the staff she had thrown in his path. He retrieved it quickly, noting that while he left her she stood motionless and did not try to run. Good. She was able to take advice when she chose which might be enough to keep her alive.

Ulf led Constance to the cart and lifted her into the back. He bound her wrists together, securing the end of the rope to the rail at the side of the cart, then pulled her cloak around her to hide her bonds from anyone who might pass by.

'Blindfold her,' Caddoc instructed.

Constance moaned softly.

'We can't let her see where we're taking her,' he explained, more for her benefit than Ulf's. 'I don't want any chance of her leading de Coudray to us.'

'How would she do that?' Osgood asked. He ripped his dagger through the dead guard's cloak, tearing off a long, wide strip that he wound tightly around Constance's eyes. He pulled her hood down across her face and spoke close to her ear. 'Once she's there she won't be leaving.'

Caddoc clenched his fists. He could not contradict Osgood's words and had no idea what would transpire, but for good or ill the decision was made.

Constance jolted around in the darkness, feeling sicker with every lurch of the cart. She had lost her sense of direction almost as soon as the cart started moving and now it no longer felt like they were on the road, but she could not be sure. She had tried tallying each time the wheel creaked a full turn, but had lost count, and with it all track of time. It was getting darker, though. The colder air that caressed the lower half of her face told her that the sun must have set.

Bound together her hands could not fully grip hold of the wooden rail and she shifted with each movement.

She wished her hands were free and she could brace herself against the side of the cart.

She wished she had crept away to safety before she had been noticed rather than drawing attention to herself trying to help.

She wished she could not clearly picture the expression on Aelric's face when she had appealed to him to save her from death.

He had considered letting the big man kill her. She had seen the temptation in his eyes before he had saved her. Aelric, the gentle boy who once had never wielded a sword. If she had not seen the scar Robert had given him she would never have believed the angry-eyed, bearded wild man could be the same person.

The cart stopped abruptly. Someone fumbled with the rope, untying it from the rail, but leaving Constance's hands bound. He took tight hold of her by her upper arms and hauled her to her feet. She wondered whose hands they were. Not Aelric—or Caddoc, as she supposed she must now think of him—she suspected he would have been gentler. Perhaps not, though. Her first hope on recognising him was that he would prove an ally. Now she was far from sure he was a friend to her at all, but his good grace was all that had kept her alive.

She was lifted from the cart, placed on her feet and turned around. A bottle was put to into her hands. Her unseen captor helped her raise it to her lips and she drank thirstily, not caring what the contents were. It turned out to be beer. The weak, sour-tasting brew she remembered from when she had lived in Cheshire before. She pulled a face.

'I supposed a fine Norman lady like you would prefer wine.' The voice she recognised as belonging to Osgood spoke scathingly from somewhere off to her left.

So it had not been him who had dragged her from the cart. She breathed a sigh of relief. Despite his harsh words he had stared at her with open hunger he did not bother to conceal and it made her flesh crawl. She was glad he had not been the one to touch her.

She did not dignify his jibe with an answer, but the idea of a warm cup of wine had never been more appealing. She took another deep swig of beer out of pride before holding the bottle out for someone to take it.

'Let's keep going,' Aelric said. 'We're leaving the cart with Osgood and going the rest of the way on foot.'

A hand took hold of her elbow and began to lead her. Constance stiffened instinctively at the unfamiliar touch of a man. Memories of Piteur leading her to his chamber reared up unpleasantly, causing her to gag. She stuck her feet out nervously, not knowing what was in front of her, and took a few shuffling steps. Her foot squelched into a puddle and she pulled it out with a cry of disgust, causing her to lose her balance. The grip on her elbow tightened and a hand rested on her lower back, guiding her onward firmly. She succeeded in taking a few more steps until her foot snagged on something in the undergrowth and she stopped again.

'You'll have to walk faster than this,' Aelric muttered in her ear. 'The others are already far ahead.'

So it was his hand at her waist. The knowledge sent disconcerting shivers down Constance's spine.

'I can't. I need my stick,' she said irritably.

'I'm not giving you something you can use as a weapon,' Aelric said with a laugh.

'What do you think I could do blindfold and with my hands bound?' Constance demanded.

'I'll help you,' Aelric replied.

His arm came around her waist. He held her close to his side and began guiding her, muttering instructions where to place her feet to avoid tangles. For the first time since the ambush she felt oddly safe. Her body relaxed as she leaned against him, but her mind whirled at the contact, sending her back into the past.

The second time they met it had been spring, not many weeks later than it was today. A time after they had settled in Hamestan, but before the thegns rose against her people. A market day filled with rare laughter and music where Constance had believed they were becoming accepted, that they could live in peace alongside each other.

There had been dancing and she'd watched enviously as the girls spun about the circle with their skirts flying, trying to ignore the stares and whispers.

Aelric had been at the centre of the knot, a set of pipes to his lips and his red-blond hair falling into his eyes. He had paused his tune as he spotted her watching and threaded his way through the circle towards her and held out his hand. When she indicated the stick she leaned on his expression hadn't been one of pity or ridicule like she was used to, but regret. Instead of turning immediately back to the dance he'd taken her hand and bowed, then walked with her through the marketplace, leaving his friends behind.

She'd fallen a little bit in love with him at that moment and now his touch was in danger of awakening something long dormant.

'Constance! What are you doing?' Aelric muttered angrily in her ear, bringing her sharply back to the present.

She realised she had stopped walking again. Disconcerted that she had been thinking of such things, she shook herself free of his hold only to find her hair tangling in a low branch. She reached her hands up, flailing around her head.

'This is too hard,' she complained. 'I keep

catching my feet and tripping. You'll have to let me see where I'm going.'

He spoke rapidly in a language she did not understand, but from the tone of the throaty, lyrical words he was swearing.

'When will you cease trying to push my tolerance? I've told you no and I've told you why.'

Constance stamped her good foot in frustration.

'Unless we're in the centre of Hamestan itself I doubt I'll recognise where we are,' she snapped, and then as an afterthought, added: 'In fact, I probably wouldn't recognise Hamestan either. I haven't been there for seven years.'

There was silence, then the cloth was pushed back from her eyes by callused hands. Even dusk seemed bright after the blackness she had been subjected to. She stared around. Aelric need not have feared that she would be able to lead anyone to them. The trees were broad trunked and towered over them with no sign of a pathway and every direction looking identical. They could have been anywhere.

'Thank you,' Constance said. She risked a smile, but Aelric remained stern faced. His eyes flickered to the side and she followed his gaze. The two other men were watching them suspiciously. Her stomach clenched as she saw the large man was carrying the body of his son. Unbidden her lip trembled. She held her hands up in front of her and raised an eyebrow at Aelric questioningly.

'I'll give you your sight, but your hands will remain bound,' Aelric said.

'Why?' Constance asked. 'I'm not going to run. I can't and even if I could your friends would cut me down quick enough.'

She raised her chin and looked at him disdainfully. 'That would solve your dilemma, wouldn't it? If I died and it was nothing of your doing, your conscience would be clear!'

Aelric bared his teeth. He reached for the dagger at his waist and she feared she had gone too far, but he cut her bonds. Blood rushed into her hands and she rubbed her wrists vigorously until they stopped stinging.

'Thank you,' she said.

Aelric ignored her. He whistled and the older man threw Constance's stick to him. Aelric pushed it into her hands, nodding curtly. 'No more delays.'

He held out a hand for her to pass by and she walked in front of him to where the other man beckoned her. Though she had to grit her teeth in determination not to show the discomfort she was in she could not prevent a wave of relief cresting inside her. Aelric had done as she asked. It was a small triumph, but it was a victory nevertheless and for the first time hope stirred inside her.

Chapter Five

'When we stop I'm going to blindfold you.'

They had been walking in silence for at least an hour so when Aelric's voice came, low in her ear, she jumped in surprise.

'Have I done something to anger you?' she asked. She tried to keep her voice steady, but the fear of being subjected once more to the helplessness of the dark caused hands of terror to grip her throat. She could think of no way in which she had disobeyed him. She had walked as fast as she was able and had given no indication she was hoping to escape. As they wound their way deeper into the forest she had given up all intention of that. Better to remain a captive than die lost in the woods.

Aelric gave her an appraising look. 'No, you've behaved as I asked, but we're closer to my camp now and there are landmarks I would rather you didn't see.'

He walked ahead, leaving her in the charge of the older of his two companions while he joined the huge man who carried the body of his son. As they walked they conferred in low voices, occasionally pausing to look back towards Constance. Once or twice Aelric offered to take the body of the boy, but the father clutched his burden tighter to him.

She glanced surreptitiously from side to side as they walked, not wanting to draw attention to the fact she was doing so. The trees were still as dense, but they had been climbing gently uphill for a while. She did not think they could be close to Hamestan and wondered where they might be that Aelric was worried she could recognise. She had given up the slight hope that she might still have a chance for freedom, but perhaps the information would come in useful in the future.

When they reached a small clearing Aelric returned to her side.

'Sit down and rest. We're going to wait here for a while. Gerrod and Ulf are returning ahead of us to take Wulf's body to his mother.'

'His mother?'

Aelric frowned. 'That surprises you?'

She nodded. She had imagined it to be just the five men who had attacked her party. She lowered herself to the ground, leaning back against a tree and stretching her legs out.

'Rollo, my bodyguard, said the forests were full of wild men but I thought there would be just men,' Constance said.

'Your bodyguard was right. There are fugitives and outlaws living all over the country, but there are women and children, too. Families without anywhere else to live.' He stared at her and his face flushed with anger. 'Did you think your brother was the only one to take the homes from people? They had to go somewhere.'

'My brother-in-law.'

Constance spat the correction instinctively, glaring at him. Aelric raised his eyebrow. It was possible that the only thing keeping her alive was Aelric's belief that Lord de Coudray would care about her safety. She wondered what her brother-in-law would say when he discovered her abduction. What of Jeanne? Surely her sister would beg Robert to act to ensure Constance's safe return?

'You say you haven't been to Hamestan for seven years?' Aelric said suspiciously. 'I think you'll find it much changed.'

'Have you been here all along?' Constance asked.

'No. I come and go. Staying in one place isn't wise. I've been to Wales and Gloucester. Colchester, too. I even saw the coast of France one time.'

Constance felt light-headed. He must have travelled almost past her doorstep to reach Gloucester, not knowing that she lived close by, spending her friendless days in misery.

Homesickness for the land she had left so long ago filled her and she gave a sniff of sadness. Caddoc looked at her strangely, then pulled his hood over his face and sat down beside her in silence until Gerrod and Ulf had vanished among the trees. No birds called in this part of the wood and the wind had stilled.

'Why aren't we going with them?' Constance asked.

'I want to keep your presence hidden if I can, so I'll take you into the camp while everyone is distracted,' Aelric replied. 'How long do you think you would live if they saw you after seeing his body?'

Constance bit her lip and looked at her hands. If she were in that position, she would want to harm anyone she could hold responsible. She rubbed her leg to try to ease the ache that gripped her bones.

'Are you in pain?' Aelric asked unexpectedly.

'No more than I'm used to,' Constance replied, indicating her ankle.

Exhaustion hit her like a fist. She closed her eyes and leaned her head back against the tree, thinking it would be all too easy to fall asleep here and not get up again. If she did, would Aelric leave her there to die or carry her to his camp? Images from the past flooded her mind, threatening to upset her composure as nothing else that day had done.

'You can't go to sleep here,' Aelric said firmly.

He nudged her in the ribs and she opened her eyes with a scowl. He passed her a small bottle and Constance took a large swig before realising it wasn't the weak beer she had drunk before but a deep, rich spirit. She coughed as the liquid hit the back of her throat and tears sprang to her eyes. She took a smaller sip that warmed her from the inside as the liquor travelled through her. She held the bottle out to Aelric who took it without a word, drank and stowed it beneath his cloak.

Constance caught flash of metal at his waist. She thought at first it was her dagger until she realised with a start it had a twin tucked into the belt beside it. He still had the dagger she had given him so long ago, and, more crucially, hers was not securely sheathed. If only she could reclaim it, she would not be in such a vulnerable position.

'If you're going to blindfold me, does that mean you plan to set me free at some point?' she ventured.

Aelric said nothing for long enough that Constance began to fear the answer. She searched his half-hidden face for recognition of the gentle boy she had known, but his eyes were iron-hard and the shaggy beard hid the lips that had once eagerly sought hers.

'I don't know. I hope you will be useful to us, but in truth I cannot say what will happen,' he said abruptly. 'The choice may not be mine to make.'

His voice was cold. Fear surged through Constance, clutching at her stomach and twisting tightly. They already had her jewels, although they could not know that, and she felt sick imagining what other uses they could put her to.

'But you're their leader,' she protested. 'They listened to you before. They would do what you decided again.'

Aelric snorted in surprise. 'Their leader? Not at all. These are free men. There are no leaders here and in any case I would not be that man.'

He pulled his hood back and fixed her with an intense expression that looked out of place on the face in Constance's memory. The Aelric she had grown fond of had been a gentle boy, serious and scholarly. He would never have been a leader. She wondered if he still played the pipe and danced, but she doubted it.

'I have not been with the men long enough to earn such a position,' Aelric explained. 'I have barely earned their trust and preventing Gerrod from killing you today may have put that in jeopardy. More so thanks to you naming me.'

'Why do you call yourself Caddoc?'

Aelric grinned coldly. 'A man must have a name and I gave up Aelric when I became a fugitive. Perhaps my new one will strike fear into Norman hearts in time.'

'How do you hope to achieve that?' Constance asked.

'Taking what is theirs. Making their lives harder. Making them wish they had never come to my land.'

He took the strip of cloth that had covered Constance's eyes and began wrapping it around his hand. He unwrapped it again, repeating the action over and over until Constance began to wonder whether or not he was aware of doing it at all. She imagined it tightening around her throat until she could no longer breathe and gave a shiver.

'You wanted to let him kill me, didn't you?' she said quietly. 'I saw it on your face.'

He tightened his fist at her accusation and Constance's stomach clenched.

'It would have made matters easier,' he admitted after a tense silence.

'The Aelric I once knew would never have contemplated letting a woman be murdered, whether for vengeance or convenience,' Constance said scornfully.

He whipped his head round. 'The Aelric you knew is dead. He died on the day my family died and I was whipped and mutilated. Only Caddoc lives now.'

'And Caddoc is a killer?' Constance retorted.

She tossed her head back. 'I should have let my brother-in-law send you to the mines if this is what you've become. I should have granted you your wish to die.'

Aelric slammed his fist against the tree beside him and he rounded on her in fury.

'What else could I have become? I left Hamestan with nothing and no one.'

His voice contained an unspoken accusation.

'You think I just abandoned you…?' she began. She was trembling again, but from anger not fear. 'Aelric, I tried—'

He cut her off abruptly. 'What I think doesn't matter now. It ceased to matter seven years ago when I left without you. My life has been hard, but I've learned to live with that. Dwelling on the past will not alter the present and I don't want to hear what might have been.'

'*Your* life has been hard!' she exclaimed. The unfairness of his declaration incensed her, but his expression was so deadly that she swallowed her explanation down.

'My Aelric truly is dead,' she said bitterly.

He jumped to his feet and towered over her, his eyes blazing. In the dim light Constance could see that beneath the scraggy beard his cheeks were red with anger. He opened his mouth, then shut it again and turned his head away.

'It's time we left.'

Constance began to rise and Aelric reached for her arms. She shrugged him off roughly and pushed herself upright.

'I don't need your assistance,' she said. She let her eyes fall on the cloth wrapped around Aelric's fist and lifted her face defiantly.

'Bind my eyes, then, and let's be off,' she said firmly.

When he did not move she seized his hands and violently pulled them towards her face, stepping closer to him as she did until they resembled lovers about to kiss. She had to crane her head upright so they were eye to eye; she had never been tall, but the difference between them had widened in the years they had been apart.

In so many ways.

Aelric shook his hands free and unfurled the cloth, his eyes never leaving Constance's. He placed his hands back where she had put them and as his fingers touched her cheeks to reach behind her head he paused. Just before the cloth took her sight Constance saw the widening of Aelric's blue eyes. The attraction he felt for her that she had seen on so many occasions filled his face once again, shedding the years from him.

She forced herself to remain calm and silent as the darkness claimed her once more, focusing instead on what she had just seen. Aelric might be as dead as he claimed to be, but Caddoc was a man. Like all men he had hungers that would need appeasing and when he touched her it had clearly had an effect on him. Her throat tightened with distaste, imagining the uses her captors might have for her. She had hoped she had put such degradation and pain behind her when Piteur died, but if it took that to keep her alive or regain her freedom, Constance would use every advantage it gave her.

Once more they travelled slowly, one of Aelric's arms around Constance's waist, the other on her shoulder to guide her. He kept her close to him with her back pressed against his chest, edging her forward and not speaking unless to give her an instruction to mind her feet or duck her head. They were still climbing and her foot slipped, jarring her knee. She sobbed in pain and without speaking Aelric lifted her off her feet. Instead of holding her as a lover might he hefted her over his shoulder so she ended up with her head and arms hanging down his back.

He moved quicker this way, his arms gripping behind Constance's knees so she did not slip. The position was undignified and she took it as a sign that he had no intention of recreating the affection they had once shared, but faced with the choice of walking or being carried she did not protest. Eventually he put her on her feet again, holding her by the shoulders until she regained her balance. He spoke for the first time.

'Keep your arms out to the side to feel your way and say nothing if you value your safety.'

He turned Constance about and took hold of her hands, extending her arms either side of her. Her fingers touched rough stone on either side. She felt upwards to discover the rocks extended higher than she could reach.

'Are we in a cave?' she asked in alarm.

'Do you think Saxons are animals?' he grunted. 'Let's go.'

He put his arms at either side of her waist and guided her forward through what felt like the narrow entrance to a tunnel. When her fingers ran out of rock and a bitter wind surged around her, tugging at her cloak, Constance stopped walking. She waited for Aelric's instructions, or for the removal of the blindfold. Neither happened, but by now her attention was on the noise that assailed her ears.

Cries of grief and anger filled the air, but above them all screams of anguish tore from the throat of a woman. Hesitantly Constance reached her hands up and pulled at the cloth covering her eyes. They were under a cloud-filled sky on a bare ridge and what she had supposed was a tunnel was the gap between two towering rock faces. It was dark now and only the half-moon gave any light.

Constance glanced towards Aelric, expecting to be reprimanded for removing her blindfold, but he was not even looking in her direction. He stood with arms folded and head lowered, his lips a thin line of sorrow.

A small cluster of men and one or two women huddled around a woman who was half-lying on the ground, clutching at Gerrod who knelt beside her. The woman's grief was so immense and all-consuming that she could only have been the boy's mother. Constance's vision blurred as her heart twisted in sickening sympathy. Instinctively she took a step forward, but felt a hand on her shoulder. She looked up and Aelric shook his head sternly. She wiped away the tears that had begun to fall, feeling her grief was out of place. Her arrival had passed by most of the people who were more concerned with the discovery of Wulf's death, for which Constance was grateful.

The man called Ulf sidled over. He muttered something in Aelric's ear, then glanced towards Constance.

'Be discreet and you'll stay safe,' Aelric replied. Ulf nodded and drew his cloak back to reveal a curved sickle at his waist. He slipped away between the rocks.

'Come with me,' Aelric instructed quietly. He took Constance's arm and led her away from the crowd towards what appeared to be a high rock face covered with trees. As they got closer she saw the branches concealed a square stone building. Aelric moved aside a large skin and pulled open a door. He nudged Constance inside the building, closing it behind them.

It smelled disconcertingly of daily life. Wood smoke overlaid the fragrance of human bodies, which in turn mingled with a lingering scent of onions and meat that made Constance's mouth water. A small fire pit provided scant heat and light, but after the bitter wind it was as welcome as any hearth she had sat beside. Whatever she had to face faded into insignificance compared to her need to rest. She limped across the room and sagged weakly on to a stool beside the fire. Closing her eyes, she held her hands out to the glowing coals, rubbing them together vigorously until her fingers moved easily once more.

She glanced around at the straw pallets littering the room and looked pleadingly at Aelric.

'I'm so tired,' she whispered.

'You can't stay here,' he said. He pointed to an unstable-looking set of steps knocked into the back wall that led to a trapdoor. 'You'll sleep up there.'

Constance stood, but her legs began to tremble and her head spun. She reeled, but before she fell Aelric's arms were around her, holding her upright.

'I don't think I can walk any further,' she gasped.

'I'll carry you,' he said. Instead of swinging her over his shoulder as he had previously done Aelric lifted her into his arms, holding her against his chest. Constance rested her hands in her lap. To put them round his neck would be too familiar and she had not forgotten the daggers at his waist. If she could somehow reach one…

Her hand crept towards his waist. As her fingertips brushed against his belly he drew a sharp breath, his head whipping down to glare at her with suspicion. She withdrew her hand hastily, abandoning all idea of stealing her dagger back.

Aelric edged his way up the narrow staircase, ducking his head to climb through the hatch. He put Constance back on her feet. The loft was filled with sacks and smelled sweetly of straw, almost like the barn where once…

No! Don't think of that, Constance instructed herself.

'You'll stay here until I can decide what to do with you. I'll bring you a blanket and some food.' Aelric's eyes flickered from her face to her body. 'I'll try to find you something more appropriate to wear, too,' he said disapprovingly.

'I'll keep my own clothes,' Constance said with dignity, smoothing her tunic down.

Aelric raised an eyebrow, then disappeared down through the hatch. Constance sat on the bare floorboards, leaning back against one of the sacks. She unbraided her hair, then ran her fingers through her it, detangling the long locks and feeling the knots of tension in her scalp start to disperse. She bowed her head and hugged her knees. When she looked up again Aelric was standing over her, arms laden. He lowered a thin straw-stuffed mattress to the floor and dropped a blanket from beneath his other arm. He handed Constance an earthenware pot that contained pottage that had a familiar flavour.

'Venison,' she remarked. 'A fine animal for outlaws to be breeding.'

Aelric smirked and folded his arms across his chest.

'What of it? The lords have so many deer they won't miss one or two, even one as gluttonous as the Pig.'

The name was what they had called Sir Robert.

'We're on my brother-in-law's land?' Constance asked.

Aelric's smile vanished. 'Not necessarily. Eat if you want it, if not there are plenty with empty bellies.'

Aelric watched as Constance emptied the bowl, his face in the dim light an impassive mask.

'Why did you weep for Wulf?' he asked once she had finished. 'You didn't know the boy. You would have fought against him if he had tried to capture you.'

'He was young,' Constance said. She pictured the sightless eyes and beardless face. 'His life was cut short and I wept for his mother. No one should have to face that grief.'

An odd look passed across Aelric's face. 'You still have a compassionate nature, I see. For young men at least. The years haven't changed you so much.'

It did not sound like a compliment.

Constance folded her arms defensively, feeling once again the sharp bite of Robert's belt buckle across her back. That had been nothing compared to the other agonies that had followed and through the fear and exhaustion she had felt since her ordeal began a new emotion stirred within her: indignation. He had talked of the hardships he had faced, but Aelric had no idea what she had endured since they parted and she had no intention of telling him now. She pushed herself to her feet and put her hands on her hips.

'The years have changed me more than you know,' she said coldly. 'I am under no obligation to share that with you and I doubt you would be interested anyway.'

'You're right,' Aelric snapped. 'I am tired and need to rest. You should do the same so I bid you goodnight.'

Constance clenched her fists at his abrupt dismissal. Seething inwardly, she turned her back and stood motionless until the creak of the stairs and the slamming of the hatch told her she was alone. As soon as he was gone she made her way to the window and began to run her fingers across the boards covering them. They were tightly nailed across and even if she could have prised them free it would be futile. She would never survive a drop from the second floor. She pressed her eye to one of the gaps, hoping to see signs that might identify her location. Pinpricks of light flickered in a distant cluster that might indicate a village, but there was nothing that helped her.

Constance returned to the mattress and lay on the pallet, listening to the sounds from below. Low, angry voices floated upwards, accompanied by the sound of crying. A child's voice rose high with confused wailing.

Her indignation flared, remembering Aelric's questioning of her tears for the dead boy. That he, who had been only a handful of years older when she intervened on his behalf, should pour scorn on her sympathy cut her to the core.

If there had been any confirmation needed that she would not be able to rely on their previous friendship to keep her safe, this was it. She still had her body, though. If she could no longer incite feeling in Aelric's heart there were other parts of his body that might respond better. Piteur's temper after a day of unsuccessful business was often eased after he had finished using her. Wrinkling her nose at the comparison, she pulled the blanket around herself, falling asleep as she tried to plan her next course of action.

Chapter Six

Caddoc hunched on the rock and stared out across the countryside. He shivered in his light wool tunic, relishing the wind that gusted around him, tangling his hair with fingers of ice.

Waking too early, he sat outside to watch the pale spring sun rising, casting light over the vale of Hamestan. It was hidden in the early morning freezing fog, but Caddoc knew the sight without needing eyes. He and his brothers had used this tower for their childhood games. He had intentionally sought out men living close to Hamestan, but it had been a cruel coincidence that the group of fugitives he had fallen in with had made their home in a location so well loved from his childhood. This tower was as close as he had been to his old home in many years. Even when it was obscured from his sight, thinking about the cruel punishment that had been inflicted on the land by Bastard William drove swords of rage through him.

He ground his heels against the rock. De Coudray's face rose in his mind, clearer after so long than those of his father or brothers, which struck him as doubly cruel. His fingers itched to slip round the Pig's neck and tighten, to plunge a dagger between the breast or slice the head from the shoulders. He never would, of course. Despite what Constance might assume, he had taken life fewer times than she would believe and never without good reason. He'd sworn the vow to her and honour had compelled him to keep it. The same honour that now compelled him to keep Constance safe even after she had chosen to stay behind rather than run with him years ago. She'd been right in guessing he wanted to know nothing of her life. Hearing how a rich woman spent her idle hours was something he did not intend to put himself through when he lived as he did.

He weighed his dagger in his hand, sighted along the tip and with a flick of the wrist sent it hurtling towards the log he had propped upright at some distance away. The dagger struck with accuracy, embedding itself into the wood. Caddoc allowed himself a brief smile of satisfaction at his skill. This morning ritual had become part of his day and years of practice had given him a faultless eye.

He sent the dagger he had taken from Constance spinning towards its twin. He retrieved both weapons and repeated the action. Twice, three times, four in quick succession; he threw and hit with both blades until the log was pocked with holes, each time imagining the target was de Coudray's heart. He pulled the weapons free and placed them side by side on the ground in front of him. He wondered if she would suspect he still had the gift she had given him and the purpose he dreamed of putting it to.

Gerrod lowered himself down beside Caddoc and they exchanged weary smiles that Caddoc knew neither of them felt. Gerrod's eyes were ringed with dark shadows and the lines on his face had deepened after the night he had spent with his wife and the body of their son.

Caddoc fastened his dagger into its sheath and tucked Constance's into his belt alongside it. He could not return Constance's to her and seeing them nestled together seemed right.

'Elga is finally asleep,' Gerrod said. 'Where did you put the woman?'

Caddoc pointed to the top floor of the tower. Wooden shutters obscured the small windows. Constance would not be able to see the sun. He wondered if she had slept at all. He had resisted the temptation to check on her in the night. Best he had as little to do with her as possible before he found himself longing for the furtive hours they had spent together.

'Whatever is in that box had better be worth all the sorrow it has caused,' Gerrod muttered. 'The woman had better be useful.'

'Osgood will be here before long with it. Then we'll see what she was protecting,' Caddoc answered. 'I should go wake her before he arrives.'

As he stood Gerrod pushed himself to his feet and barred his way.

'I think I'll come with you.' He folded his arms, his face stern. 'Aelric.'

Caddoc opened his mouth to protest, but Gerrod leaned in towards him.

'You can deny it as much as you like, but she called you by another name and it was one you recognised. I want to know why a fine, *Norman* lady such as she claims to be calls you by a name you claim not to know. I don't trust her and I'm beginning to doubt you.'

Caddoc clenched his fists, then released them. Gerrod was a giant of a man. It would do no good to antagonise him unless Caddoc wanted to be on the receiving end of a beating.

'The name was mine until I was exiled. My father was Thegn of Hamestan until de Coudray took his lands and title. I gave up my name when I ran to Wales and took shelter with Emrys of Arllechwydd, my mother's uncle.'

'You've been lying to us about who you are?'

Gerrod growled. 'Why didn't you admit to your name?'

Caddoc sucked his teeth.

'I have grown used to the new one in the seven years I've worn it. I am a fugitive.'

'We all are, lad,' Gerrod said. 'What makes you think the Pig will even remember you after this time?'

Hate filled Caddoc's veins, threatening to consume him. He was unsure what was worse: that he might still be hunted, or that he was so inconsequential as to be forgotten. He lowered his head.

'My father fought to the last. I ran. I'm not worthy of the name he gave me. It burns me inside to know what de Coudray did. What he's still doing to my home. I want de Coudray dead, but Constance was right seven years ago and it still holds true now. I would need an army to get close to him. I can't do it, so I hurt him how I can, when I have the opportunity.'

Gerrod snorted angrily. 'And what is she to you for you to refer to her in so familiar a manner?'

Caddoc swallowed the lump that unexpectedly filled his throat and glanced towards the tower. Constance had been nothing to him for years. She should be nothing now, but his heart had quickened when he put his arms around her and he could not forget the delicate cast of her jaw or the watchful brown eyes that had captivated him so long ago. He was getting himself more tightly wrapped in a net with everything he said.

'I came across her in Hamestan, but I haven't seen or heard of her in seven years.'

He wondered for the first time where she had been. Not Hamestan, unless she was lying, which he doubted. She must have chosen the convent over him, he thought resentfully.

'You came across her?' Gerrod glowered. 'You would go to the trouble you have gone to for a mere acquaintance? Don't try to fool me, lad.'

Aelric bit back his indignation. After his loss Gerrod did not deserve lies to compound his grief and of all the men in camp he was most likely to keep Caddoc's secret.

'I was hostage in her brother's house. Naturally we met. We became friends, then more than friends.' He stared at his hands, losing himself briefly in the memories of Constance's kisses. Her touch had burned his soul whenever they met and brought heat to his cheeks even after all this time.

'We were lovers. Only one afternoon before my father rose up in rebellion. She saved my life. I don't know how or why she came to be travelling with what de Coudray values so much. It may be a coincidence, but I want to find out.'

'Perhaps Wulf was right after all and it was

the woman that de Coudray wished to protect,' Gerrod said.

'Possibly,' Caddoc agreed. 'Or something else I can use against him. I can't forget what he did to my family. One day I'll have my revenge.'

'One day?' Gerrod asked. 'My son is dead because of what we did yesterday. How many days do any of us have?'

Caddoc rested a hand on the big man's arm. 'I grieve for Wulf as you do and the plan to ambush de Coudray's men was not mine.'

Gerrod stared out across the plain below. The mist was lifting, giving them glimpses of bare wasteland and burned-out buildings where once fields of crops and dwellings had stood.

'The best way to avenge your son's death is to discover what is afoot and use it against the Pig,' Caddoc said.

'I don't care any longer about intrigue or revenge, all I want is the means to fill my belly.' Gerrod said gruffly. 'Do you think we can use the woman? Will de Coudray pay for her safe return?'

Caddoc shrugged uncertainly. The rancour in Constance's voice when he had mistakenly called the baron her brother did not imply a loving relationship. On the other hand, years ago he had listened when she begged for his mercy and Constance had risked freeing him when no other person dared intervene. Perhaps de Coudray was more indulgent to his pretty sister-in-law than towards anyone else.

Gerrod stared him down. 'Let's go and find out,' he said grimly. 'For her sake I hope he will because, your lover or not, I'll be more than happy to send the Pig her head after letting Osgood have his fun with her for a day or two.'

Caddoc's stomach clenched. He hoped this wasn't Gerrod speaking but the grief.

'You don't mean that.'

'Why not? Her cursed people have made us suffer enough. What would she care about what happens to us?'

Caddoc looked into his friend's eyes.

'She wept for your son.'

Gerrod's eyes moistened. Caddoc looked away, ashamed of how he had briefly been jealous of the sorrow Constance had shown over Wulf's death.

Gerrod strode into the tower, moving quietly through the still-sleeping figures. He picked up a low stool and a rush light, then made his way up the staircase to Constance's prison. Caddoc followed, tensing. He checked his dagger was in the sheath as he followed the older man, hoping he would not have cause to need it.

Constance was kneeling by the window, face pressed to the cracks where the wood did not quite meet. Her body was shrouded in the blanket he had given her, but her hair was loose and fell almost to her waist, a dark cascade that gleamed chestnut where small rays of light stole through the window coverings. She turned as they entered and looked at them warily, her eyes black smudges in the dim light set into a face as pale as watered milk.

'You won't find out where you are by looking through there,' Caddoc said.

She said nothing.

'Did you sleep well?' Caddoc asked.

'No,' Constance replied coldly. She gestured around at the bare floorboards and thin mattress. 'Did you really expect me to?'

'I regret we cannot give you furs or feather pillows,' Caddoc said drily. How luxurious her life must usually be if that was her first concern. 'We live modestly here and without the comforts your people expect as their birthright.'

'I don't expect them,' Constance answered. Her lip twitched. 'What gaoler provides such luxuries to a condemned prisoner?'

'Don't say such a thing!'

After Gerrod's threats anything Constance might do or say to put further ideas in his head were unwise.

'Isn't that what I am?' She leaned back against the wall, as close to the light as she could. 'If not, then tell me how long you intend to keep me here before releasing me.'

'Until I can decide how best to make use of you,' Caddoc answered.

Constance looked him in the eye. Her gaze was filled with hatred and Caddoc found it impossible to believe she had once looked on him with affection.

'My brother-in-law is a powerful man. When he discovers I have been abducted he will raze the forests to find me. If you release me now, you might live.'

Gerrod had been silent, standing beside Caddoc, but now he walked to where she sat. He swung the stool around in front of him with an exaggerated flourish and sat on it heavily. Constance flinched as the stool leg came towards her, her hands crossing protectively in front of her chest. She was clearly anticipating further violence on top of yesterday's rough handling. It knotted Caddoc's stomach in shame to see.

'My son died yesterday,' Gerrod said without preamble. 'Your bodyguard murdered him trying to protect something. What is it that de Coudray has?'

'How do you know what we were carrying belongs to Lord de Coudray?' Constance asked.

'We knew you were coming,' Gerrod snapped.

'The Pig has hardly kept it a secret that he was awaiting the arrival of something important.'

Constance stretched her legs out, crossing the twisted foot on top of the other, and placed her hands in her lap. Her expression became contemplative.

'It was us you were waiting for? Not just any travellers who passed by?'

Caddoc nodded in confirmation.

'What did you believe it was?' Constance asked. She sounded puzzled and her forehead wrinkled. If she was pretending not to know, her act was convincing.

'We don't know,' Caddoc admitted. 'Something valuable though. Jewels or gold.'

'Or a new bride,' Gerrod said, leering at Constance. 'Is that what your purpose to him is?'

'Lord de Coudray has a wife,' Constance said.

Gerrod smirked. 'Not any more. She died of the flux not three weeks past.'

'You're lying,' Constance whispered. Her cheeks paled further, if such a thing was possible, and her brow furrowed. She struggled to her knees and looked from man to man. The implication of what she had learned struck Caddoc.

'Why do you care?' Gerrod sneered. 'What does the lady's death mean to you?'

'She was my sister.'

Constance hurled herself towards the men with

a cry, fists aloft. Caddoc seized her before she could reach Gerrod. He pushed her arms downwards, trapping them against her sides with his arms locked around her. Instead of struggling she went limp in his arms, her body shaking.

Caddoc had encountered death on many occasions and the final spasms of a body nearing the end of its life were familiar to him. Constance reminded him of that now. Without intending to he shifted his arms, one in the small of her back, the other with a hand resting on her neck beneath her flood of hair, and realised they were no longer imprisoning but comforting her. Something inside Caddoc fluttered like a weak bird. He realised it was his heart.

'You didn't know she was dead?' he asked.

Constance looked at him with eyes that glistened. 'My brother-in-law has told me nothing. Tell me it isn't true,' she entreated.

Her eyes were large and dark with flecks of honey lightening them. Caddoc had forgotten how long her lashes were.

'It's true,' Gerrod muttered harshly.

Constance gave one loud, gulping sob of distress. Caddoc tightened his arms, drawing her head on to his shoulder, and stroked her hair. She shifted slightly and her breasts brushed against his chest, causing all manner of unwanted sensations to assault him. He had held her closely the previous day, but now he was acutely aware of curves that had barely begun to develop when he had known her before. He slipped a hand downwards to rest on her lower back.

'Stop that noise, you silly girl,' Gerrod barked. 'You're not the first person to lose someone.'

Constance drew a shocked breath. Caddoc tightened his arms around her, anger flaring at Gerrod's callousness. He expected her to begin crying once more, but she blinked to clear her tears away and stood motionless in his arms.

'You're right,' she said. She turned a baleful look on Gerrod. 'It was simply the shock of finding out in such a manner.'

Caddoc tilted her chin so she was looking at him.

'Why did your brother-in-law not tell you?'

Constance's eyes slid to the window.

'We do not speak,' she said.

'You said the Pig would raze the forest to find you,' Gerrod muttered.

'I lied.'

Caddoc had to strain to make out her words and could hear the apprehension in her voice. She twisted the edge of her blanket between her fists and her lower lip began to quiver. She bit it to stop the trembling and Caddoc was gripped by the unexpected wish that it was his lips trapping hers.

'I'm afraid I will not be as much use to you as you may have believed.'

Behind her Gerrod scowled dangerously.

'He's still your family,' Caddoc said.

Constance's mouth twisted into a grimace. 'If you're hoping to appeal to his sense of kinship, it will be futile.'

Her eyes flashed with something akin to hate and Caddoc felt her body tense in his hold. He let go of her and stepped away. Constance leaned against the wall, looking weary though the day had barely begun. The conditions she was being kept in must be far from what she was used to. He felt a stab of sympathy, until he reminded himself that what must seem squalid to her was normal for him and countless others who had been displaced so she and her kind could live in comfort.

'The panniers contain my property,' Constance said. 'The box holds my dowry and legacies from my father and husband.'

'Your husband? You are married?' Caddoc asked. His stomach lurched. He had not imagined Constance married, but it made sense. While he was running for his life she had followed the path set out for rich and well-connected girl.

'My husband is dead,' she answered curtly. She folded her arms and jutted out her jaw, her eyes moving from one man to the other. 'You can take everything. I won't need it. I intend to enter a convent as soon as I am able. Take what you want, only give me my freedom in return.'

'What if we want you?' Gerrod growled. 'We already have your gold. What else do you have to bargain with?'

Fear crossed Constance's face. Her hands moved to her cloak, pulling the edges tighter over her breasts in a manner that told him she had given thought to what else they might take.

'Nothing,' she admitted quietly.

Gerrod caught Caddoc by the arm and drew him to the top of the stairs.

'You heard what she said, she's no use to us.'

'We don't know she's telling the truth. Let's wait at least until Osgood gets here.'

'She's turned your head,' Gerrod sneered.

Caddoc narrowed his eyes angrily.

'I just think there is sense in taking the treasure and not risking drawing attention to ourselves.'

'Don't think you can fool me. I saw how you held her. You were having a good feel while you were stopping her getting to me.' He grinned nastily. 'I don't say I'd blame you, lad, she's comely enough, but why should we show her any mercy?'

'It's not mercy, but sense,' Caddoc insisted. 'If we kill her we've lost any chance of bargaining with de Coudray. We're not murderers.'

Gerrod looked at him scathingly. 'We'll leave

her be for now. When Osgood brings the box we'll find out if she's telling the truth.'

He stomped down the stairs out of sight, pulling the trapdoor closed behind him. Caddoc turned back. Constance was still by the window where he had left her.

'Why didn't you tell me the truth before—about your brother-in-law not caring?'

She eyed him with disdain. 'Why do you need to ask? I would have said—or done—anything to remain alive.'

She moved to him. He expected her to stop, but she continued until they were almost touching, causing his throat to tighten. He wanted to hold her more than he had expected. His body cried out for her, but allowing Constance to once again command his affections seemed ludicrous and would end in nothing but misery.

'Thank you for what you did,' she said shyly.

'I told you your life would not be at risk,' he reminded her. 'I keep my word when I give it.'

She raised her head until she was looking at him closely. Now his vision had adjusted to the gloom he noticed faint lines at the corners of her eyes and a solitary crease in the centre of her forehead from too much time frowning.

She was regarding him with equal intensity.

'What is it?' he asked, unnerved by her scrutiny.

'I didn't mean defending me against your companions or keeping me alive,' she said. She lifted a hand, which she placed hesitantly on Caddoc's chest. He should have removed it or stepped beyond her reach, but he didn't. Beneath his tunic his skin fluttered, raising goosepimples as if reacting to an unnoticed breeze.

'I meant how you held me when Gerrod told me of my sister's death,' Constance murmured. 'I wasn't expecting your kindness. I've done nothing to warrant it.'

It had surprised Caddoc, too, but he accepted her thanks with a slight smile.

'I know how it is to lose people I love. I wish you could have found out in a kinder manner. You've lost your husband and now your sister.'

He laid a tentative hand on her shoulder to console her and was surprised to feel the tension she carried.

'I've known so many deaths I barely know how to grieve any more,' she said.

She raised her head. Her lips were slightly parted, smooth, and temptingly close to his. Another step forward and he would be able to kiss her with the slightest tilt of his head. His chest felt tight where her hand rested and he covered it with his own in case she was about to withdraw.

He took the step, parting his lips in anticipation.

Behind him the trapdoor thumped open and Osgood's voice hailed him.

'I've brought the strongbox. Let's see what other prize we've won ourselves!'

Chapter Seven

Constance jumped, just as Aelric jerked away from her touch. She had time enough to see the flash of disappointment that crossed his face before the familiar watchfulness returned to his eyes.

'Good. I was beginning to worry you would never arrive and we'd be giving board to this one for the next ten years,' Aelric said harshly with a jerk of his thumb towards Constance. His sudden animosity was startling. She hoped it was a performance for the sake of his friend.

'You can relieve yourself of that burden at your earliest convenience,' she said tartly.

He waved a hand with a hiss to silence her. She quailed at the prospect of ten years' captivity. Ten days would be a hardship enough, but any longer than that would surely drive her to madness.

Osgood peered around Aelric and spotted Constance. He had clearly not seen what had almost happened between them. Aelric's broad figure must have masked her from view of the hatch. Osgood wrinkled his lip, then his eyes took on a greedy gleam and he licked his lips slowly.

'Who said you could speak, woman?' he grunted. 'Keep your mouth shut until you're told otherwise.'

Constance bit back a retort, still bristling at the reference to herself as a prize. She bowed her head and folded her hands in front of her demurely. She was confident she would appear composed and modest, but inside her heart was beating with an unnerving intensity that had little to do with Osgood's impudence.

She glanced at Aelric again out of the corner of her eye. Yesterday she had been overwhelmed with terror and noticed only the ragged beard and tangled hair. She hadn't appreciated fully how much he had changed in seven years until he had taken her tenderly in his arms. Gone was the scrawny boy whose legs and arms appeared overgrown and ill fitted to his body, and in his place stood a broad-chested man; tall, muscular and handsome.

She had not been wrong in guessing he was still attracted to her. What she had not expected was to feel that interest stirring inside her as if she was sixteen once more. She smoothed the hair back from her cheeks, feeling heat where her palms touched her skin.

Aelric turned his back on her. 'Bring the box over here,' he instructed.

As Osgood carried the small chest under his arm and placed it in the centre of the room. Constance tried to catch Aelric's eye, but to no avail. He kept his face carefully averted from her. Perhaps he was already regretting what they had nearly done. She had not intended to approach him when she did, but he had held her with such tenderness she had been unable to resist her impulse. The risk had been great, but if they had not been interrupted Aelric would have kissed her, she was certain. Perhaps the men would be satisfied with her jewels and would set her free without her needing to resort to such tactics a further time.

Gerrod came back into the room, closing the hatch behind him, and the three men stood over the strongbox. Constance joined them, taking care to keep her distance from Osgood. She could not forget the way he had looked at her yesterday or when he came in today. He wanted her. She had seen it in his eyes the way she had recognised it in Aelric's, but Osgood's expression chilled her, making her remember the expression Piteur always wore before forcing her to submit to him. There would be no kindness in Osgood as a lover.

Her stomach clenched. She moved closer to Aelric, drawing reassurance from his presence.

Osgood knelt and pulled at the iron lock on the chest, but it did not open. He thumped the top with his fist making it wobble.

'It's locked!'

'Of course it will be locked,' Aelric said scornfully. He cast a glance at Constance, the first since they had pulled apart with such haste. 'Did you expect the lady would travel without her valuables carefully secured?'

He gave the strongbox a light kick that had no effect in the slightest. It was taller than it was wide and fell on to one side.

'We'll have to break it open.'

'My bodyguard had a key,' Constance said, 'but you never bothered to search him.'

She took a moment of satisfaction at the dismay on their faces. They began to speak all at once, shouting over each other as to who was to blame for such an oversight. Constance watched them with growing contempt. Norman or Saxon, men were all the same: casting blame and brawling.

'I have a key,' she said quietly.

Osgood was the first to realise she had spoken. He pointed a finger at her accusingly.

'What did you say?'

'I have a key of my own.' She lifted her head haughtily. 'The chest was sent by Lord de Coudray, but do you think I would hand over the only key to someone I knew nothing of?'

'You had better not be tricking us,' Gerrod said darkly.

In answer Constance reached beneath the neck of her tunic. A cord hung down between her breasts, plaited silk so fine it had been missed when Osgood searched her. Perhaps he would have discovered it if he had not laid his hands on her breasts and uncovered her secret. She dangled it in front of their eyes, perversely enjoying the look of surprise that crossed their faces as they viewed the two keys, one for her strongbox and the other for her chest.

Aelric caught her eye and his expression was a mix of outrage and a glint of humour. He held his hand out, but she ignored him and knelt beside the chest, inserting the correct key into the lock and twisting it open.

She pushed the chest towards the men without bothering to look inside. Her legacy from Piteur did not matter and all the ornaments in the world were nothing compared to her freedom.

Aelric shot a look at Constance that chilled her. He threw the lid back. Osgood swore. Gerrod thumped his hand against the wall. Aelric's face was unreadable.

'Is this some form of a jest?' he said coldly. He folded his arms and glared at Constance. 'I would have expected you to have more care for your well-being.'

'It's all I have,' she said desperately. How could it not be enough for men who had nothing of their own? 'You can take everything.'

'Everything of nothing?' Gerrod growled.

Aelric carefully turned the strongbox around so Constance could see the contents. She gazed at it in disbelief, even taking hold of it and pulling it towards her to make sure she was not imagining what she saw, but there was no mistake.

It was empty.

'Is this a trick?' Gerrod growled.

Constance tipped the chest towards her and turned it round and round, examining each side and hoping desperately that it would turn out to be the wrong box. She knew as she did it that she was not mistaken; her key still protruding from the lock was evidence of that, as were the initials of her brother-in-law burned into the oak lid and etched on to the iron lock.

'I don't understand,' she murmured. She raised her eyes to find the three men staring down at her grimly.

'Don't you?' Aelric asked quietly. He folded his arms, his eyes boring in to her, his mouth a grim line. Only a short while before he had been about to kiss her and she had believed some of his old affection had been rekindled. Now he stood beside her other captors, clearly demonstrating his allegiance. Fear coursed through Constance. If he did not believe her, then what hope did she have of convincing his companions that she had not played them false? She saw her prospects of freedom melting like spring snow.

'No! I'm telling you, it should be full,' she declared.

Aelric tilted his head to one side, looking disappointed as much as disbelieving. Constance peered inside once more in case the act somehow made the missing contents reappear. It remained dreadfully empty.

'Well, not *full*,' she amended, 'but there should be rings, a brooch, a bracelet, a purse with coins. It shouldn't be empty.'

'So much for one woman,' Gerrod growled. 'Your husband must have been generous indeed!'

Aelric's head jerked up at Gerrod's words.

'You believe me, don't you?' Constance whispered, hearing the desperation in her voice. 'I've never lied to you.'

'I don't know,' he said slowly.

'Where is it all, then?' Osgood said. 'What did you do with it?'

'Me?' Constance could not prevent a laugh erupting from her. Serious at her situation was, to be accused of stealing her own property was absurd. 'Why would I do that? And when could I have done it?'

Her voice was louder and shriller sounding with every question. She could feel the blood racing through her veins, pumping faster until her heart hammered painfully in her chest.

'Before we attacked you,' Osgood grunted. 'To trick us. You could have left them somewhere on your route to go back for later.'

'What purpose would there have been for me to do that?' Constance cried. She pushed herself to her feet and put her hands on her hips, glaring at the men, unable to believe their stupidity. 'You might just as easily have found the other key on Rollo's body and emptied it before you brought it here.'

Osgood's expression was outraged and he let loose a long string of obscenities, casting aspersions on Constance's parenthood, character and anything else he could think of. Constance let his insults wash over her, eyes on the strongbox that was as empty as her heart was of hope.

'I want my freedom more than I want any riches,' Constance said when he eventually fell silent. 'I told you I would give you everything and I meant it.'

'I believe her,' she heard Aelric say. 'There would be no sense in anything else. She didn't know we were coming for it.'

'Then who took them?' Osgood asked.

Constance lifted the lid once more, wrinkling her brow in puzzlement. 'He's right. Where did everything go?'

Aelric sat back on his heels beside her and folded his arms. 'Tell me everything that happened as you travelled,' he said.

Constance closed her eyes, picturing the route they had taken. The start of the journey seemed so long ago now, another lifetime rather than the two weeks it had taken. Rollo, the bodyguard, had brought the box and two keys. He had watched over Constance as she packed her belongings and kept one key for himself. In case hers was lost, he had explained. Four of them had set out together, joining other travellers on the roads, frequently meeting the same people at hostels or inns.

'My clothes and linens, everything that I own, came with us on a cart as far as Stafford. We stayed the night in Westune at the house of William de Warenne. That was where we met with the monk and swapped guards. Rollo insisted we left the cart to be taken more slowly by two market traders who would be passing through Hamestan,' she recalled. 'And...'

She gave a cry of annoyance and turned to face Aelric.

'That evening Rollo met someone he knew. A servant travelling with his master, Guy de Brançoise, from Shropshire. I was enjoying listening to the bard, but Rollo sent me up to the bedchamber because he said he wanted to do business.' She huffed at the memory. 'I thought their meeting was a coincidence, but he must have taken everything out then and given them to his associate.'

'Rollo was your bodyguard,' Aelric mused. 'The man who ignored your plight in favour of defending the strongbox from Wulf. Why would he do that if he knew it was empty?'

Constance's heart fell. She had been sure that was the answer. She looked at Aelric. His eyes were bright with interest and for a moment they were allies puzzling out the mystery.

'Perhaps he believed he had left something inside,' Constance suggested. 'The next morning he was furious that the traders had left so early before he could speak to them again. Or perhaps in the confusion he had forgotten. After all, we were not expecting to be ambushed!'

'I think you were,' Aelric said, glancing towards Osgood and Gerrod. 'Or at least, your bodyguard knew there was the possibility. It was common knowledge that you were arriving. I don't think that was accidental. De Coudray had made sure word had spread that Rollo would be travelling and bringing something valuable. It wasn't too hard to discover by which route you were coming.'

'Then my brother-in-law is responsible,' Constance said. 'He told Rollo to remove the jewels. He used me as a distraction while the real things of value went separately!' She bunched her fists in anger, certain now that she had reached the truth. 'He stole everything and left me to risk danger!'

'Unless you are the thing of value?' Osgood sneered.

'I don't think so. I am of less use to my brother-in-law than my jewels,' Constance said bitterly. She passed a hand across her eyes wearily. 'I am less use to you also.'

Aelric opened his mouth to speak, but then closed it again and looked away.

'And I wish we had saved ourselves the trouble,' Gerrod thundered. 'First you tell us you are of no worth to de Coudray and now we discover you have nothing of value either.' He shot her a look filled with loathing and turned to Aelric, who was staring intently at the box on the ground.

'My son died for nothing,' Gerrod muttered bitterly.

Constance's cheeks flamed. The boy's face flashed into her mind, along with those of the other men who had died with him. Were the monk and the guard still alive in the forest or had they joined the number of dead? Anger overtook her fear, giving her strength she had not possessed since her capture. She took a step towards the men, past the box.

'Your son died because you attacked me,' she exclaimed. She threw her hands up in exasperation, no longer caring what effect her words might have. The big man opened his mouth to speak, but Constance advanced towards him once more, words spilling out of her as she pointed an accusing finger in his face.

'Your son was a thief! You're all thieves. And murderers. None of this would have happened if you had stayed within the law. He would still be alive and I would be home.'

Her throat seized on the word 'home'. She had not been going home. There was no home she belonged to. No one who would greet her arrival with pleasure. No one to mourn her if she never arrived. Once more the cloisters called enticingly to her. The energy left her as suddenly as it had arisen and she dropped her hands to her sides, standing silently as Gerrod towered over her. He suddenly seemed much larger than he had previously. Out of the corner of her eye she could see Aelric, moving in front of Osgood to prevent him stepping forward, hands raised in warning.

'Within the law?' Gerrod spat out. He moved towards Constance. She feared he would strike her and raised her hands as a shield above her head, but Gerrod pushed roughly past her and with a mighty kick he splintered part of the board away from the window. Light flooded into the room through the thin gap, causing Constance to screw her eyes up at the unaccustomed brightness.

'Look at what your King commanded be done to our land,' Gerrod commanded. 'Look what your lord brother-in-law has done. We have no choice to be within the law. Your people drove us outside it when you raped our country. We have no homes to go to. Your soldiers saw to that.'

He seized Constance by the shoulder, twisting her around. He forced her to her knees facing the window, pulling her hair back so she looked into the light. She had lived with violence daily and had trained herself to endure it without complaint, but since Piteur's death the need had ended. Now she was once more faced with it and her mind revolted at the thought of more. She drank in the light, wondering if her outburst had signed her death warrant and it would be the last time she saw the sky. She was not sure if the emotion that flooded her was panic or relief.

'Gerrod, enough!'

Aelric's voice was a roar of rage. The pressure on Constance's hair lifted so suddenly the absence was almost painful in itself. She let out a sob and sagged forward, hands outstretched.

Hands lifted her to her feet once again, though gentle and supportive rather than aggressive. One arm came about her waist, the other across her chest, a hand on her shoulder rigid and firm, compelling her to remain upright when her body wanted nothing more than to sink to the ground. She did not look around, knowing it would be Aelric who held her. None of the other men would care whether she was in discomfort or not.

She looked out of the window as Gerrod had instructed. Tears blurred her vision, obscuring the view over a wasteland of dull greens and brown earth. Of rising hills and a flat plain. From the level of the trees she got a sense that they were somewhere high up, but nothing more. A short while before she would have searched for any sign of recognition, but her location no longer mattered to her. She would never leave her prison alive.

'Are you trying to get yourself killed?' Aelric hissed in her ear.

His body was so close as he held her that she could feel the heat radiating from him. His angry breath lifted the hairs on her neck and she was filled with the unexpected wish that they had not been interrupted and she had succeeded in kissing him. Doing it might never have secured her freedom, but she would die with the memory of his lips on hers one last time.

'Do what you will,' she sobbed. 'I don't care any more.'

Constance wiped her eyes with the sleeve of

her tunic. She lifted her face to the sky and closed her eyes.

'What do you mean, you don't care?' Aelric said suspiciously.

'I can't live in this nightmare any more,' Constance whispered. She bit down on her lip hard before continuing, tasting the blood that she drew. The iron bitterness sent a shudder through her. 'I've been struck, bound and blindfolded, dragged through the countryside and imprisoned. And for what? An empty box and a handful of deaths that need never have happened.'

She pulled away from Aelric, who let her go without resisting, his eyes never leaving hers. In the morning sunlight he was as pale as a wraith. She stared from one man to the next, taking them all in as she spoke, her hands held out, palms up in supplication.

'My entire family are dead and my brother-in-law will not care if I die. I matter to no one. I don't know where my jewels or money are and I don't care. Kill me, violate me, or set me free. You're going to do one or the other eventually, but I cannot stand the waiting. Do it quickly and put an end to this.'

She dropped to her knees; no longer brave enough to stand before them. Footsteps sounded on the wooden floorboards, then a crash as the trapdoor slammed shut. When Constance raised her head she was alone once more. A sweat of relief broke out across her body and her limbs began to tremble. She staggered across to the thin mattress and slumped down on to it, lying on her side so she could face the hatch. The empty strongbox was within her reach. She pulled it closer, wrapping her arms around it like a child with a doll, dreading the hours to come.

Chapter Eight

Constance must have slept because when she opened her eyes next the light was fading. The box had fallen from her grip as her arms had become limp, but she was still lying in the same position. The release of the tension that had been growing inside her since her captivity began had sent her deep into oblivion and her body felt more rested than after the previous night.

She was still lying facing the hatch when it opened and Aelric emerged from the floor below. Constance pushed herself on to one elbow and stared at him silently. He closed the hatch with care to do so quietly and crossed the room to crouch down beside her. He carried something in his hand, a glint of metal. At first Constance feared it was a knife and that he had come to slit her throat, but as he held it out she realised it was a goblet. He reached into his sleeve and produced a chunk of bread that he placed on the floor beside her. Constance stared at it.

'If you're feeding me, does that mean I am to live for now?' she asked warily. She lifted the goblet. 'Or is this the means to my end?'

Aelric bared his teeth in a snarl. He slammed both fists on to the floorboards.

'Don't jest about such a thing! It's wine.'

He freed it from her fingers and took a swig, wiped his hand across his lips and pushed it back into her hand. She placed the goblet on the floor beside the bread. Aelric ran his hands through his hair, twisting it into knots.

'What did you think you were doing earlier?' he raged. 'Provoking their anger in such a way?'

'Should I have stood by meekly and allowed them to accuse me of stealing my own property?' Constance retorted.

'Yes! Unless you were willing to deal with the consequences of what you said.'

Constance glared at him, saying nothing.

'Did you mean what you said about wishing us to kill you?' Aelric raged. 'Because you have no idea how close you came to losing your life today.'

Constance sat up and hugged her knees close to her chest. His ferocity had been unexpected and her pulse was racing. She reached for the goblet and sipped slowly.

'I meant it,' she said quietly.

Aelric's face twisted, his forehead furrowing and his lips pursing. He sat alongside her and drew his feet up, resting his elbows on his knees and his chin on his elbows.

'Why?' He sounded calmer. Interested in what she might say. 'Do you really value your life so little you were prepared to throw it away?'

'I was prepared to die rather than remain a captive for ever,' Constance said coldly. She narrowed her eyes, staring at him in challenge. 'You once told me that death would be preferable to a life of slavery.'

'You've never been a slave,' Aelric said scornfully.

'I was a wife. What's the difference?' Constance said in an undertone.

She hugged her knees and closed her eyes, reliving nights she had hoped to banish from her memory for ever. When she opened them again Aelric was staring at her with an expression that sent shivers deep inside her.

'I have no home. I am as much an exile as you, but at least you have your companions here. I've never been brave enough until now to see that you were right,' she sighed.

'Perhaps I was wrong to say that,' Aelric muttered. 'Do you still mean it?'

Constance felt her lip begin to tremble. 'I don't

know,' she whispered. 'I was being escorted to Hamestan against my wishes. I didn't want to go there. I don't want to remain here. I hate the choice not being mine to make.'

Her eyes began to smart as the irony of her situation hit her. She rubbed them with the heels of her hands. Aelric edged closer.

'When you told us to kill you…' He looked down at his hands, then back to Constance. 'You also said "violate". Is that what you expect us to do? Is that what you think Saxon men are like?'

'It's what all men are like,' Constance spat out. Her hands moved to the neck of her tunic, high enough to hide the scars beneath and feeling the ghosts of Piteur's fingers pulling at her flesh.

'If he had the chance, your friend Osgood would have me on my back quicker than I could blink. Or on my knees in front of him!'

Aelric jerked his head at her crudity, snorting with disgust that came as a surprise to Constance. Perhaps he never demanded of women what her husband had forced her to do, or perhaps it was the idea of her doing it that repulsed him. The hunger she'd noticed in Osgood's eyes had also been clear to see in Aelric's. She found herself wondering for the first time how many women had been in his life since they had parted and the stab of jealousy took her by surprise.

'Osgood won't touch you,' Aelric said, his

voice low and determined. He placed a hand on her arm, squeezing gently. 'No one will.'

His certainty enveloped Constance like a fur mantle. She took a breath and leaned towards him. This could be her only chance and she did not think there would be interruptions this time. Aelric had closed the trapdoor quietly and his movements suggested he intended his presence to go unnoticed.

The sun was already beginning to set, turning the light orange as it crept through the gap in the window boards. Constance studied her companion. In the twilight Aelric's blond hair and shaggy beard glowed, lending his blue eyes an intense brightness. His face bore lines and his eyes were wary and ringed with shadows, but the cheekbones that had once seemed too angular now suited him. The neck of his tunic was slashed deep and her fingers itched to touch the thin covering of fine hairs visible across the V of his chest.

'Why did you come up here?' she asked softly.

'To bring you food,' he answered. 'Before anyone else returned.'

'Just that?' Constance breathed.

He looked at her questioningly.

'There is nothing else you wanted from me?' She shifted on to her knees, ignoring the twitching pain that shot through her leg, and faced him. She wanted no man to touch her. Anticipating doing again what her husband had subjected her to set her stomach churning, but the hope of buying her freedom in any other way had vanished. If she had to do this, she was glad it was Aelric who she had once loved and whose touch was not completely unknown to her. She lifted a hand and placed it on his chest. Her fingers trembled against muscles that tensed under her touch.

'Nothing I can offer you?'

Aelric's heart was a steady drumbeat beneath her palm. Raw yearning was emblazoned on his face, but he remained as unmoving as a statue.

'What are you doing?' His voice was suspicious. Constance cringed inwardly and swallowed.

'I'm offering what I know you want. What all men want?'

His face darkened. He scrambled to his feet, arms crossed defensively. 'And in exchange what do you expect?'

'Nothing,' she lied. She stood to face him, staring into his eyes. 'I'm scared and alone and may die tomorrow. Why shouldn't we take pleasure in each other's arms?'

Aelric turned away and Constance's heart sank.

Whatever she was doing, she must be doing it wrong, or she had been mistaken and he was not interested. She had no experience of seduction. Her husband had never bothered with such preliminaries. He had simply instructed her what to do, with the back of his hand or his riding crop always waiting for her if she did not comply quickly enough.

She tried to recreate how she had felt with Aelric seven years ago. How they had passed from quick, furtive kisses into something more frenzied and uncontrollable but the memories or feelings would not come and she did not know how to continue.

'I thought you wanted me,' she said, her voice cracking. She made a sound that began as a sigh of despair and ended in almost a sob of humiliation. 'I was mistaken.'

Aelric swept his head round. Constance bent her head, letting her hair fall forward across her face to hide her embarrassment. She felt Aelric's fingers moving through her hair and brushing it back behind her ears. He cupped her chin and lifted her face. His eyes were full of hunger.

'We loved each other once, didn't we?' she asked in a whisper.

'Did we? What did we know about love?' The corner of his mouth twitched. 'We were barely more than children, just waking up to what our bodies sought.'

It had been love to her. She had recklessly given herself to him then, heedless of the consequences and to hear him dismiss it as nothing more than the lust all men felt cracked her heart.

She swallowed down her grief and continued with her plan.

'What does your heart want now?' Constance whispered. 'What does your body want?'

She reached a hand to his chest once more, spreading her fingers wide. She felt the intake of breath, saw the pulse at his throat quicken. His hand sought her waist, tugging her closer until they were face to face. He bared his teeth in a grimace that could have been passion or hatred.

'I want you,' he growled. 'But this will not end well. It can't.' His voice had an edge to it she had not heard before, but which spoke of danger. She knew then she had him.

'I risked shame and ruin to be with you years ago,' she said, goading him. 'What would you risk to be with me now, or is Caddoc too much of a coward?'

She had barely finished speaking before his mouth was on hers and he was bearing her downwards to the floor.

He had reservations still, but the instant their lips touched, fire coursed through Caddoc. Constance gave a small squeak of surprise that only intensified Caddoc's excitement. He dug his fingers into the loose fall of silken hair at each side of her head, pressing his palms against her temples and weaving his fingers through the strands so she did not pull away.

Memories he had suppressed for years flashed through his mind. Of Constance shy and smiling, blushing in the shadowy cow barn as she guided his hands around her waist, of himself trembling with longing for the ultimate pleasures she had granted him and which she was now once again offering willingly.

They were kneeling together on the bare floor, close to the thin straw mattress. He glanced toward the trapdoor, confirming he had closed it behind him. In the tower below them his companions would be resting or talking. No one had seen him come up here. They did not need to stop at a kiss. Their eyes met and Aelric had the strangest sensation that they were preparing for combat.

He closed his eyes, giving his imagination free rein to indulge the craving that he had tried to ignore since he had first recognised Constance in the forest. He had truly meant it when he told Osgood that no one would use Constance for his pleasure. He himself would never have touched her but for her insistence and now he had begun he could not bear to stop. The pressure was building within him, demanding a release one way or another, and the prospect of a sweetly willing woman meant his resolve was weakening the longer she was in his arms. It seemed fantastical that after so long she should still want him, but then she was a widow and must miss the comfort of lovemaking.

'Is this really what you want?' he asked through clenched teeth, his lips brushing against hers. 'If it isn't, then stop me now because I tell you I will not ask again.'

'I don't want you to stop,' Constance whispered. Her voice was urgent and breathy, warm against his cheek. She gazed at him through half-lidded eyes.

It was all the answer Caddoc needed. Overwhelmed by his need to possess her, he pressed his body fiercely against Constance. Heat spread from his groin outwards as she pushed back against him, her hands clutching at his waist. She found the hem of his tunic and her hands dove beneath, causing him to draw a sharp breath. Her fingernails were long and scraped against the muscles of his chest.

Caddoc ground his teeth as white-hot lust riddled his body like a fever. It had been too long since he'd had any companion in his bed and his desire was so acute it was bordering on painful. By the time his lips were on hers once more he could scarcely draw breath. This time he forced her lips apart, tongue hard and demanding. He met no resistance as her tongue met his eagerly. The kiss was unlike any he had experienced.

Harsh and angry and unsettling, more like a fight than anything bordering on affection, but the taste of her drove him wild. If this intimacy they had fallen into was combat, then Constance was the only opponent Caddoc wanted and he was determined that he would be the victor.

He dropped his hands from her hair, knowing she would not move her head away, and wrapped his arms round her slender waist. Constance tilted her hips, wriggling until she was free of the hose she wore, in the process brushing against Caddoc in a way that stopped the breath in his throat. Months of pent-up frustration flowed through his veins until he believed he could wait no longer. He dug his fingers into the hair that fell loose down Constance's back, grabbing handfuls and burying his hands deeply as he pulled her with him. They slid down on to the straw mattress, Constance spreading her legs as Caddoc settled himself in between them.

His lips travelled down her throat and she moaned softly, slipping her hands under his tunic once more. As her cool, sure fingers began to slip to his back Caddoc tensed. The first woman he had tried to bed since his flogging had screamed in disgust at his mutilated back and refused to bed him. He could not bear Constance to touch the twisted and puckered flesh.

'Not there,' he said roughly.

Constance said nothing and slipped her hands around his neck, but as her fingers brushed against the scar de Coudray had left on Caddoc's flesh her eyes widened. No other woman had been able to compare his body before and after the disfigurement it had suffered. Revulsion at what he had become threatened to overwhelm Caddoc, destroying his fervour. Before he lost his way completely he seized Constance's wrists, feeling the blood flowing through them with a steady rhythm. He guided her hands firmly away from his body down to her side. When he removed his hands she remained motionless.

He tugged his breeches down with one hand then pushed Constance's short tunic above her waist. He paused as the palm of his hand skimmed across the soft roundness of her belly, feeling her tremble under his touch.

'Do it,' Constance commanded.

As she spoke she turned her head to the side and her eyes were hard. There was as little tenderness there as there had been in her voice. Caution told him to stop, despite her declarations otherwise, but by that time Caddoc was too far along the path to obey.

Without speaking he entered her. Constance gave a gasp, her body going rigid. Her eyes remained fixed on some point in the distance and she bit her bottom lip. Caddoc took his weight on his elbows and bent his head to kiss her, but Constance lay passive beneath him, hands never straying from where he had placed them and her body barely moving in response to his rhythm.

In handful of thrusts he was spent. It was over almost before Caddoc knew it. Momentarily weakened by the passing tremors that always followed lovemaking, Caddoc sagged down on top of Constance. He reached a hand instinctively to her cheek to caress her, but withdrew it. His lip curled as he considered how inaccurate the word was to describe what had just passed between them, comparing what they had just done with the tender and innocent kisses from so many years ago. Then their caresses had been sweet and exciting, promising a future of love.

This was the hollowest act he had ever committed.

Constance shivered and turned her head forward once more. She was not looking at him, but something or someone far away and her eyes were hard. There had been no tenderness involved in what they had done this night, only ugly passion, anger and frustration.

Disgust at himself—at both of them—washed over Caddoc. He rolled away and pulled his breeches back up, then sat up. Beside him Constance said nothing and gave no indication that she was even aware of his presence. Whatever she had hoped to gain from what they had done she did not look as though it had been achieved.

'Is that what you wanted?' Caddoc asked, more abrasively than he intended.

'Didn't I please you?' Constance asked. Her face contorted with misery.

He shook his head in disbelief. How could she think that such an empty act could please him? Clearly it had given her no satisfaction. Whatever her motives had been it had not had anything to do with him.

Constance rolled on to her side with a gentle sigh, facing away from him. Her bare legs were crossed at the ankles and her tunic skimmed her rounded thighs. Ordinarily such a sight would be enough to excite Caddoc, especially if the woman in question was in his bed, but he felt as unmoved as if he was staring at an effigy.

'Why did we do that?' he asked.

Constance sat up. She crossed her good leg beneath her, the twisted foot sticking out in front. She pulled the tunic down over her knees to give her a semblance of modesty that to Caddoc's mind was unnecessary given what they had just done.

'I told you before,' she said, twisting the hem of the tunic around her slender fingers.

'You were lying.' Caddoc said. 'You said we should take pleasure from each other, but I've bedded drink-addled Welsh whores who showed more enjoyment than you did.'

She sat forward, her hand jerking up to strike him, but she hesitated. He almost willed her to make that move, but she lowered her hand and did not answer, biting her lip once more.

'Is that what you've spent the last seven years doing?' Constance asked quietly.

'What I've done, or who I've done it with, is no business of yours,' Caddoc spat out. There had been women, of course, but not many and even with the commonest woman he had paid to satisfy him, the act had never been this empty.

'I hoped to please you,' Constance said, her voice devoid of emotion. 'That perhaps there was still some of what you once felt for me.'

He knelt in front of her and took her by the shoulders. 'Why do you care about that?' Caddoc asked. 'We haven't seen each other for years and by rights, what I have made you endure since meeting again should earn your hatred, not love. What do I mean to you now?'

Constance's eyes were hard, displaying precious little affection. A sick feeling began to grow in Caddoc's stomach along with a suspicion of what he meant to her, or at least what he represented.

'I hoped if I could please you perhaps you would look more kindly on me,' she whispered.

'Did you think you could buy your freedom in such a manner?' he asked, not really wanting to hear the answer. 'Rutting like an animal?'

The slap came from nowhere, across his cheek with a strength that he would not have expected. Used to reacting instantly, he seized hold of Constance's wrist before it had finished the arc back down. He held it tightly as she pulled away, noting absently that the pulse was far faster than when he had been about to bed her. At least this emotion was genuine.

'Never do that again.'

He let go of her wrist and she dropped it into her lap.

'Is that why you did it? Tell me the truth,' Caddoc demanded.

Her face was wraithlike, dark eyes made darker by the shadows that encircled them, holding his gaze with an honesty that had been missing until then. It tore deep into his guts to see this lent her face much more beauty than any of the coy smiles and shy glances she had employed before.

'What if I did?' Constance said coldly. 'I have no other means to buy it and I have no weapons to fight my way free. If that makes me no better than one of your whores, then so be it.'

Caddoc spat out an obscenity in Welsh. Constance flinched and whipped her head down. A tear splashed on to her tunic. Worms of guilt writhed in Caddoc's gut.

The room became stifling, the walls constricting him. He pushed himself to his feet. Without looking back he walked to the hatch and wrenched open the trapdoor. Constance made no move to stop him so he lowered himself through and pulled it shut.

Chapter Nine

The room below was starting to fill as people came in for the night. Gerrod and his wife were sitting quietly in one corner, arms around each other and heads together. A younger woman was tending to the pot over the fire, her daughter on her hip. Life and company did not appeal after what had just taken place, but Caddoc wanted some solace from the anger that bubbled inside him. He found what he was looking for, tucking the wrapped bundle under his arm.

Ulf had returned from Hamestan and was playing a game of jacks with Osgood. They had a pile of tally sticks and looked engrossed in a game that would go on long into the night. Ulf caught Caddoc's eye and gave a wary half-smile. Caddoc jerked his head towards the door, indicating Ulf to follow. He skirted round the edge of the room, keeping to the shadows, and left the building.

Stars were beginning to appear in what promised to be a clear sky. A half-moon cast light over the plains below and the frost was enough to take his breath away. Caddoc felt his way to the edge of the rocky outcrop and sat down with his back to the tower. As he waited for Ulf to join him he unwrapped the *crwth* that he had brought with him. He looked at the instrument without seeing it, his fingers tracing the spirals on the wooden board. He laid the bow beside him on the calfskin and plucked a string that in the silent night sounded harsh and tuneless. His fingers found their place easily and he ran through the first part of the accompaniment to a melody he loved. Tonight the music brought him no comfort. He cradled the instrument lovingly, but his inspiration left him for the first time.

He could not lay the fault at her feet, but what had happened with Constance was to blame. He'd slept with other women who had tried to use their sex to gain an advantage—usually some triviality such as a pretty ribbon—but never in the manner Constance had gone about it.

Her eyes. That was what chilled him most; the way she had gone blank as he touched her, going to a place where he did not exist. He could not forget the utter lack of emotion in her expression. What she had offered had been no part of her, but something separate.

And through it all her eyes had remained open, dry and empty.

The memory was enough to make him weep with frustration.

Eventually Ulf came and sat alongside him.

'It's good to see you safe,' Caddoc said. 'What news from Hamestan? Has de Coudray discovered his missing sister?'

'I expect so, though I didn't see him in person. Rollo's brother was waiting for him in the inn, angry at the delay.'

Ulf gave a rattling cough and spat over the edge of the ridge. 'Osgood told me there was no treasure. Was it the woman all along?'

Caddoc sucked his teeth thoughtfully. The empty box, the bodyguard rushing to defend it, and Constance herself. The whole affair gnawed at him like a maggot.

'It wasn't her. I think she was a diversion. Something he was happy to sacrifice while he sent the treasure another way.'

'What are you going to do with her?' Ulf asked. 'Gerrod would still happily slit her throat and Osgood thinks we should sell her to a brothel. Just imagine what a high-born woman like that would fetch. We could live like lords for a year on what we'd earn!'

Caddoc hissed him into silence, revolted at the thought of Constance enduring such indignities.

He owed her no protection, but could never condemn her to that life. He'd rather see her dead before that.

'I'll think of something.'

But what, and when? Gerrod and Osgood would not be put off for ever and it was a wonder they had managed to keep her presence secret. The women in the camp would welcome a slave to make their lives easier, but he doubted a cosseted Norman woman would survive long under such hardship.

He stared down over the edge of the ridge to where Hamestan lay, concentrating on the shadows in the distance. If he turned around his eye would be drawn to the window on the second floor and he did not want to think of Constance. She should be lying on the bed, warmed by the afterglow of lovemaking and the heat from his own body, not crying alone. He should be drowsing in her arms, not sitting on a barren rock in the cold. He bunched his fists in frustration, half-planning to return to the room and demonstrate what a night as his bed partner should involve, but the coldness on her face and the sting in her words held him back. She had not been concerned with pleasure or the comfort of his arms, only what her body could buy her.

'I knew bringing her here was a bad idea as soon as I saw it on your face,' Ulf muttered darkly.

'Saw what?' Caddoc asked.

'What I see on your face now. I know who she is, too, though it took me longer than you. I never understood what you saw in a lame girl like her. One of *them*, too. Edgy she was, always watching and alone. A quiet one.'

'Maybe that's what I liked,' Caddoc said. He had dreamed about her and pined for her for too many years to recall, but the timid, innocent girl whose face filled his mind in the dead of night bore no resemblance to the hard-eyed woman who was prepared to bargain with her body in such a cold way. What had happened in seven years to transform her so completely?

Ulf shrugged and coughed again. The cold winter had not been kind to him and he was growing older. 'I know why you can't decide. I know what she did for you.'

'You were there at the hanging?'

He had not seen Ulf until his third return to Cheshire, two years after his exile, and they had never spoken about what had happened on that day.

'Do you think I would have let you do something so foolhardy if I had been? Your father would have haunted me for eternity,' Ulf exclaimed indignantly. 'I heard afterwards what you did. It was the talk of Cheshire for weeks.'

Caddoc ground his heel into the dirt. 'My father would have been ashamed at what I've become. He was a warrior. I've done little to avenge my family and I'm no closer to succeeding. I thought this was my chance.'

'Your father loved you and wanted you safe. He always saw your mother in you more than your brothers.'

A lump filled Caddoc's throat. His mother, who had never lost the lilt of her childhood tongue, had been gentle but sickly with pale red hair that had left its trace on Caddoc's own. Her death the year of the invasion had been unexpected to no one. He'd inherited his love of music from her, too. Caddoc wrapped his *crwth* back in its skin and folded his arms around it protectively.

Caddoc bit a fingernail, imagining the future stretching out ahead of him, unchanging, filled with defeat and bitterness, cold and hunger. He could return to Wales, plead for Emrys' favour and live out his days in exile. De Coudray would still be alive, holding the land that should belong to Brunwulf's sons. Hamestan would remain under the yoke of his enemy for ever and Constance would…

What would she do? Enter a convent as she had suggested or remarry? Perhaps she would do neither, but would continue to live under the Pig's protection.

'If you know what happened, you know why I

can't let them kill her. I owe my existence to that woman in there. I am under obligation to her.'

'You need to make a decision soon,' Ulf prompted.

'Is it mine to make? I'm not the leader here. I never was intended to be one,' Caddoc said. 'My father had three sons to follow him into battle or to rule and they all died with him.'

'Then let them do what they will with the woman,' Ulf suggested. 'She can't mean anything to you after this long and you surely mean nothing to her.'

Caddoc shook his hair out of his eyes. Ulf was right, there was no room for tenderness in what he needed to do. To allow the growth of the affection that Constance had sought would be deadly for him. His resolve strengthened tenfold. De Coudray would pay for what he had done and anything he had felt for Constance would not stand in his way. If she could not be of use, then she had no worth to Caddoc.

'I'll wait until light,' he said, 'then I'll do what I have to do.'

Morning brought frost and the scent of promised snow. Constance woke when it was barely light and lay awake, huddling beneath the thin blanket with the useless strongbox beside her. She kept her eyes tightly shut in an attempt to ward off the day and relived the events of the previous night over and over, wondering how it had gone so wrong.

After Aelric had left she had given fully into despair for the first time since her captivity had begun. She wept until the tears stung her cheeks, thinking of the man who she had thrown herself at, had once loved, and who had looked on her with such contempt. This morning her head felt light and her mind dreamlike. A proper bed seemed something from a dream, warm food an impossibility, freedom even further beyond her reach.

Her body ached from sleeping on the thin straw, but to this was added the discomfort she felt inside. She had endured worse indignities and greater pain, but the soreness she had not experienced since Piteur's death was an uncomfortable reminder of her failure to win Aelric's favour. He had wanted her, she knew that, he had said so himself. Why, then, had he been so angry, even before he discovered her reason for seducing him?

He had been fierce at first and she had feared the cruelty that her husband had inflicted, but it had not come. She had expected what they did to be endurable but nothing more, but Aelric's kiss had taken her breath away and made her blood pound in a way that no other had. She could have stayed in that kiss forever, freezing time if it was possible. She had responded in kind, but when he had made it clear she was to lie still, as Piteur had frequently commanded her, she obeyed instantly and instinctively. And still this had not seemed to please him. She must have done something wrong, but could not think what and it had all been in vain.

Her stomach gave a lurch that was not altogether unpleasant as she remembered the strength of the embrace Aelric had held her in. She had not expected to enjoy the experience, but had found herself not wanting him to end their kiss. His sinewy frame was deceptively slight, hiding muscles that were hard and powerful. He was lean as he had always been, but without the thickness of chest and burliness that would turn into a paunch such as Piteur had had and Hugh was starting to get.

A jolt shot through her and she almost gasped aloud. How had she forgotten about Hugh? She could have used his name to bargain with. More than that, with all that had happened she had forgotten the reason she had agreed to return to Hamestan. If she could persuade Aelric to aid her in assisting Hugh, she might yet have one last chance to secure her safety.

The trapdoor creaked open and a footstep fell on the loose board. It was Aelric. She recognised his tread before she opened her eyes and wearily raised her head.

He stood over Constance, saying nothing. His face bore none of the disgust or resentment it had the previous night. He wore his cloak hood down and edges slung back to show the tunic and surcoat he wore beneath. The matching pair of daggers was sheathed at his waist and he had a coil of rope slung across his shoulders.

He revealed no emotion. Terror seized Constance at what his intentions might be. She struggled to her feet, ignoring the knots sending sparks of pain shooting through her neck and back. Before Aelric had the chance to speak she held her hands up and took a step towards him.

'I have something else to bargain with,' she said hurriedly. 'I can give you what you really want.'

'More than you gave me last night?' Aelric refused to meet her eyes, keeping his gaze slightly averted. 'Do tell, please.'

She ignored the scorn in his voice.

'The means to take your revenge on my brother-in-law.'

Aelric narrowed his eyes and pursed his lips. He tilted his head to the side and waved a hand as if he was a lord granting permission to a courtier. Constance let her breath out. She had bought what might be her only chance of surviving.

'I have reason to believe Lord de Coudray is involved in a conspiracy.'

She saw a flash of interest cross Aelric's face before he buried it deep within him.

'Why are you telling me this?'

'Because if you release me I can find out if it is true. I could tell you and you could reveal it. You could take your revenge legitimately and have him brought to justice through the law.'

'Why would I trust Norman law? When has that ever been kind to me or my people?' Aelric scoffed. 'I want the Pig's body at my feet, not in the Hundred Court.'

When he spoke of Robert's death his eyes burned with alarming intensity. He had kept the promise she had exacted from him, but with his weapons to hand he resembled the ferocious warlords who had fought against William's army and she was gripped with a dread that he would once more seek to avenge his family.

'You vowed you would not seek to kill Robert. It's better than no revenge,' Constance said. Her eyes were drawn back to the daggers. She bit her lip. 'Or a meaningless gesture he would not care about.'

'You would be happy to assist me with bringing about his ruin?' Aelric asked. 'It is you who commanded me not to seek revenge, but you would turn traitor to save yourself?'

She flushed scarlet and spun around as his accusation struck her to the core.

'I offered you myself before I thought to offer you him!' she snarled into his face. Anger flooded her, hot and rapid, filling her veins. She grasped his hand to better force her point and his arm jerked. She withdrew, folding her arms about her body. Aelric's eyes followed her movement.

'Do you feel no shame for what we did last night?' he asked. His jaw was tight. Judging her, as if he had any right to.

Constance lifted her head. She had spent the night tearing her conduct apart in self-recrimination, but while Aelric spoke with such derision she would admit nothing. As she watched Aelric fold his arms across his chest, it hit her that her failure to buy her freedom was the least of them. She would never reveal to him what his touch might have awakened in her.

'I only regret that it did not have the desired effect,' she said coldly.

'So now you would betray your brother-in-law to a Saxon and an outlaw in exchange for your liberty?' Aelric asked. He met her eyes for the first time, raising an eyebrow in surprise.

'I wished long before I met you that Robert wasn't my kin. I have no loyalty to my brother-in-law, nor any love.'

Aelric looked mistrustful. Thoughts of the

wrongs Robert had committed filled Constance's throat with bile: injuries to her and the death that would never be forgiven or forgotten. It was a crime against Aelric that he did not even know Robert had committed. She wrapped her arms tight around her belly and thought of the dreadful secret that had wearied her heart for almost seven years.

The need for vengeance that lived in Aelric's blood dwelt also in hers and had since the grey-clad mother superior at Brockley had explained why Constance had been bleeding in such agony when her monthly time was still two weeks off. It should matter to Aelric. Her loss was his also and he should have the right to add that to his account against Robert, but she could not bear to tell him. If she was about to die as she dreaded she was, her secret could die with her.

'Whether either of us like it or not, your country is my home too now,' she continued. 'I would help a good man uncover the wrongs of a wicked one if it meant the world was better for all of us.'

Aelric's head snapped up. His mouth twitched at one corner.

'Am I a good man, Constance?'

She had been thinking of Hugh, of how together she and Aelric could present any evidence to him. The question, voiced softly as if he was talking to himself, was unexpected. She looked at Aelric and realised she did not know the answer.

'You were once,' she replied. 'Only you would know what you are now.'

She walked past him, sat back down on the mattress. Aelric's eyes followed her movement and his lips parted, a hunger flashing across his face. She blushed as she pictured once more what they had done there. She drew her knees up, hugging them to her chest, and let her hair fall across her face.

Aelric's face darkened. Instead of answering he crossed to the window and looked out through the gap Gerrod had kicked free.

'Is what I have told you enough to buy me my life?' she asked. 'There is nothing else I can say or do.'

'Your life?' Aelric asked in confusion.

Constance glanced down at the knives at his belt, the rope over his shoulder. Chill fingers ran across her scalp and down her back.

'Aren't you here to kill me?' she whispered.

'What?' Aelric spun around. He looked astounded. 'Is that what you think I am here for? Am I a murdering savage in your eyes?'

Constance gestured to the weapons. 'Then what are you going to do with me?'

'What you wanted,' Aelric said.

He crossed rapidly back to where she sat, his

cloak billowing behind in his wake. Constance's anxiety began to flicker and swell like a flame catching alight. Did he mean to take her once more as he had last night? The memory of his lips on hers was strangely enticing. She tilted her head back, heart beginning to race.

'It will please you to know that the sacrifice you made last night was not futile,' he said curtly. 'That's why I am here this morning. I'm setting you free.'

Constance sagged with relief and disbelief. Her vision blurred. She put her face in her hands and took deep breaths until she was able to master her emotions better. He had not been insensible after all.

'Thank you.' She sighed in relief. 'Aelric, I knew—'

'You knew nothing,' he interrupted, his voice harsh. 'Don't thank me. Keeping you here is becoming more troublesome and costly, and brings us no advantage.'

His eyes fell on the strongbox and he kicked it into the corner of the room. 'We're leaving now.'

'So soon?' It was still barely light.

'Would you prefer to stay?' Aelric asked. His voice was urgent and his eyes flickered towards the trapdoor. A suspicion crept into Constance's mind. She stood up and reached her hand lightly to his shoulder. He pulled away as if her touch burned his flesh.

'You haven't discussed this with the others, have you?' she asked.

Guilt crossed his face, replaced quickly as he set his jaw firmly. 'No. They have their own opinions on what should happen to you that would weigh on my conscience if I allowed it to happen. I want you gone before the matter can arise.'

His voice carried an air of menace and Constance felt the blood drain from her cheeks.

'They still mean to kill me?'

'Gerrod does. Osgood would sell you to the brothel. I assume you wish for neither of those fates.' He looked her up and down and his lip curled in scorn. 'Unless you would happily sell your body to anyone else who might pay for it?'

Constance gave a low exclamation of disgust that appeared to have no effect on Aelric other than to make him turn away.

'Gather anything you have,' he said. 'I want you gone.'

As he spun round his cloak parted, giving Constance sight of his hands. They were bunched into fists, the knuckles white, and she realised with shock he was furious, but working to control his anger.

There was nothing to pack. Constance was already dressed and wearing her cloak for warmth. Pulling on her boots took no time at all. While she did this, Aelric stood with his back to her, peering down the hatch to the floor below.

'I'm ready,' Constance said quietly.

'Keep quiet and stay beside me while we leave the tower,' Aelric instructed.

Constance took a final look around the room that had been her prison, relief mingling with a confusing heaviness in her heart.

She had got her freedom as she had wanted it, but not in the way she had envisaged. Aelric had let her go not because she had awakened his love, but because he despised her for what she had done and could not bear the sight of her any longer.

Chapter Ten

They moved stealthily through the tower and on to the ridge. Caddoc feared he had not been quick enough to remove Constance from the building before her presence was noticed. He should never have delayed by listening to her words. Words which now itched his brain like a hive of bees.

She had been serious about handing over the Pig's secrets to him. The thought that he was not mistaken in his belief of de Coudray's treachery excited him beyond belief. He blinked to clear the temptation from his mind. Even if she were able to discover something the blood chilled in his veins at the idea of her putting herself in danger. Besides, he wanted more than the Norman justice she had mentioned. He wanted the vengeance his vow to Constance had denied him.

To his relief only a handful of people were there to witness Constance's departure. Ulf sat outside one of the small huts, sharpening his short sword. He met Caddoc's eyes and nodded, then continued with his task. When Caddoc turned back to Constance he saw she had stopped and was looking around at the camp, her face solemn. Gerrod's wife, Elga, and her friend were kneeling in the clearing, scraping at a deer hide with sharp, flat stones. They stared openly at Constance. Elga's eyes were wild and dark, her skin sallow. The loss of Wulf had hit her hard and she was discovering more consolation in a skin of sour wine than in Gerrod's arms.

Hoping Gerrod had kept their secret from his wife, Caddoc slung a careless arm around Constance's shoulder, leering down at her and letting his hand stray towards a breast.

'These French whores are indecently cheap.' He laughed. 'It's even worth the trouble of smuggling them here.'

Elga's shoulders dropped and her face became contemptuous. As Constance passed by Elga spat on the floor and followed with a stream of insults in their native tongue, then went back to her task. Caddoc glanced at Constance. Whether she understood the words or merely the sentiment he was unsure, but her already creamy cheeks paled even further.

Instinctively Caddoc moved in front of Constance, taking her by the arm and turning her away from the sight of Hamestan lying below. As he directed her through the passage that separated the camp from the rest of the forest she stopped abruptly.

'Why did you call me that?' she asked angrily. Her eyes were unusually bright and the soft hollow at the base of her throat was tight. Was she trying not to cry? 'You have no idea how desperate I was to do what I did!'

'You told me you regretted nothing,' he blurted out.

Constance deserved no pity, but equally no censure. She had used him, but equally he would have felt no qualms in planning to use her if he had found a way. If she was shamed by what she had willingly done, that was for her to live with, but he decided he would not condemn her for what she had done. He ignored the guilt that gnawed at him as he wondered what it had really cost her to throw herself at him.

'Would you prefer me to tell them the truth of who you are?' he asked, a little more gently.

She folded her arms and glared at him, biting her lip in a manner that drove him to distraction. His chest filled with irritation at her obstinacy and he mirrored her stance, feeling the heat rising to his throat and neck.

'What do you expect me to do, Constance?'

he thundered. 'I am trying to walk a fine line between proving my loyalty to the people I live with—the people to whom I owe my allegiance—and keeping you alive. A matter that you seem determined to make harder at every turn.'

'And why are you doing that?' she spat out.

'Because I am in your debt and I told you I would keep you safe!'

'Then it is just as well we will be free of each other before long and your obligation will be at an end,' she muttered, turning her back.

'We agree on that, at least,' Caddoc replied in an undertone as bitter as hers.

The journey was uncomfortably silent. Constance said nothing as Caddoc blindfolded her before leading her out of the stone passageway, but the resentment that filled her eyes weighed as heavy as a rock in his stomach long after he had covered them. He removed the cloth as soon as he dared, knowing she would be unlikely to find her way back to the camp and ignoring the knowledge that this saddened as much as relieved him.

He watched her as she walked, wincing as the long trek clearly hurt her twisted foot. She made no complaint, which doubled his sense of remorse. If he had chosen, he could have taken her to the boundaries of Hamestan itself much sooner than he intended to, but he retraced his steps, led Constance in circles and doubled back, the precaution instinctive.

The sun was high overhead when he led her to the edge of the forest.

'This is where we part,' he said.

She stared off through the thinning trees to where a rough, rutted path led away. Caddoc would have expected her to look more relieved than she did. She looked back at him with the wide, deep brown eyes that he knew would haunt his dreams for the rest of his life.

For one wild moment Caddoc imagined taking her with him to Wales as she had once claimed to want, but she had chosen years before to stay and marry someone else. And married well from the treasures she had described. She was on the other side of the war and out of his class. There was no way their lives could meet. Constance had simply realised that a lot sooner than he had.

He swallowed as regret threatened his composure. Regret that they had spent so little time together, with such a gulf of time between them. Regret that he could not keep her and that she would not wish him to even if that were a possibility.

She spoke, her voice not much more than a whisper.

'I may never see you again.'

Constance reached her hand to his cheek, brushing softly against his beard as she spread her fingers wide. They were slender icicles against the heat of his flesh and the pang of longing that ensued almost doubled him over. The thought of separating for ever hit him harder than when she had not gone with him seven years previously. He covered her hand with his and pressed it tightly, then firmly placed it down by her side.

'We parted once before. We can do it again,' he growled.

He would not meet her eyes, but he could picture the soft honey flecks amid the brown.

'I'll have to bind your hands now,' he said gruffly, covering her hand with his. 'It must look like you escaped or you will have too many questions to answer.'

He looped the rope around her wrists, drawing them together. The coils of rope fell loose about her hands.

Constance frowned. 'It will have to be tighter to look convincing.'

'It will hurt,' Aelric said.

'It will be a pain that passes.'

Constance pushed her hands towards him, insistently. She was right and he pulled the rope tighter as she instructed, crossing it between the coils. She stifled a small cry of pain as the rope bit into her wrists. Tears welled in her eyes.

She blinked and let them fall down her pale face where they met other tear-tracks in the grime on her cheeks. It would only make her appearance more dishevelled and her story of escape more credible.

Caddoc took her by the shoulders, his hands firm. He turned her towards the track, savouring this last touch that sent heat rushing along his arms, up to his brain and down to the parts that cried out for a second chance at satisfying them both.

'There's a village not far down that road. You'll come to it before too long and without any danger if you keep walking straight. You should manage that without your stick. You're on de Coudray's lands, but the people will look after you and take you where you need to go.'

She twisted her head round to glance over her shoulder at him. He held her firmly, refusing to let her turn fully. If she brought her lips within his reach, he would be lost.

'There's nothing more to say,' he said. 'Go now while you can.'

He dropped his hands, turned his back and strode into the forest where the trees were thickest. He watched from the undergrowth, keeping pace with Constance as she began to walk.

She took a handful of faltering steps at first like someone in a dream, but as she reached the path she stopped abruptly and lifted her hands to her face. Caddoc's heart lurched as he realised she was wiping away more tears. In the fine mist she looked small and unreal against background of the trees, her tousled dark hair and brown clothing seeming to make her a part of the wood itself. She brought to mind a spirit from the childhood stories his mother had told, though he doubted any of the fair folk had looked so beguiling.

Constance turned and looked behind her and he dropped hastily to his belly in case she saw him, but she continued to circle. Caddoc held his breath in case she turned herself around and started in the wrong direction. He had no intention of revealing his presence to her unless absolutely necessary, but if it came to it he would set her back on the path.

There was no need as she soon began walking towards the hamlet. Caddoc pushed himself upright and followed. She moved slowly, but as the track widened she became faster. When she first glimpsed the roof of a cottage she stopped and gasped loudly enough for Caddoc to hear from his hiding place. He remained still as she ran towards the safety of the dwellings.

'Please, will someone aid me?' she cried. 'For pity's sake, anyone!'

Before long her cries had drawn villagers from

their tasks. Caddoc tensed and notched an arrow in his bowstring. He had come across one or two of the people here and trusted they would aid Constance rather than do her harm, but if they didn't he was ready to act. Constance sagged to the ground, the composure she had displayed for so long finally giving way to loud sobs and Caddoc's fears were unfounded when an older woman drew Constance into her arms with loud exclamations of comfort.

With difficulty Caddoc wrenched his gaze away from the scene and turned deeper into the woods. He could not risk being discovered if the men decided to search the forest for Constance's abductor. He left her there, in the arms of others, receiving the comfort he could not give.

Voices assaulted Constance from all sides, questions firing at her like a volley of arrows.

'Who are you?'

'Where did you come from?'

The villagers huddled close around, their presence overwhelming after the days she had spent in seclusion. She pushed her tangled hair out of her eyes and stared around. The villagers were mainly women. Only one or two men stood there and they carried tools they had not bothered to lay down when she interrupted their tasks. Were the rest of the men working in the fields or had they fled and taken refuge in the wild as Aelric and his companions had? She held her bound hands up in entreaty.

'Please, free me.'

'Did you come here alone?' asked a male voice from behind her. 'Who brought you here?'

Other questions followed. She had to force down the fear that her answers would somehow displease her interrogators. Her departure from the camp had been so rapid she had not considered how exactly to explain what had happened to her since her capture. She would have to create a convincing story before she encountered Robert, who would surely be more intrusive than this. She could barely stammer out her words through the sobs. Her accent clearly marked her as an outsider. The men in particular furrowed their brows darkly.

'We should search the woods in case there are others.'

'No!'

If they discovered Aelric they would surely harm him. She calmed herself. It would never happen. Aelric would have been long gone by the time she had reached the village. 'I ran, but no one followed. Where am I?'

'Enough now! Let the poor child alone. Can't you see she's been tormented enough?' The older woman who had taken hold of Constance when she had stumbled into the clearing pulled her closer into an embrace.

Constance nodded gratefully. The sensation was of being cradled once again like a child. She leaned her head against the woman's scrawny breast, the last of her strength ebbing. One of the few men, old and bent over, brought a knife and cut the ropes from her wrists.

'We call this place Aldredley,' he said gruffly.

Constance flexed her hands and whimpered as feeling flooded back into them, burning like fire. Aelric had taken her at her word and bound them tightly. She refused to think of the way his eyes had briefly flashed with remorse and instead watched as rough, red wheals formed, standing out against her pale flesh. The man with the knife ran his twisted fingers over the marks, his calloused hands uncomfortable against her sore skin.

'Which devil did this to you?' he asked.

Constance opened her mouth to answer, then closed it again. Aelric had instructed her to lay the deed at the door of Caddoc the Fierce, but even naming him caused her heart to twist.

'I don't know their names,' she sobbed. 'They wouldn't tell me.'

'They've injured you!'

A sallow-faced woman her own age pointed to Constance's foot, which stuck out to the side, the ankle twisting outwards. In the hose with no skirts to disguise it, the deformity appeared more crooked than usual. She became conscious of it in a way she had not in Aelric's company and drew her legs close to her.

'It has been like that from birth,' she said. 'No one did that to me.'

The woman stepped back hastily; worried such proximity might twist her own limbs. Constance drew her knees up. Her leg throbbed painfully and she would suffer when she tried to walk next.

'Did they mistreat you otherwise?' the woman who held her asked in a gentle voice.

Her sharp, black eyes travelled down Constance's body, scrutinising her dishevelled appearance and man's attire. They came to rest on her lower half where they lingered long enough on Constance's belly for her to understand what she was being asked. Her hands slid instinctively around her body in a gesture of protection.

'No one hurt me,' she whispered.

Not in that way at least, she thought bitterly. Thinking of Aelric's contemptuous expression as he had left her in the night, she burst into tears once more. The knowledge that Aelric could not wait to be rid of her cut deeper than any pain he could have inflicted with a dozen knives or swords.

'I need to get to the house of Lord de Coudray,' she said.

Her words produced a further ripple of disquiet from the people clustered around her. Constance bit her lip in worry at the effect the mention of her brother-in-law's name created. These people were Saxons. Why should they aid her?

'We have little to do with the baron,' the man who had freed her muttered.

The woman hushed him.

'Guillaume will be back tonight. He can go tomorrow and take a message.'

Constance furrowed her brow in confusion at the unexpected French name.

'My husband,' the woman explained. 'He's a farrier.'

Seeing the surprise Constance failed to hide, the woman gave a smile that made her lined face look younger than her greying hair suggested she was. 'Not all of us hate all of you. Some of us have learned to get along when the need strikes.'

Constance blushed. Her lip began to shake as her heart gave a throb of sadness. A Norman married to a Saxon woman and living alongside the people he had conquered. Could that ever have been her and Aelric if events had taken a different turn so many years ago? Robert would never have allowed it. Now she would never see him again. She began to cry in earnest.

The woman patted her hand comfortingly.

'I am Edyt. You can rest in my home until

someone comes to fetch you,' she said. 'Let's get you inside.'

The men helped Constance to her feet and under Edyt's direction led her inside one of the huts. Edyt motioned towards a low stool leaning against the wall and Constance lowered herself on to it. Edyt ushered the men out, closing the door behind them. Constance sat passively while the other woman clattered pots and pulled herbs from hooks hanging from the eaves. The single small room was shadowy and airless, the fire smoke stinging Constance's eyes, but it was quiet and comforting after the noise and brightness outside.

Edyt ignored Constance as she stirred a small pot over the fire, humming to herself. Presently she poured the contents into a wooden cup and held it out to Constance.

'Drink this.'

Constance took the cup and sniffed. The steam was fragrant and made her eyes water. She recognised mint among the other, unknown, pungent scents.

'What is it?'

'Herbs that will help you sleep.' Edyt narrowed her eyes, then turned away and began to prod the sparse fire. 'And they can prevent a child sticking in the womb. If such a thing was required.'

Constance sat forward, clutching the cup between her hands. 'I told you no one harmed me in that way.'

'Then the herbs will merely help you sleep,' Edyt answered, her back still to Constance.

Apprehension surged through Constance. What if she was with child? The possibility had not even crossed her mind when she had seduced Aelric. She counted rapidly on her fingers, hoping she had not been caught. She remembered the losses she had suffered, both recent and so long ago, and drained the cup, shuddering at the bitter taste.

Edyt faced her once more. Her eyes fell on the cup in Constance's hands. She lifted her chin and gave a thin smile of understanding. Constance looked at her feet, shame crashing over her.

'How did you know?'

'I wasn't certain, but you would not be the first to deny such a thing happened. The shame should not be yours, though, but the men who forced you into such an act.'

Tears stung Constance's eyes. She put her head in her hands to hide her face.

'I didn't want to do it,' she mumbled.

She was lying though. Since Piteur's death she had determined to forswear any intimacy with a man, but once the notion had entered her head she set her foot on the path willingly. No wonder Aelric had mockingly called her a whore in front of Gerrod's wife and no wonder he despised her for what she had provoked him into doing.

'He never forced me. I chose to do it. He would never have touched me otherwise.'

Her conscience would not allow Aelric to be branded a defiler. He had not been the one to initiate the act, but she would never forget how, as soon as their lips had touched, he had become the same rough, unstoppable force her husband had been.

'When my Guillaume first came to the village five years ago he was looking for work. He sharpened my knife, but I had no money to pay him with,' Edyt said. 'Fortunately we women have another purse that does not run short of what it can supply. We do what we must.'

Despite her shock at the crude honesty of Edyt's words Constance giggled. It burst out of her, went on for far too long and became too shrill, but she felt helpless to stop it. The heat from the fire combined with the effect of the herbs made concentrating difficult. She gave a long yawn. Edyt motioned to a rush mat by the fire.

'Rest now. Whatever you've suffered is over with. You'll never have to face your tormenters again.'

Constance slipped to the mat and curled up, warm for the first time in days. Her head was spinning, dulling her senses. Edyt was right. She was free and soon would be in Hamestan, yet her heart was heavy. The Aelric she had once loved was gone for ever and Caddoc despised her, so why did the idea of his absence cause her so much grief? Bewildered by the emotions racking her, she fell asleep.

Chapter Eleven

Constance's disappearance had been discovered by the time Caddoc returned and was met with more anger than he had anticipated. Gerrod was waiting at the entrance to the rock passageway, arms crossed and face thunderous. He held the thin, long-bladed knife he used for butchering. Ulf and Osgood stood behind him, both holding short swords: a makeshift court or a party of executioners?

'So you came back. I half-thought you'd both be gone and that would be the end of it,' Gerrod muttered.

Caddoc eased his hands out from beneath his cloak to show he was unarmed.

'Keeping her served no purpose,' he said calmly. 'Now we can put that behind us and decide what to do next.'

'We could have been rich men!' Osgood exclaimed. He waved his sword aloft. 'She'd have fetched a fine price to the right buyer.'

'More than your conscience is worth?' Caddoc asked. 'Not enough to buy mine.'

Osgood bared black teeth and Caddoc was filled with a rush of repugnance.

'You should have told me what you planned, lad,' Gerrod thundered.

Caddoc folded his arms and mirrored Gerrod's stance.

'Perhaps, but we've been going round in circles since she arrived. This ended the matter quickly.'

'Ended?' Ulf's head shot up. 'How?'

His expression was a punch to Caddoc's guts.

'Not like that!' Caddoc exclaimed. That Ulf could think him capable of cold-blooded execution was sickening. Constance, too, had believed this morning he was capable of killing her. Was that what he had become?

'I set her free.'

Ulf nodded, approval replacing the shock on his face. Caddoc's heart felt too heavy to care. Though the return from the village had taken a fraction of the time travelling with Constance had taken, he was weary. All he longed for now was something warm to eat and solitude where he could dwell on the feelings Constance had aroused in him.

Dwell, relive and banish for ever.

'If you feel I have betrayed you, I will leave here, if you wish. You owe me no shelter and I owe you nothing in return, but I'm a quick hunter and a hard worker as you know.'

The men exchanged a glance, knowing that he spoke the truth.

'How can you be sure she won't betray us as soon as she gets to the Pig?' Gerrod asked. 'What if she realises how close she's been all this time?'

Constance's eyes filled Caddoc's mind. Her offer to hand him the means to see Robert in disgrace had been real enough. He believed deep inside that their identities, such as they were, would be safe with her. He shared none of this with his interrogators.

'She wouldn't know where to look. I led her in circles, then left her close to the village of Aldredley.' He scratched his beard and considered for a moment. 'Just to be certain I'll go back in a day or two and ask around to make sure she said nothing. Ulf can come with me. He knows people there.'

Ulf agreed and Caddoc's anxiety eased a little. It would give him the opportunity to confirm her safety, too, as much as the villagers would be able to tell him.

Gerrod stood aside and gestured for Caddoc to pass between the rocks. As he walked his hand felt for the twin daggers. It was unlikely they would strike him down from behind, but until he was in the open of the clearing he would watch his back carefully.

As he made his way inside the tower something occurred to him and he paused.

'Who discovered she was gone?' he asked Ulf in a low voice.

'Osgood. And by his expression when he came down it was just as well she wasn't there.'

Ulf rested a hand on Caddoc's arm and watched as the meaning of his words sunk in. 'You did the right thing. Perhaps it is in you to be a leader after all.'

Ulf ambled off, leaving Caddoc standing alone. He went inside and helped himself to the scrapings from the pot over the fire. It was almost empty. Tomorrow he would go hunting once more. A young deer, or even a brace of conies, would help regain Gerrod's trust.

He took his bowl to the fire and stared into the flames, barely noticing what he ate. His life before Constance had been thrown into it had been simple. Survive without capture, earn what he could and, if that didn't happen, eat what they could steal. It had been hard, but the path was laid out. Now he couldn't see him ever reaching that level of peace again.

Why had she offered to betray her brother-in-law? She had been desperate to gain her freedom, he had proof enough of that, but there had been a real animosity in her words. What did she hate him for? There was so much Caddoc did not know of her life and he found himself wishing he had asked, but it was too late for such regrets now.

Thanks to the concoction of herbs Edyt had given her Constance slept more deeply and easily than she had done for years, not even being aware of the arrival and departure of Edyt's husband. According to Edyt she had lain so still throughout the afternoon and night that the older woman had become concerned she might never wake.

Despite her ordeal and the fact she would have welcomed protection, the next morning Robert—grudgingly by Guillaume's account—sent only an ox cart and driver to collect Constance from the hamlet. They covered the distance with maddening slowness, Constance keeping a wary eye on the woods as they passed through. It would be extremely bad fortune for a further ambush, but she had not forgotten Aelric's explanation of how they had been aware of her arrival. She wished she had her dagger or even her stick that she had left behind.

It was not a long distance. Constance could have ridden there in half the time. She resolved to return to Aldredley herself once she was recovered and thank Edyt. She would rest for a few days, but after that there was no reason why she could not beg a horse or mule and ride back to the village. A day or two should see her well enough for that.

Constance had been barely conscious when she had been taken from Robert's house to the convent in Brockley so long ago and her memories of that time were muddled. She was not aware they had arrived in Hamestan until the ox driver tugged on his reins and pulled the beast to a standstill. She looked around her in interest at the changes she saw. The building was larger and grander than when she had departed seven years previously. A high wall encompassed outbuildings and offered protection and in Constance's absence a second storey had been added with a staircase leading up to the door. Robert had clearly prospered in the years she had been absent.

Robert greeted her arrival with belligerent hostility. He came from within when the driver knocked on the large oak door, but moved no further than the top of the staircase. He stood with one hand on the hilt of a sword that was buckled at his side and looked down at Constance sitting in the cart.

'Get down and come inside. I don't intend to stand here waiting in the cold air.'

Guillaume, who had accompanied Constance

to Hamestan on Edyt's orders, helped her down and gave her his arm as she climbed the steps. As she dropped into an awkward curtsy in front of her brother-in-law a momentary pang of sadness enveloped her. This had been Aelric's house. He would recognise it even less than she did and she was thankful he was determined never to set foot in Hamestan. She pushed him from her mind. No such man existed. Not for her and certainly not for Robert.

'Good day, my lord,' she said. 'It is an honour that you receive me in person.'

Robert snorted rudely. 'Honour, nothing! I wanted to make sure you arrived this time.'

Blushing with embarrassment, Constance turned to Guillaume, standing a little way behind her, and smiled. 'Thank you for your kindness. Will you take a drink before you return to your home?'

Robert snorted once more. 'See how she behaves as chatelaine!' he exclaimed to no one in particular. 'Making free with her hospitality at my expense. No, he will not take a drink. He doubtless has work to do. Make your goodbyes and come inside. We have things to discuss.'

'His lordship is right. I must leave now if I am to get back to Edyt before dark,' Guillaume said.

He bowed deeply to Robert who barely acknowledged the civility and swept inside. Constance held her hand to Guillaume.

'I won't forget your kindness, or your wife's. I will come back to visit.'

Guillaume bowed his head, then left.

Alone, Constance took a deep breath and clenched her hands, knowing she could no longer delay entering the house. Robert's attitude had been what she had expected. She smiled humourlessly to herself, wondering if, in years to come, she would look back on her time in captivity as a brief interlude of peace before the company she would have to endure in Hamestan.

The inside of the house was as changed as the outside. The fire pit had gone, replaced by a large hearth at one end that even on the mild day burned fiercely. What had been bare walls now hung with brightly coloured tapestries. Stairs at the far end led to a gallery that had not been there when Constance left. A maid was sweeping the old rushes into a pile while another carried dishes from a table to the room that had once been where the family slept. The smell of roast meats drifted to Constance's nose and her belly tightened painfully. She had declined the thin barley broth Edyt had offered her that morning when she realised it was the only food the woman possessed.

Robert was standing in front of the fireplace, hands behind his back.

'Come here, girl,' he commanded. Then to the servants, 'Out!'

The girls hurried out, eyes on the floor. Biting down her annoyance at the way Robert addressed her, Constance crossed the room. Robert gestured to one of the two chairs close to the fire and she sank gratefully down. Instead of sitting opposite her Robert began to circle around the chair.

'You were expected two days ago. I received no message until late last night when that man appeared and told me you were found wandering in the forest alone.'

There was no concern in his voice, only anger. He stood behind her and rested his hands on the back of the chair, leaning over her.

'Tell me what happened,' he instructed. 'Where is Rollo?'

'Rollo is dead,' Constance said quietly. 'One of your guards, too. We were ambushed.'

She watched carefully to see what effect this news would have on her brother-in-law.

The redness of his face deepened. She could see why Aelric and his companions referred so contemptuously to Robert as 'the Pig'. Since she had last seen him he had expanded like a bladder filled with air. Wet circles ringed the neck and armpits of a heavy, fur-trimmed jerkin, his chin rolled into his neck and his lips appeared permanently moist with saliva. Compared to the lean and half-starved villagers she had seen his frame appeared a living insult to their hardship.

'Rollo was an able fighter,' Robert mused. 'I am surprised. You were allowed to live, I see.'

This was the part Constance had rehearsed. Her story needed to be truthful enough in case the monk and guard had survived to be questioned, but she was unwilling to lead Robert towards Aelric and his men.

'When they realised I was a woman they planned—'

She broke off and wrapped her arms around herself protectively.

'They said I would fetch a good price in the brothels of Wales. They were going that way when they fell on us.'

'They?' Robert asked. 'How many? Who? What happened to Rollo's body?'

He hammered out questions, walking around her chair. It was more unsettling than the shouting interrogation Gerrod had subjected her to.

'I don't know.' Constance wept. She found the tears she had hoped to conjure came easier than she expected. 'It all happened so quickly. They bound and blindfolded me. I couldn't tell how many there were. We travelled by cart for a day. At night we stopped by a river. I slipped away while they were drinking and waded across, then ran until I could run no further. I had almost resigned myself to dying in the forest until I stumbled into the village yesterday.'

'It was that easy!' Robert remarked.

'It was not easy,' Constance snapped. She brandished her wrists to reveal the welts on them, glad she had insisted Aelric tighten the rope. 'I ate nothing and slept on the bare ground, terrified of being recaptured or eaten alive by wild animals.'

Robert frowned. He walked to the fire and jabbed violently at the logs with the iron. When he turned back his eyes were narrowed and more pig-like than ever.

'You have not asked where your sister is,' Robert said.

Constance closed her eyes, realising she had made an error. It should have been the first thing she asked. That her grief came after her dismay was something she would have to think on later when she was alone.

'I overheard the men who abducted me saying Jeanne has died.' She looked back at Robert, her eyes blurring. 'Is it true?'

'Yes, of the winter flux,' Robert answered. He did not look like a grieving husband ought to, but this did not surprise Constance. Another reason to despise him. Her own grief felt dull, like an aching tooth rather than a sharp wound. Perhaps so many losses had hardened her so that Jeanne's death after an absence of so many years could barely touch her heart.

Robert's eyes narrowed. 'What did these men know of my affairs? What are you keeping from me?'

'I've told you everything I can,' Constance said. 'They talked of who owned the land and that your wife had died. They did not know who I am so I suppose they saw no reason to hide it from me.'

'What else did they say of me?'

His face was growing redder with each question and Constance feared he might have a fit.

'Nothing,' she faltered. 'At least, not that I could tell. It was hard to understand their accents, but I recognised your name.'

Robert began pacing around the room, hands behind his back.

'I have enemies. If I find out there is anything you haven't told me…'

'They talked of going to Wales via Shrewsbury. I think they had been tracking us since we left Westune.'

Robert gave a start and looked about to speak, but a servant appeared at his shoulder.

'A cart has arrived bearing Lady Arnaud's chest.'

'Good. You aren't fit to be seen dressed like that,' Robert sneered, looking her up and down.

Constance jumped to her feet. Fresh clothes had never seemed more appealing. The urge to rid herself of the filthy hose and tunic was unbearable. She was caked with mud and could still smell the straw from the bare mattress. Worse than that, underlying it the scent of Aelric still lingered, torturing her with something she could never have.

'I'll come down,' she said.

'No need,' Robert answered. He addressed the servant. 'Have it taken to my chamber.'

'My chamber, surely,' Constance said.

Robert drew his lips back in a forced smile. 'Of course, though your room is not fully prepared yet. It will be safe in mine.'

Banging and footsteps announced the arrival of the men. The chest was brought in and Constance walked to stand by it.

'Rollo decided it was best if we travelled separately from the chest,' she remarked.

'I know,' Robert said. 'It was on my instruction that he did so. It is fortunate that I did or you may have been left with nothing but the rags you wear.'

She smiled and spoke in a careless manner. 'The men who attacked me broke open the strongbox. It was empty.'

A flash of hate filled Robert's eyes. The final confirmation that she needed. When the box was opened it would contain the missing jewels and money. His face was scarlet, but if Constance could face down Gerrod she could face Robert.

'I would like it opened now,' she said.

'Do you have the key?' Robert asked, smirking.

Constance shook her head, stomach twisting. Her moment of triumph when Osgood had brought the strongbox had turned on her. The key was back in Aelric's camp along with that of the strongbox.

'I can fetch a chisel from the blacksmith's, milady,' the servant interjected. 'He could force the hinges.'

Robert looked like he wanted to strike the man dead with the tool he mentioned, but in front of the two traders and Constance he could do nothing but agree.

The tool was brought and the deed done. The smith threw the lid back and as Constance had expected, carefully placed among the folds of linens and dresses she discovered the missing objects. Her eyes met Robert's.

'How fortunate that Rollo acted so cleverly and moved everything valuable here.'

'Indeed.' His eyelid twitched. 'I shall allow you to keep your money in my own strongbox. I do not doubt my servants' honesty, but it is better to be careful.'

Constance nodded reluctantly. It was on her

lips to accuse him of using her as a distraction. If she had not survived, her jewels and money would doubtless have found a permanent home in Robert's coffers. He knew she understood that, but there was nothing Constance could say that would not be an outright accusation and provoking him so openly would be foolish when she was friendless in his house. Instead she gathered the topmost girdle, shift and kirtle. She picked up the leather bag she knew contained her father's brooch and other favourite objects, rings and a bangle or two. She determined to wear these at all times rather than let them out of her sight.

'With your permission I will bathe and change now.'

Robert spread his hands wide. 'Of course. Leave the chest here and I will have it taken to your room once you are ready.'

'May I have something to eat and drink?' she asked. 'I have barely eaten in the past days.'

'If you are to live under my roof I suppose I must feed you,' Robert grumbled.

Constance flushed at yet another sign of Robert's hostility. She stood and faced him.

'If you begrudge the idea so much, then why did you order me to come back? I would gladly have not come,' she said sharply.

'You will take your place in my household because that is the fitting place for you as a member of my family,' Robert answered firmly. 'Now, I have work to do. The servants will give you anything you require and show you where you may sleep.'

Constance nodded, bunching her fists to stop her hands trembling. Robert climbed the staircase and slammed the door to the upper room. Constance stared into the fire, barely noticing the flames. When the maid brought a dish of mutton she ate without tasting, her stomach churning. Servants hung curtains and filled the bathing tub with steaming hot water and soon she lay submerged, eyes closed and thinking of nothing but the comfort and pleasure of being clean once again. The composure and ease of mind she had feared was gone for ever began to return. When she emerged from behind the curtains, freshly dressed in a warm wool gown, she discovered Robert waiting.

'When you ran you managed to save nothing but yourself?' he asked.

She raised her eyebrows at his callousness, then composed her face. What had he expected her to do?

'My mind was not on retrieving my property.'

Robert frowned. He muttered something unintelligible beneath his breath and walked away without another word. Constance watched him go, her mind alive with curiosity.

Robert had been furious to learn his name had been known, but she had detected anxiety beneath his ranting. Could there be a connection between his fear of enemies and what Hugh D'Avranches had tasked Constance with finding out? She was more determined than ever to uncover anything that might harm his name.

It was Hugh to whom she must pass information and Hugh she must turn to for aid if necessary, but as she followed the maid through to the sleeping quarters she felt the ghost of Aelric walking beside her in the home Robert had taken from him, crying out for revenge. She wished fervently it were he who would be her protector and friend.

Her ordeal had taken more of a toll than Constance had realised and for the rest of the day and that following she did little but sleep and think, sitting by the fire in the empty hall. Robert was mercifully absent until nightfall on business he did not divulge. At night she lay awake on the narrow bed that she had last occupied seven years before. The last time she had slept in this bed Robert and Jeanne had been the other side of the dividing curtain. Now Robert occupied the gallery room and Constance's bedfellows were the female servants. It was a relief not to be close to him, but her task would have been easier if she was able to gain access to his private papers.

On the third morning Constance woke with a determination that she had not previously felt. The sun was warm for the first time that year and after eating ravenously she dressed carefully, adding her favourite jewellery for safekeeping. She made herself familiar with every room in the building, identifying the possible places where Robert might have hidden any evidence. She climbed the stairs to Robert's private quarters and cautiously pushed open the door.

'What do you want?'

Robert's voice made her jump. She had thought he would be out as usual.

Wiping her suddenly clammy hands on her skirts, she bobbed a curtsey and backed out. Robert rolled himself from a chair and strode towards her.

'I wish to borrow a horse and visit the people who helped me. I want to repay them for their kindness.'

Her intention was met with sneers but her legs went weak with relief that he had not suspected her presence for other motives.

'Your tenderness is misplaced. They live on my land and were doing their duty to their lord and master. Anything less than that would have seen them in the stocks for the insult to my rank and yours.'

'Nevertheless I wish to go riding.'

Robert folded his arms and spread his legs, filling the doorway.

'You always did like to roam. Go out, if you must. But any ill that befalls you will be on your head, not mine.'

He went back inside, slamming the door. Constance made her way to the kitchen. She would take some food at least. Robert would not miss that. The morning was bright and she could be there and back before he even demanded her presence again.

Chapter Twelve

Caddoc and Ulf approached Aldredley cautiously. They arrived at the middle of the day, when the sun was high. Most of the inhabitants would be at work in the fields and there would be few people to notice their arrival. The two men were known a little, and while the villagers had no love for their new Norman masters, it was never a good idea to risk discovery.

They kept to the woods until the houses and barn were in plain sight, then crossed from the thick bracken undergrowth to the rutted path where Caddoc had left Constance only a couple of days before. He glanced keenly towards the village square before catching himself and shaking his head at his own foolishness. She would be long gone by now. A good thing, too, because in the nights since they had parted she had invaded his sleep with more relentlessness than her countrymen had torn through England.

Creeping closer, Caddoc watched as a pair of old women crossed from the well to one of the low houses. A grey palfrey he did not recognise stood tethered to a post, but there was no sign of the Frenchman he knew lived with one of the women. An old man was bent over a log, chopping ineffectively with an axe. The village appeared peaceful.

'I think we're safe,' he murmured to Ulf. 'Be quick and careful. Find out what happened to the woman if you can, but mention no names.'

Pulling his hood further forward to hide his mutilated ear, Caddoc strolled down the path and into the village. Their arrival went unnoticed at first, but before long suspicious eyes followed them. Ulf pushed his hood back and smiled in greeting at faces he recognised, which relaxed as they recognised him in turn. Caddoc stood back and watched before moving further into the village.

'Lord Brunwulf!'

The heat drained from Caddoc's body. He turned slowly, hand reaching for his dagger.

'You are mistaken.'

The man who had spoken words that pierced his heart was the old man who had been chopping wood outside the shack.

'Too young.' The man sighed. 'My eyes are failing and my mind is confused. But one of his sons?'

Caddoc pulled the cloak around him tighter. 'Brunwulf and his sons were hanged,' he said.

'Aye, do you think us here could forget that, with the rogue who sits in his place? We regret his passing every day. Brunwulf was a fine man. His sons, too.'

Caddoc ran his hands through the knots of his hair, troubled by the mention of his father.

'Life is hard since the Normans came,' he agreed. He sat down beside the man. 'You have one living here, I've heard.'

'Aye but he was never a fighter, you could tell. He was a bondsman. Now he's at peace and fights no more.' The old man wiped a hand across bleary eyes. 'If they were all like him the world would be a better place.'

Caddoc pondered his words. How many across England had done the same? How many had taken English wives, or English husbands for that matter? A pit of loss opened in his belly that threatened to suck him in. He glanced towards the axe embedded in the log. The old man had made little progress.

'Let me help you,' he offered.

The man waved a hand and grinned.

Caddoc shrugged off his cloak and, noting how warm the day was becoming, his heavy wool tunic, leaving him the thinner lower layer. That would stay on so no one would see the scars beneath. He shoved his sleeves above his elbows and picked up the axe. Splitting the logs was the exertion his body needed and each strike brought him greater satisfaction, blotting out his frustration. Before long his muscles were aching and sweat that ran freely down his back. When done, he carried the logs to the old man's shack.

'This should see you right until the weather gets milder,' he said with a smile.

The man took Caddoc's hands.

'Thank you for your kindness. We're not venturing too far into the forest at these times. From what I've heard the woods are getting wilder. More so than even you make it.'

'How so?' Caddoc asked.

The old man sucked his few remaining teeth. 'There's more than you living there, or travelling through. Evil men who'd torment anyone they come across. Not three days past we had a slip of a girl stumble in who'd been wickedly treated and was lucky to escape with her life.'

Caddoc's throat tightened. 'Tell me more.'

The old man sucked his teeth once more.

'A Norman she was. Dark-haired and pale. On the scrawny side.'

Caddoc bristled at the disparaging description. Pale or not, Constance was still as beautiful as she had been at sixteen and how else would she have appeared after days of imprisonment? He resisted his impulse to defend her. He told himself it was the safety of his men he needed to know, but knew that concern was secondary. He wondered ruefully when Constance's well-being had become so vital to him.

He listened as the old man described Constance's arrival and questioning, waiting to hear a description of himself or one of the men. He slid his eyes to where Ulf was talking with a pretty girl who was beating sheets in a tub outside a cottage. If they needed to leave in haste, he was easily to hand. He need not have feared as the old man's story tailed off.

'Did she say where she had been taken? Or who took her?'

Once again the old man sucked his teeth.

'Not within my hearing. The girl denied it, but most likely she'd been used for some foul means. Old Edyt took her off and will have seen her right if that was the case.'

Caddoc's lip twitched. The knowledge that Gerrod's camp was safe made him breathe easier, but references to Constance being 'seen right' filled his mind with horrific images.

'Where is this Edyt? What passed between them?'

'Her husband took the girl to the baron's house. He's the Frenchman, so would be welcome where we are not. As for what passed between them, only Edyt will know that and she keeps her secrets well.'

Caddoc's shoulders dropped. He had the information he needed. Constance was safe in Hamestan, back among her countrymen. The man suddenly started forward, gesturing over Caddoc's shoulder.

'That's Edyt and that's the girl herself!'

Fire coursed through Caddoc's veins. He turned sharply and indeed, she was there. Constance walked alongside a woman who was bent at the neck, but it was difficult to tell who was supporting whom.

Caddoc realised he had begun to tremble and when he bunched his fists his palms were damp. That the mere sight of her should have such an effect on him was astounding. He took a step closer to view her better. The two women paused. Constance was standing side on to him, listening to the old woman and nodding gravely to what she heard.

She looked different. He could not have expected her to remain in the same filthy clothes, but he had not imagined her as she was. Her cheeks had gained colour that they had been lacking and the blue-black shadows around her eyes had begun to diminish. Her hair was pulled back beneath a veil, but Caddoc could still see the dark coils looping around her ears and providing a frame for the jaw that was set firm in determination. She wore a dress of green the colour of summer leaves. It was gathered with a girdle, drawing his eyes downwards to her slender waist and the swell of her breasts that had only been hinted at beneath the man's tunic she had worn as a disguise, which was now obvious to anyone who looked. And Caddoc was looking all too closely, drinking in the sight.

Constance smiled and Caddoc's face softened in response, but at that moment she turned slightly towards him and stiffened, her shoulders rising as though she had been stabbed. Her hand flew to her mouth and her eyes widened fearfully. Caddoc was instantly alert, his hand reaching for his dagger as he prepared to seek out the source of her distress before he realised he had no need to search. He was the cause.

Constance whipped sharply round, calling to mind a doe startled by the hunter. Caddoc knew he should let her go, but the need to speak to her overruled his sense.

'My lady, wait!'

She halted, but her body was still tense and ready to flee at any moment. Caddoc remained where he was, sensing that if he stepped towards her she would go for ever. He held his hands out, palms up to show they were free of weapons and in a gesture of supplication.

'I only wish to speak to you. Grant me a moment of your time, please.' He spoke rapidly in case she decided to leave, but she whispered something to the woman by her side who had been staring at Caddoc with undisguised animosity. The woman fell back and he walked towards Constance, palms still outstretched. His pulse rate had just about returned to its regular rhythm by the time he joined her, but as she raised her eyes to his it lurched into double speed again.

'I only want to see that you are have recovered.'

'From the ordeal you subjected me to?' she asked scathingly. She pulled the edge of her veil forward defensively. 'How many gaolers would be so considerate? As you can see I am well.'

Three rings ornamented her fingers. An enamelled brooch nestled on her breast and a jewelled pin held her veil fast at the side of her head. She wore enough finery to feed this village for a year. She had lost no time in presenting herself as the wealthy lady she undoubtedly was.

Constance's eyes travelled across his face, then downwards. He realised with a start that she was examining him as closely as he had scrutinised her. Caddoc became conscious of how unkempt he was in his worn tunic, clinging to him with the sweat his labour had created. The gulf between them widened further.

'Why did you come back here?' he demanded.

A faint pink blush spread across her cheeks. 'I came to bring them a gift to repay their kindness.'

'What did you bring?' Caddoc asked out of curiosity.

The colour in her cheeks deepened to a flush that matched the red of her lips. 'Bread, ale, mutton. My brother-in-law would give me nothing more, but they have so little and were so kind to me.'

She looked so ashamed at the meanness of her gift that Caddoc's throat tightened. He folded his arms. 'I told you that you would find Hamestan a different place to the one you left.'

Constance's face fell. She waved an arm around. 'I thought your life was harsh because of the way you lived, but theirs is equally poor. It's the same in the other places I passed through. It's no wonder you hate us for coming here.'

Caddoc looked at her with scorn rising in his throat. 'And yet you come here flaunting such finery so openly.'

Boldly he took hold of her hand, lifted it and stroked his thumb across the surface of the three rings. She began to pull away, but he held steady.

'Did our ambush teach you nothing about guarding yourself?' he snapped in a rush of frustration.

'I don't wear them to flaunt them!' Constance muttered.

Violently, she pulled her hand away and folded

her arms across her body. The gesture forced her breasts closer together. Despite his anger Caddoc could not take his eyes from them. Why had he not taken more time or care when Constance had been in his arms. A body like hers called out to be caressed and explored at length, not casually and quickly used. It was little wonder their time together had been so unfulfilling for both of them.

'I prefer to keep my possessions where I know where they are. Wearing them is the safest way I can think of.'

Something in her tone of voice set Caddoc's senses alert.

'Why so?'

She wrinkled her forehead and wrung her hands together, glancing around fearfully.

'Tell me,' he prompted. When she did not answer he looped her arm through his.

'If you try to take me again I'll scream,' she warned.

Caddoc's lip curled. Her reaction was unsurprising after the way they had parted, but hurt none the less.

'You have nothing to fear from me. I am more in danger when a word from you could put my neck in the noose.'

'You think I would do that!' she exclaimed.

'It's no worse than what you think me capable of,' he sneered. He scuffed his foot angrily in the dirt.

'Once we would never have suspected the other capable of any injury.'

'That was long ago. We aren't those people any more.'

Constance glanced over her shoulder to where Edyt stood. The woman gave a curt nod and turned away.

'I'll tell you, but not here,' she said.

Still holding Constance's arm, Caddoc began strolling towards the stream. Constance limped slightly as she leaned in against him, shoulders and arms touching. But for the expression on her face they might have been a pair of lovers strolling as they once had. With any other woman he would have chanced an arm around her waist. He'd held Constance so close before, but when no longer abducting her and forcing her through the woods the gesture felt too intimate. He noticed what he had missed before.

'You haven't replaced your stick,' he remarked. She looked up at him and for the first time since they had met, she smiled.

'After going without it for so long and walking so far I decided I would try for longer. I can't walk far before my leg hurts, but I think I can do well enough for short distances.'

She spoke with pride. Caddoc had not realised

how living with the twisted foot affected her beyond the difficulty in walking. He decided they had gone far enough if that was the case. He stopped by the stream and helped Constance sit on the grass, which was comfortably dry.

'Tell me what's troubling you,' he commanded. 'It's plain on your face something is.'

Her eyes flickered from side to side. She looked mistrustful, but when had he given her reason to be otherwise. After a pause that went on far too long for Caddoc's liking she spoke.

'Soon after I arrived at Lord de Coudray's house my chest was brought. He didn't want me to open it, but I insisted. Guess what I found?'

The answer was obvious now, given what she was wearing, but Caddoc supplied it anyway.

'Your missing jewels?' he murmured.

'Yes!' Her eyes shone with indignation, giving her face an edge of beauty.

'Did you challenge him?' Caddoc asked. His skin prickled at the thought of Constance confronting the Pig and he was suddenly fearful. He resisted the urge to wrap her in his arms, assuming she would not welcome his touch. 'He is a dangerous man to cross.'

'I know,' she said, her voice anxious. She glanced down, her brow furrowing momentarily. 'I said nothing, but I made sure I kept my most treasured pieces with me.' There was a rebuke in her tone.

Caddoc's conscience pricked that he had immediately ascribed the worst motives. She wore her jewellery not through flamboyance, but for safekeeping.

'There's more.' She bit her lower lip before continuing. 'I went to bathe and change into fresh clothes soon after I arrived. My chest was searched while I was absent.'

Caddoc blinked to rid himself of the image of Constance bathing, her naked flesh slick and speckled with water droplets that called out to be licked away.

Control yourself, man, he commanded.

Anyone would think he was seventeen again, pulling her by the hand into the cowshed to shelter from the rainstorm and stealing a kiss. She was within reach if he wanted to kiss her now. He imagined what her reaction might be, of a repeat of the revulsion she must have felt when he touched her before. He pictured himself doing it anyway with such care that would break through the shield of ice that encased her until she melted in his arms.

'How can you be sure?' he asked when he had mastery of his voice again.

'Dresses were beneath shifts. Things were not folded as my maidservant had done before I left

Bredon. Small details that would not be noticed unless I was looking for them.'

'But nothing was missing? Why did he do that?'

'I think he was searching for something else.'

Her wide brown eyes were thoughtful.

'I told you Rollo had tried to see the traders again, but they had gone? What if he had something else to put in the chest, but failed to do so?'

'What of it?' Caddoc asked.

'Robert asked if I had taken anything when I escaped. He was annoyed that I hadn't. Perhaps he thinks something is still in the strongbox. Do you still have it?'

Probably he did. He had not been back into the loft since Constance had left it, not wishing to dwell on the memories the room evoked and it was small enough that lying in the corner it might be overlooked.

'I haven't touched it and I doubt anyone else will have,' he answered.

'Can you bring it to me?' she asked.

Caddoc looked at her in surprise. 'Why? It was empty.'

'What if it wasn't?' she said. 'Or perhaps there was something on the outside we failed to spot. We weren't looking for anything other than what we expected to find.'

She sounded eager, already imagining a discovery. Caddoc half-hoped she was right.

'What would you do with something if you found it? Give it to de Coudray?'

Constance snorted. 'Of course not! I have a powerful friend who could see him brought to justice.'

'A Norman friend? A man?' Caddoc felt once more the heat of desire, mingled now with a touch of jealousy.

'Yes, the man I promised to help uncover what Robert is involved in. He won't act without proof.'

Caddoc watched her closely as she spoke. Her jaw was set and her expression dark. Even during her imprisonment she had not shown such animosity toward her captors.

'I want to know why you hate him,' he asked.

'Does it matter? I have my reasons.' Constance held his gaze, daring him to push her further. 'It's enough that my enemy is yours, surely.'

She was under no obligation to share her motives, so despite his curiosity he bent his head in acceptance.

Constance pushed herself to her feet and brushed her skirt down.

'I have to go. Robert knows I have come here, but will be expecting me back before too long. He was angry enough even at that.'

'Constance, don't defy him and risk yourself,' Caddoc said. He stood and turned her to face him. 'I will be too far away to help if you need my aid.'

She raised her eyebrows in astonishment, then a faint smile crept across her face. She blinked it away and her eyes hardened.

'If you wish to help, find the box and bring it to me.'

She walked away.

'I've told you I think you are wasting your time with that,' Caddoc called after her.

She looked back over her shoulder. 'Then don't come. I shall return here five days from now. If you choose not to help me that is your decision, but it might be the only way I can discover what I need to know.'

This moment could be the last time he would see her unless he found what she wanted. She was wasting her time, but he already knew he would be waiting for her on the appointed day. He let her go three paces before he called her name.

'I'll do my best, but I cannot promise it will still be there.'

Her smile lit his day. He chased after her and placed his hand on her shoulders, aware of her sharp intake of breath. This simple sound was enough to drive him out of his mind and he would have kissed her there and then if Ulf had not begun to walk towards them. He waved a frantic hand and Ulf retreated to wait beside a cowshed.

Caddoc led Constance to her palfrey.

'I'm glad I saw you again,' she said as she

unhitched the animal's rein. 'I would not have wanted to part as we did.'

Caddoc lifted her on to the horse. His hands lingered on her waist and he spread his fingers, feeling the soft flare of her hips. She covered his with her own, squeezing gently, then removed them, not unkindly.

'Take care and don't travel without an escort or guard,' he said sternly. 'I didn't go to the trouble of freeing you from captivity to have another wild man lay claim to you.'

Her eyes widened in alarm, then she dug her heels into the horse's flanks and cantered away. Caddoc watched her go, regretting his words. He'd come close to building some trust between them and to mention her capture had sent it crashing down again. Moreover, the thought of anyone, wild man or other, laying claim to Constance was something he did not wish to ponder for fear the jealousy would consume him.

Chapter Thirteen

Constance rode hard until she was out of sight of Aldredley, far enough away to ensure she could not have been followed. Once she was certain she slipped from her mount and leaned against a tree, head back and eyes closed. A soft breeze played around her and she tilted her head further back to better allow the air to cool the burning of her throat and cheeks.

Seeing Aelric had caused a jumble of emotions she could not untangle without more consideration than she dared give them. Her initial fear at seeing her former captor had given way indecently quickly to the heart-racing desire that his appearance had caused. She should have baulked at his clothing sweat-stained from wood chopping and hair in the customary tangle, but the sight of the tunic clinging to his sinewy form and the heightened colour in his cheeks had reached deep inside her, demanding she submit to what her body craved.

When he looked at her his eyes had burned with the same intensity she felt inside. He had wanted her. She had seen it on his face as he walked with her, just as she had seen it during her seduction in the tower before he became angry, but to feel such a powerful craving herself was far too disconcerting. She fanned herself rapidly with the fringe of her veil until her cheeks cooled and she could breathe without her throat tightening.

She set off for Hamestan, wanting the days to pass quickly until she could return to discover if Aelric had done as she asked and brought the chest. To put herself in his path again would be to throw herself open to temptation once more. Sense told her to stay away, but she could not do that. Five days would give her long enough to subdue the traitorous yearnings that disconcerted her so much. Her promise to Hugh meant she had to discover what secrets Robert was keeping. Aelric would be the means to that end, nothing more, she told herself. Nothing more than that.

When Constance arrived back at Hamestan she discovered it was market day. Traders called their wares, children lingered with keen eyes near the stall selling pastries and a piper played while his scruffy dog danced on its hind legs to a smattering of applause. The sight drew a smile from Constance, but the music plunged her into sadness as she remembered Aelric playing in the same place. She could not imagine the angry-eyed man joining in something so light-hearted now.

To her surprise Robert was in the square. He was not the type to enjoy the amusements afforded by a fair or market day. Previously she had never seen him attend one, or walk willingly among his tenants. As she studied him his presence became clearer. He was walking from stall to stall, inspecting the goods and talking to the stallholders with a severe expression. The four foot-soldiers at his heels were the only indication of his rank, but the fact he kept them so close was a sign of something else. Fear for his safety? A need to display his power? She wasn't sure, but seeing him so closely guarded reconfirmed her belief that Aelric would never succeed in getting close enough to do what he craved.

She dismounted and led the mare round the edge of the marketplace. Robert saw her and cocked a finger to beckon her over. Boiling inwardly at the curtness of his gesture, she hitched the horse's rein to a post and threaded her way through the crowd.

'So you're back from your journey,' Robert remarked, ignoring her curtsey. 'Not using your stick?'

'I find I am stronger than I used to be,' Constance replied. She looked around her. 'I did not expect to see you here.'

'I am checking they are accounting for everything they sell,' Robert said, peering suspiciously at a pie seller's tray. He held an arm out and nodded curtly to Constance. 'Walk with me now you are here.'

Swallowing her dislike, she took it and walked alongside him, the bodyguards following close behind.

'I don't trust half these vagabonds not to try a deception when it comes to paying me what they owe,' Robert growled.

'How could you be sure?' Constance asked. Their clothes were old and the people themselves had the gaunt, half-starved look she had witnessed in Aldredley. The lives of everyone she encountered appeared equally barren and full of suffering. 'None of them look particularly prosperous.'

'They could pay more. I draw in barely any taxes,' Robert grumbled. He scratched his swollen belly. 'I raise a miserable amount, barely enough to live on. I told D'Avranches last time I saw him that they could pay more, but he refused to consider it. I'd squeeze them if I was in his position.'

Constance wrinkled her nose at his greed and callousness.

'You have seen Lord D'Avranches recently?'

Robert curled his lip into a crafty sneer. 'No, he's too busy considering how to manage the troublesome Welsh than to pay his vassals such attention, but he'll be making his tour of his empire shortly. Better for him if he stayed out of the way of men who have more important work to do than pay courtship to him.'

For the first time since returning to Hamestan Constance's senses tingled with anticipation. His contemptuous manner was no proof that Robert was involved in intrigue, but the disparaging terms in which he spoke of Hugh left her certain he had no loyalty to his overlord. She was so busy speculating what he might be planning that she missed Robert's words, only heard her name in raised tones. She looked at him questioningly.

'Is your conscience satisfied by your act of charity?' Robert said.

'It is for now,' Constance answered. 'I was glad to be able to repay their kindness.'

'You seem remarkably keen to waste your time and wealth on these people. Did your husband sanction such generosity of nature? It would surprise me greatly from the Piteur I knew.'

Constance's flesh crawled. She had always wondered if Robert had been aware of Piteur's nature before she was bound to him by marriage. Hearing the cries her sister had muffled in the night, it would not have surprised her to learn the two men were kindred spirits. She gave thanks briefly that Jeanne was at peace and could no longer suffer torments at Robert's hands. It struck her that Jeanne must have left possessions behind her. A cloak, perhaps, or warm shifts that would go some way to make the lives of Edyt and the village women easier. She must search them out before she returned to Aldredley. It would provide a perfect reason in case Robert became suspicious.

'I intend to return to the village soon,' she said.

'You'll be returning nowhere,' Robert said firmly.

'But I must! I promised.' Tears prickled Constance's eyes at this unexpected barrier to her plan. She blinked them away fiercely before Robert could see the effect he had caused. 'There is good I can do to these people. I will not spend my days idly doing nothing.'

Robert drew closer to her. His breath was sour on her face. 'You won't be idle. You need to give your attention to running my household. My wife's passing has left my servants in disarray. You've run your own home so you'll be capable of taking her place.'

His pig-like eyes narrowed as he gazed at her in a manner that sent chills through Constance. For one horrific moment the worst possible meaning to his words flashed through her mind before she succeeded in calming herself. He was referring to the role of chatelaine; that was all.

'I am willing to manage your affairs, but I see no reason why I cannot come and go as I please,' she said.

'I have not got the resources to spare to escort you about the countryside,' Robert answered. 'I see you went without an escort or chaperone today. It is unfitting behaviour for a young woman, especially a widow who should be mourning her husband.'

'There was nothing to mourn,' Constance spat out. She removed her hand from Robert's arm. They had completed a circuit of the square and were close to where Constance's horse waited. She crossed her arms and faced Robert with what she hoped was a calm expression.

'I can travel alone as I did today. I am not a maiden with a reputation to be ruined. It isn't far and the road is good. There is no reason why I cannot carry out what you wish and have my own diversions, too.'

'I want you to stay inside the manor grounds,' Robert said.

'Am I a prisoner?' Constance asked.

Robert's jowly chin jerked up. 'No, but I order you to remain here where I can ensure you are safe.'

'Then I am a prisoner,' she muttered, turning away.

'I am not an unreasonable man. You may come as far as the marketplace, or down to the river,' Robert said. 'I expect your obedience, Constance. You won't have forgotten what happened when you last left my house without my permission.'

Quickly he raised a hand to head height, palm outstretched. Constance flinched and Robert smiled in satisfaction at the sight, then lowered it again.

'I won't disobey you,' she said through clenched teeth.

'See to it you don't. You were fortunate to escape with only a beating last time. If I had known then you had released my prisoner, I would have seen you in irons as a traitor.'

Constance bit back her hatred, anxiety twisting her stomach. She clenched her fists, concealing them in the folds of her dress. It would not do for Robert to start thinking about Aelric in case his part in Constance's capture became known.

'Did you ever find the boy?' she asked. 'He must have been recaptured quickly enough.'

Robert curled his lip. 'No, I never found him, but a scrawny weakling like that would not have survived long on his own. I'm surprised he lasted ten strokes without dying halfway through. I should have let him fight me. It would have been better value as entertainment for the crowd to watch him bleed out. Most likely he was taken by slavers or died face down in a river somewhere. You cost me money that day by setting him free. Money you can repay me by your work.'

Constance breathed easier. It was good that Robert believed Aelric dead. She regarded him quietly. He was burly and taller than Aelric, but flabby, whereas Aelric had developed strength and muscles that had taken her by surprise when she touched him and caused the confusing sensations that beset her. Perhaps it was not so unlikely that Aelric might triumph, assuming he could get past Robert's guards.

'I have visitors arriving soon and there is much to be done,' Robert said. 'Return to the house and speak to my staff regarding meals to be prepared and accommodation. Perhaps in a month or two, if you have pleased me, I will see the way to letting you visit your friends again.'

'You do me such a kindness,' Constance said scathingly.

'I see marriage did not teach you manners,' Robert growled. 'Perhaps another husband will succeed where your first failed.'

Constance's blood ran cold.

'It is not my intention to remarry,' she said, unhitching the horse's reins. 'I intend to take my vows at Brockley as soon as I am able.'

If only she could bring that day forward and reach the sanctuary of the convent now. She must discover what she could for Hugh as soon as possible, then beg him to aid her as he had promised he would.

'If I say you will remarry then that is what you will do,' Robert said. 'I have connections that would benefit us all by an alliance. I am your protector and know what is best for you.'

She had assumed he was talking hypothetically, but now it became clear why Robert had insisted she return. There had never been any intention in his mind that she could leave after a year. He had spun a web and she had walked willingly into it.

'I will not stand for that,' she protested. 'Lord D'Avranches will support me in that.'

'D'Avranches's opinion is of no consequence to me. He has his own matters to attend to dealing with the Welsh. He will hardly risk antagonising one of his tenants-in-chief to placate a mere woman.' Robert's eyes narrowed. 'Besides, there is no guarantee he will keep his position longer than his predecessor. Our King is fickle with his favours and harsh to judge those who fail him. When I find you another husband you may leave my household. Someone will have a use even for a cripple such as you.'

Constance closed her eyes, fear and disgust overwhelming her. She could not endure marriage to another man of the sort Robert would find. She would run tonight. Back to Aldredley where Edyt would surely keep her safe until Aelric arrived.

And then what? Beg him to take her with him? Go back to the camp where she was among enemies and live as a fugitive as they did for the remainder of her days? That would never work. Robert would know where to look and Aelric had made it clear that her presence in the camp was unwelcome. He desired her, but he did not want her.

She was alone here and friendless and had no option but to submit to Robert for the time being until she could find another solution. She bowed her head meekly, hating herself for her cowardice.

Robert snapped his fingers at the guards who had been following at a discreet distance. They stood to attention.

'Escort Lady Constance back,' he instructed. 'I have further business here and I would not wish her to be unattended.'

He walked away, leaving Constance shaking. She mounted her horse; glad she would not have to walk back as her legs had turned to liquid. Her reaction to Robert's threatened violence had been instinctive and genuine, but she felt no shame. Let him think she was in fear of him and he was less likely to watch her. She would run his household as he demanded and in the process search for the evidence she needed to see him at Hugh's mercy, but a month or two would be too late. Aelric would have returned and found she had not come. He would think she had chosen not to because she did not care to see what he had found. The thought that he was so close but beyond her reach was enough to bring tears to her eyes and she travelled back to the house blinded by tears.

The dreaded demands on her body aside, Piteur had left Constance alone to run his house as she saw fit and the long years of commanding a household had left her an able and efficient manager. Robert's servants, who had become lax since Jeanne's death, were soon working tirelessly. One crucial result was that Constance had access to almost every chamber in the house, save Robert's own. She took every opportunity to search for anything that might be considered incriminating, but found nothing other than lists of guests, three names appearing on five occasions. She doubted Robert would leave letters detailing a conspiracy in clear sight, but even so it was better to occupy her mind than imagining Aelric waiting for her.

Robert's visitors came and left, a huddle of men who eyed her with suspicion whenever she approached. She sat silently during mealtimes, watching carefully for any indication that one of them might be the husband she feared she must take, but none paid her more attention than another. After she retired to bed each night she often heard voices raised in argument, but could make out no distinct words.

Sleep eluded her, not least because whenever she closed her eyes Aelric was there, his lips on hers and his hands roving across her body in a manner that had never happened during their blundered coupling in the tower or their hasty, fumbling adventures in the past. When she did sleep she awoke wrapped in the bedsheets, fevered and craving something she could not name. It was as though her body had broken free of her mind's control and was demanding gratification she was unable to grant.

Her frustration grew until the day came and passed when Constance should have been meeting Aelric. Though her face betrayed no outward emotion, inside Constance screamed and raged with sorrow.

She would never know if he had gone to the village and he would never know she had been prevented. He would believe she had changed her mind, just as he believed she had years ago. She hugged herself tightly, slipping her fingers beneath the neck of her gown to her shoulders, running them across the scarred flesh where Robert's belt had cut deeply. If only Aelric had seen the scars she bore he would never have resented her not meeting him.

* * *

When Constance had counted seven days since she had last seen Aelric she could bear it no longer. She threw down her embroidery with an irritable sigh, causing the young girl she had selected as maidservant to jump in alarm. She had not left the confines of the house for days, venturing only to the courtyard. She had seen no purpose in going anywhere, but today the spring sun was warm and she felt the urge to be among people. It was market day again and she decided to walk into the town and remind herself that life continued outside the walls of the house. She bid the maid fetch their cloaks and together they prepared to leave.

Robert was in the Great Hall, feet stretched out by the fire.

'Where do you think you're going,' he barked.

'To the market,' Constance answered. 'I have my maid to escort me.'

She steeled herself for his objections, but he merely sniffed and demanded she bring back a couple of fowl for the guests who would be arriving later that day.

Once more the town was filled with people visiting stalls, making purchases and exchanging greetings. The warmer weather appeared to have lifted everyone's moods despite the poverty that they lived with. It was the first time Constance had really observed what had changed in seven years and she was surprised by what she saw. The marketplace had been open, but was now enclosed on all four sides. Buildings had grown larger and a new forge stood beside the ovens, replacing the old hut that had stood there. One sight sent a chill running through her. The gallows stood where they always had. She looked away, Aelric's screams filling her memory. She turned to go, the day spoiled.

A hunched beggar swathed in rags squatted against the wall by the well. As Constance walked past the man clutched at the hem of Constance's cloak with filthy hands. She recoiled and attempted to pull free, but her assailant held tight.

'Does the lady have a heart kind enough to spare anything?' he croaked in a beseeching voice.

Constance stopped struggling. Her instinct was to brush him off, but as she recollected the hardship she had seen since returning compassion prevailed. She slipped him a penny. When she pressed the coin into his hand the beggar clutched her wrist tightly and spoke in a voice she recognised.

'Thank you kindly, mistress.'

Constance stared down into Ulf's face.

'Why are you here? Is everything all right at the camp?' Visions of Robert discovering the hiding place and the ensuing slaughter filled Constance's limbs with lead.

'The camp is safe, but our friend with two names was expecting you. He sent me here to keep watch to tell you he's waiting where you used to meet.'

He dropped her hand and shuffled away, leaving Constance standing open-mouthed staring after him. She raised a hand to her cheek that was suddenly pale. Around her people carried on their business unaware of the whirlpool of emotions spinning around Constance's head. She slipped the maid a penny.

'I'm going to the river to pick flowers. Go buy yourself a ribbon or sweetmeat.'

It took time to reach the old cowshed on the bank of the Bollin and her ankle was beginning to throb, but the idea that Aelric might be waiting meant the journey passed unnoticed. As her feet travelled the old, remembered path her mind spun with a turmoil of memories.

She paused outside the low building. It had been old seven years ago and it was a wonder it still stood here, forgotten. No men worked in the fields, no animals grazed outside and the beams were beginning to rot. Her hands began to tremble as she reached to run her fingers over the rusty iron door handle. It crossed her mind this could be a trap and that she was once more throwing herself into captivity, but she dismissed it as foolishness. Aelric need not have let her go and she would have been easy enough to abduct from Aldredley when they had met. Besides, a treacherous voice told her, wouldn't she willingly take captivity at Aelric's hand over the same conditions with Robert?

Cautiously she pushed open the door and slipped inside.

Chapter Fourteen

Caddoc waited in the near darkness, reclining against a wall in the corner beside the door, legs crossed and face concealed by his hood pulled low. In his dark clothing he was confident he could remain unseen if anyone beside Constance entered and if he didn't then the stout stick that lay beside him would have to ensure his presence remained a secret.

The weather had turned warm and the small shed was stifling despite the thin tunic he wore. Dust motes hung in shafts of sunlight and he watched them drift lazily to the floor. He had arrived before sunrise and was prepared to wait until darkness when Ulf would join him. He had told Ulf they would leave then, but Caddoc knew that he would wait longer if necessary to see Constance again.

Even if Ulf found her there was no guarantee

she would come. He settled back against the wall and closed his eyes. Old straw had rotted into the earth, but the cowshed still smelled the same as it always had. He never imagined such a scent could evoke the memories it did.

The creaking of the door opening jolted him alert in time to see a slim figure enter and close the door quietly. Constance unpinned the veil that covered her hair and throat and took a step into the centre of the shed. She sighed; clearly thinking she was alone until the sound of Caddoc shifting made her jump.

'Aelric?'

He pushed himself upright. She reached him at the same time as he stood and threw herself against him, burying her head in the warm curve of his shoulder and flinging her arms about his neck. Instinctively he wound his arms around her and held her tightly. She was warm and smelled of roses. Her breasts were soft, pushing against his chest, and his body began to react in the most predictable way. He could have stayed like that for ever, but his low laugh of surprised delight caused her body to tense and the spell binding them was broken. He clasped his arms around, enjoying the sensation for a moment longer, before Constance squirmed free and stepped back. Her cheeks flamed alluringly.

'Forgive me. I don't know what I was thinking,' she said awkwardly.

Caddoc waited until his heartbeat had slowed to the customary rate.

'What sort of man would demand an apology for such a greeting?' he asked, fixing her with a bold stare. 'Do you think I am carved from rock?'

His words were a joke, but there was no mockery in it. All the same her blush deepened, spreading to her throat and disappearing beneath the neck of her gown. She took another step away from him.

'Where is the chest?' she asked abruptly.

'You assume I have it?' Caddoc asked. He swallowed down his disappointment that this was her first care.

'Would you have come otherwise?' she asked, stepping further from him.

He was as convinced as ever that there was no point, but had agreed to bring it solely for the chance of meeting her again. It irked him that the mystery mattered to her more than his presence did. He drew a deep breath, determined to match her coolness towards him.

'I apologise for making you walk so far, but this is as close to Hamestan as I am prepared to venture.'

'So you have the box? I hope you would not risk yourself without good cause,' she said.

'There would have to be a compelling reason to bring me here,' Caddoc agreed. He lifted his gaze to meet hers. She stared back in a manner that caused his stomach to begin a slow tumble. She could not be feeling what he was or how could she remain so aloof?

Constance turned abruptly and walked away from him. He watched her examine their surroundings. It was here they had met in secret, the lonely girl and angry boy. Where they had talked of dreams and ambitions that would never be fulfilled. Where he had first slipped his hand about her slender waist and drawn her close, becoming more daring than ever before, and she had willingly allowed him further and further indiscretions.

Emotions threatened to overwhelm him. How could what they did in the loft be so empty and shaming when the same act so long ago had been sweet with all the frenzied passion and desire only a youth could feel? He knew the answer. She had not wanted to do it and had been bargaining under duress, not giving herself willingly. Would it be more fulfilling now she no longer felt she had to buy her liberty? He felt himself begin to stir as he considered it. His body felt acutely sensitive, every nerve awakening, and he was filled with longing to find out.

Perhaps Constance was thinking of the same

memories, but with a different recollection because her shoulders tightened and she would not meet his gaze when she finally turned around.

'How long have you been here?'

'Since before dawn.' When Caddoc answered his voice sounded oddly muffled. He cleared his throat and began again. 'I went back to Aldredley as you asked me to. I waited for you until nightfall, but you never came.'

'I wanted to come, but Robert would not let me leave the village,' Constance answered. Her voice was high with frustration and tears rose in her eyes.

'I was right to be concerned for you.' Caddoc's lips twitched at the vastness of the understatement, thinking of the suspense and agonies he had gone through and how only Ulf's sensible words had prevented him rushing straight to Hamestan Manor in search of her.

Constance wiped tears away fiercely before they settled on her high cheekbones. Caddoc raised a hand to assist, but drew back, knowing such a gesture was too intimate. How hard had she tried to keep their assignations either seven years ago or more recently? He was watching her reaction closely, arms folded across his chest.

'He prevented you?' Caddoc asked quietly. 'Did he hurt you?'

He took a step towards her, but Constance

wrapped her arms about herself, creating a barrier he dared not break.

'Robert said it was too dangerous for me to leave the house. That there are too many dangerous outlaws crawling about the woods,' she explained, raising an eyebrow. 'After what happened on my journey here I could hardly contradict him without raising his suspicion too much. You said the same yourself last time we met.'

Caddoc glanced to the doorway. 'Where does he think you are today?'

'Still at the market, I suppose,' Constance said in a carefree manner that did not seem entirely convincing. She was deeply unnerved by something. 'He allows me the freedom to walk into the town and down to the river. I am not a prisoner in the house, but he knows I could not go too far on foot.'

Caddoc reached out and touched her shoulder, closing his hand gently around it. She jerked away, but then her body relaxed and she leaned her head down so her cheek was resting on his hand. Caddoc turned her to face him and found himself level with her warm brown eyes.

'Constance, are you being mistreated?' he asked anxiously.

Her eyes creased at the corners. She smiled for the first time at the fierce concern that filled his voice and the fingers that gripped suddenly tighter. He wanted her so deeply the need was like an open wound, but beneath the lust he was discovering a further urge—to guard her from harm.

'No, he's as rude and boorish as ever he was, but he does not hurt me.'

Caddoc relaxed his grip. Constance covered his hand with hers. The touch of her cool fingers on his skin sent ripples of desire along his arm, spreading through every part of his body. It tugged at his groin, but more unsettlingly it continued in a direct line to his heart.

'So you are safe?' he asked. 'And happy?'

'Happy? No,' Constance replied. She removed her hand from his and began twisting her fingers together, pulling at the loose edge of her long veil. He wondered if she was even aware she was doing it.

'My sister is dead, as you told me. Robert expects me to act as his chatelaine in her place.' She jutted her jaw out. 'He likes me to be modest and silent and wait on the guests who visit him.'

Caddoc bunched his fists at the image of Constance submitting to the Pig's orders in the home that should have been Caddoc's.

'He treats you like a servant?'

Constance raised an eyebrow. 'He treats me as any man treats the women in his household. Someone to smooth over difficulties and ensure his reputation as a host is not damaged. I don't object as it gives me the freedom to move around the manor house and discover what I can.'

'Do you think he suspects you are working against him?' Caddoc asked. 'Could that be why he prevented you from returning to the village?'

'He suspects nothing,' Constance said. 'He prevented me for the sake of spitefulness because he did not wish for me to help Edyt. As long as he believes that is the only reason I wanted to leave my plan is safe.'

Her eyes blazed and she wrinkled her brow. On any other woman it might have looked ugly, but her temperament was too strong to be marred in such a way. Powerful emotions suited her face. Anger, indignation…or passion.

'And you have discovered nothing that might harm him?' Caddoc asked.

She furrowed her brow, a slight crease forming between her arched eyebrows. They were standing close enough together that when she gave a deep sigh of dissatisfaction her breath kissed his cheek. He took a small step closer to her, until there was barely any space between them.

'He has visitors. Men who come to the manor house. Often they seem to be arguing, but stop as soon as I approach.'

'Men?' He was surprised at the jealousy that surged through him. 'Do you know any of them?'

'No.' Her voice was too firm, her answer too

quick and decisive for Caddoc's comfort. It was a matter she must have considered. He reached out his hand once again to draw her into the protection of his arms, but stopped himself.

'I do not want to know any of them.'

She turned her gaze on him, long lashes rimming the brown eyes, and a flash of fear rose and fell in them. He gave in to the impulse he had been denying and reached out, drawing her to him and enfolding her tightly in his arms. She gave a small gasp of surprise and did not respond as she had when she had first hurled herself into his arms, but she did not resist.

'I fear for you,' he said.

'You don't have to.'

As she spoke she laid her cheek against his chest and Caddoc became acutely aware of the intensity of his heart beating within its cage. If she could hear it beneath his flesh, would she understand what the sudden rapidity signified? He was torn between wanting her to know what effect she had on him and reluctance to deal with the enormity of what might result if she did.

Constance took another deep breath, causing her breasts to lift and push against Caddoc. When she exhaled the sound was ragged in her throat.

Caddoc tucked a hand under Constance's chin and lifted it until their eyes met, trapping her gaze and refusing to allow her to break free. Her lips trembled and she pressed them firmly together to better hide whatever emotion was racing through her.

Caddoc placed his hands either side of her face, fingers spreading across her cheekbones. A thrill of anticipation began to race through him, but as he dipped towards her she leaned back, a shield coming down across her eyes.

'I cannot stay here any longer. My maid will be waiting,' Constance said. 'Show me the box, please.'

Caddoc could have wept with the frustration at her abrupt change of topic. He had already succeeded in keeping her with him longer than he ever expected, but there had been a reason she had come. Once he gave her the box she would have no further need of him. She would be gone from his life so, ignoring the reservations he felt, he leaned forward and kissed her anyway.

Aelric's lips were firm, his beard and moustache teasing Constance's sensitive skin as his lips claimed hers. It was the briefest of kisses, but seemed to last for ever. He pulled away before she had really had time to appreciate what he had done or respond as her body told her she should, but the pressure lingered long after.

He stepped back and released her from his arms.

'Forgive me,' he said, echoing her earlier words. 'I don't know what came over me.'

He did not sound, or look, apologetic in the slightest. She didn't know whether to be offended by the liberty he had taken or relieved that he was unrepentant. All she understood was that the longer she spent in the airless, gloomy cowshed, the greater the trial to her self-possession. From her unseemly behaviour in hurling herself against him to the moment he drew her into his arms she had been picturing him kissing her and much more. She suspected it would be a different experience to the harsh, unemotional act they had committed before. The knowledge frightened her more than it excited her. It had taken more strength than she thought possible to break away from him and turn her mind back to the reason she had come.

'The box?' she asked, swallowing down her desire.

Aelric's expression darkened. He nodded his head towards the corner of the shed.

'Over there,' he muttered.

She raced to where he indicated and knelt to uncover the box where it was concealed beneath old straw. She glanced up at Aelric. His face was solemn, his blue eyes hard as ice.

'Did it cause you trouble to bring this?'

'It's hardly cumbersome,' he said. 'I'm stronger than I look.'

She'd insulted him somehow. 'That isn't what I meant.'

He knelt beside her, long legs bending under him.

'The men are still angry I let you go. I made sure they did not see me leave with this.'

Constance pulled the box towards her. It felt heavy in her arms.

'This has to be the answer. If Rollo knew the box was empty why was he trying to protect it?'

Aelric shrugged.

Constance examined all faces, but there were no particular marks. The lock was unremarkable. She put her hand inside and felt about. Her hand touched the bottom sooner than she expected and she pulled it out again slowly, measuring the height with her arm. It came to just below her elbow.

'I don't think this is right,' she mused. 'It seems bigger on the outside.'

She held it out to Aelric who examined it closely, suddenly interested.

'A hidden compartment?'

He ran his fingers lightly over each surface, then probed each hinge and ornamentation with careful fingers. Constance knelt beside him, shoulders almost touching. She felt her way around the iron corner coverings and when her fingers brushed over a nail that was slightly raised she pressed it. There was a barely audible click from inside the box. She smiled at Aelric in glee. His face echoed her triumph, but his eyes were full of disbelief as he took the box from her.

'You didn't think we'd find anything,' Constance said.

Aelric sat back and ran a hand through his shaggy hair. 'No I didn't,' he confessed.

He'd come anyway, though, because even the slightest chance to ruin Robert was too much to resist for him. She could hardly criticise him for that when she had pinned her hopes on such a small thing, too.

'If you're right, Rollo replaced your jewels with something important, but not anything that would cause suspicion if it was found.' He raised an eyebrow. 'Here, my fingers are too big, see if you can free it,' he said.

Constance put her hand inside the box, feeling for the loose panel. She wriggled a fingernail underneath the base that had lifted slightly, but paused before pulling it free.

There would be nothing there. Or there would be something that would help her achieve her goal. Either way there would no longer be a reason for her to meet Aelric again. They could be nothing to each other after they parted today. Prolonging this encounter would only make leaving more tortuous, but how could she hasten their departure?

Aelric placed a hand on her wrist, preventing her from pulling the wood free.

'What will you do with it, if there is something that could harm your brother-in-law?'

'I'll pass it to the friend I told you about,' she answered. 'To Lord D'Avranches of Chester. It was he who asked me to try discover what Robert is doing.'

'He's using you as a spy! A fine friend to put you in danger while he is safe in so far away in Chester!' Aelric said scornfully.

'There are places I can go that he can't. He cannot be seen to become involved without evidence,' Constance said calmly. Aelric's jealousy was oddly exhilarating until the true reason hit her.

'Of course, you must hate Lord D'Avranches as much as you hate my brother-in-law.'

To her surprise Aelric shrugged.

'I dare say he's no worse than Edwin who my father owned fealty to.' He smiled to see her surprise. 'Men of my status have always bowed to someone. I don't object to that. It was losing my father's land that cut deep.'

His hand tightened momentarily on her wrist. His thumb caressed the soft flesh over her pulse, creating such tremors that it was a relief when he released her. Constance pulled the flap of wood loose and upended the box. Something fell into her lap.

It was a fold of parchment with a small but heavy object wrapped inside. Aelric reached across and unfolded it to reveal a small circular brooch with deep carved patterns and a red stone set in the centre.

'This is what Rollo was protecting?' Constance asked in surprise.

'It isn't one of yours?' Aelric asked.

She held it to the light. 'It hardly looks valuable. Certainly not worth losing his life over.'

She reached for the parchment.

'It's a poem. Or a song, perhaps, but I don't recognise it.'

Aelric ran his eyes over it, holding it steady in her hand. Constance tried to ignore the tingle that ran through her at his touch and instead concentrated on the writing. She read it aloud.

'The metre is clumsy and the rhymes contrived,' Aelric said scornfully.

'I was hoping for a list of names, or details of a plot. There is no evidence this was even intended for Robert,' Constance murmured. Her shoulders dropped in defeat.

'There's nothing here worth the trouble we've gone to.' Aelric sighed. He pushed himself to his feet, then held a hand out and helped her stand.

'I'll keep looking,' she said obstinately.

'What you are doing is dangerous,' Aelric said. 'Stop risking yourself and let me deal with de Coudray.'

His voice was harsh and the ferocity that had been absent all afternoon was suddenly apparent on his face, erasing all tenderness.

'How?' she whispered.

'Your way has proved fruitless. I would be the threat he fears, if you freed me from the vow you placed me under,' he snarled.

It was on the tip of her tongue to consent to his demand, but agreeing to that would be to send him to his death at the hands of Robert's guards and would put an end to any hope she had of gaining Hugh's assistance.

'I will not do that.'

'You would put yourself in danger, but will not let me take my chance?' Aelric clenched his fists. He turned away, kicking old straw across the floor in frustration. His shoulders rose and fell as he attempted to master his emotions.

'You are not the only one he has wronged. I have my rights, too,' Constance said.

He spun round to stare at her, face contorted. He was still holding the parchment and screwed it into a ball, throwing it to the floor with unexpected violence.

Silently Constance retrieved it and smoothed it flat, eyes blurring as she read the words again.

In this place where they had been everything to each other, seeing Aelric so casually dismissing the song was yet more proof that the boy she loved no longer existed.

'I remember you used to write songs. When you would play music and sing,' she said quietly.

He gave a sharp intake of breath. 'Do you suppose an outlaw has time for such frivolity?'

'But you loved it—' she began sorrowfully.

He cut her off with an abrupt wave of the hand. 'There is no room in my heart for feelings.'

The pain in his voice made Constance long to reach out and comfort him, but he bunched his fists, his face contorting with rage.

'My life is hard and brutal. All I can think about is the vengeance I crave, which you have robbed me of with the vow you made me swear.'

He put his hands on her arms and drew her close, but without the tenderness he had before. He stared deep into her eyes, his own the violet of a thundery sky.

'Take your chance, if you must. But I may be too far away to come to your aid if needed.'

He stormed past her, pushing the door open and slamming it harshly, leaving Constance stunned in his wake.

Chapter Fifteen

The journey to Aldredley took Caddoc the rest of the afternoon, even striding out in an attempt to rid himself of the jumble of emotions his encounter with Constance had raised. Constance had talked of her rights, but no resentment she might hold towards her brother-in-law could come close to the severity of his own grudge. If she had been so cosseted in her marriage that Robert expecting her to act as chatelaine offended her, then her troubles were light indeed.

He paused as he reached the stream that ran alongside the village, his mouth dry. He dropped to his knees to gulp handfuls of cold, clear water into his mouth. He ran his hands across his sweat-covered face and beard, sluicing his head and scrubbing vigorously until his body at least was cooler. His temper remained as hot as the unexpectedly warm day.

His argument with Constance had provoked such a desire for Robert's death that his determination to keep his vow was sorely stretched. He stood before crossroads that he had not expected to encounter. Far from a quick and easy way of inconveniencing the baron, Constance's abduction had made life infinitely harder. He needed to decide whether to remain in the camp and resign himself to his life, taking petty acts of revenge against Robert, or leave Hamestan and put Robert and Constance behind him for ever. The third choice—the desire that screamed inside him to be sated—would damn him in Constance's eyes.

The sun was level with the top of the trees. He could make it back to the camp before nightfall, but would be travelling for the most part in dusk. He found the old man whose wood he had chopped still sitting outside his hut. From all appearances he might not have moved in the intervening days.

'May I beg refuge for the night? A barn or shelter I might sleep in?'

The man wrinkled his face and peered at him.

'Brunwulf's boy?' he asked.

Caddoc was about to deny it as he had before, but instead he drew himself up and looked the man squarely in the face.

'I am.'

Was he imagining the glint of tears in the old man's eyes, or were they simply pale and watery as the eyes of so many elderly he had seen?

'I knew when I saw you before. I'm glad I lived to see this day. Take my bed for the night, my lord.'

Caddoc held the old man's hands and pressed them tightly. Such a sign of devotion was alarming when he had done nothing to earn it.

'I'm not your lord and I would not deprive you of your bed. Anywhere will do for my needs.'

The old man cocked a thumb towards a low barn on the edge of the clearing. It looked in worse condition than the one he had left outside Hamestan, but would keep him dry if a sudden shower came on them in the night.

'You will help us, my lord, won't you?' the man begged, clutching at Caddoc's hands.

'I'm not sure I am capable. I'm not my father,' he answered, his stomach twisting.

The man gestured to the ground. Caddoc sat beside him and listened to rambling tales of his father's greatness as a thegn, which were undoubtedly polished by the passing of the years and comparison with the Pig until he might have believed Brunwulf to be a living saint. Perhaps it had been foolish to acknowledge his identity, but the admission was unlikely to reach de Coudray's ears and the old man's pleasure lifted Caddoc's heart and gave him some much-needed solace after the quarrel with Constance.

Listening to the old man describe Brunwulf's honour and steadfastness racked Caddoc with further indecision. He would be consumed with shame for ever if he broke his vow, but what use was honour when everyone who might judge his lack of it was dead?

When he was able to gain his liberty he made his way towards the shelter, but stopped as he recognised another traveller who had entered the clearing.

'Ulf!'

His conscience pricked. He should have waited in the cowshed outside Hamestan as agreed, but he had stormed out without a second thought to Ulf's existence. Besides, how could he have remained where Constance was after the words he had so harshly struck her with?

He strode to Ulf and clasped him by the wrist.

'My apologies, I should have waited—' he began.

'I guessed you wouldn't be there when I saw Lady Constance,' Ulf interrupted.

'When she went to the cowshed?' Caddoc asked. It had taken Ulf longer than expected to reach the village if that was the case.

'When she returned to the town.' Ulf's expression darkened. 'What did you do to her?'

Caddoc's throat tightened. Constance could not have lingered long if she had crossed paths with Ulf. Had some misfortune befallen her in that short time?

'Nothing. What was wrong with her?'

'Well, she looked angry enough to kill, but sad enough to die and her eyes were red. I don't think she even noticed me on the path.' Ulf folded his arms and stared accusingly at Caddoc. Caddoc mirrored his stance.

'We didn't part on good terms, but it was her obstinacy that is the cause of that.'

Or had it been his declaration he would take no further interest in what befell her? His stomach writhed, but he pushed the quarrel to the back of his mind.

'We can stay here tonight and bed down in the straw,' he said, pointing to the barn. 'I'm afraid our bellies will be empty, though.'

Ulf grinned. 'Not necessarily. Your lady has a generous heart, broken or no.'

He held up a penny, but Caddoc barely noticed it, too stricken by the thought of Constance's heart. Did he really have the capacity to break it, and if so, why did that fill him with elation rather than guilt?

Ulf ambled away to find the cottage he had visited the last time they had been there. He whistled and the girl appeared. Caddoc watched as they spoke, then Ulf ducked inside the house and returned a short while later with two eggs, a piece of bacon fat and a triumphant smile on his face. For a moment Caddoc was filled with envy at the ease with which Ulf conducted his affairs. His friend was older and far from handsome, yet his manner seemed to draw women to him. But then Ulf would never seek to aim at such a high target as a noblewoman.

'Tell me what happened with your lady,' Ulf prompted as they ate.

Caddoc chewed the morsel of fat, giving him time to frame his answer. He told Ulf of the discovery of the brooch, his voice rising in impatience as he spoke of Constance's insistence that it must mean something significant.

'She clings to the hope that the Pig may be crushed by means of law. Perhaps in the world she inhabits that might be the case, but it isn't enough for me. I would have his head, but she refuses to let me take my chance. She thinks I will fail, that I'm too poor a fighter to succeed.'

Ulf spat out a piece of eggshell.

'I doubt you could get close enough to the Pig to end him, but wouldn't you rather die trying?'

Caddoc laughed.

'You've been listening to too many ballads and sagas if you think that is how life works.'

'You don't believe what you sing? Not that you do much nowadays, I've noticed.'

Caddoc rubbed his eyes wearily. Twice in one day he had been called to reckoning on that score.

'Songs are a diversion from the truth.'

'Why does it matter what the lady believes anyway? You owe her nothing.'

'I made a vow to her when we parted seven years ago that I would not spill de Coudray's blood. I asked her to release me from that vow and she refused.'

'Then you might as well believe in ballads as truth,' Ulf scoffed. 'What is more important to you? A promise you made to a foolish girl—a Norman one at that—or putting an end to the man you hate and who makes so many lives unbearable?'

Caddoc fingered his dagger that slept as always at his waist, Constance's nestled alongside it, a familiar feel as his own and one he had become accustomed to far too quickly. What was holding him to his vow? He had repaid the debt he owed Constance for freeing him when he had interceded with Gerrod to spare her life. They were equal now. The only thing holding him was his own conscience. That, and the knowledge that to break his word would cut him off from Constance and any hopes he might have for her for ever.

* * *

He was woken the next morning by cries and angry shouting. Ulf snored beside him until Caddoc nudged him awake. Cautiously they drew their hoods over their faces and eased the door open. A tremor of anger stabbed Caddoc at what he saw, flooding his limbs with burning oil and causing his hand to reach instinctively for the daggers.

Two soldiers were moving from building to building, pulling the villagers into the square. He exchanged a glance with Ulf.

'Is it us they're looking for?' Ulf murmured.

'I doubt it. De Coudray does not know of our existence. They'd have no reason to search here,' he replied.

Unless Constance had betrayed them to her brother-in-law. Willingly or unwillingly, that was the question. He did not know which would be worse to discover.

'We need to run,' Ulf growled.

Caddoc put a hand to his friend's chest to prevent him from bursting out of the shed.

'We'd be cut down instantly. Let's wait for our moment and slip away quietly.'

The soldiers had brought nearly all of the villagers out now. They huddled together, looking fearful but resigned to what was happening. This was not a new occurrence to them.

'We've paid what we owe. We cannot pay any more,' the old man was pleading, to the agreement of his neighbours.

'His lordship says you'll have to. He needs money.'

The speaker was dressed in a heavy fur-trimmed cloak.

Taxes. Caddoc's lips curled. Simple greed was all that was at play here. His shoulders relaxed.

'Let's go,' Ulf whispered.

Caddoc nodded. They slipped out of their hiding place, but as he turned to go the sound of laughter stopped him in his tracks. One of the soldiers had kicked down the pile of logs Caddoc had chopped. They spilled across the ground.

'We'll take these as payment. Any hens you have, too.'

Caddoc's face flushed. Without considering the consequence he marched across to where the huddle of villagers stood.

'Lord de Coudray has forests full of wood. Let him gather his own.'

The tax collector stared at him in astonishment, then spat on the ground before him. Caddoc squared up to him. He was taller than the Norman and his wild hair and beard must have made him appear astonishing because the man blinked in surprise.

'Who are you?'

'My name is Caddoc the Fierce. I've killed greater men than you for much less than this. Leave these people alone.'

Out of the corner of his eye he saw Ulf appear, heavy stick in hand. A couple of the younger men from the village were edging forward. Caddoc bared his teeth. The pent-up frustration and impotence he had been fighting to control came to the fore and he snarled. He almost willed the man to command his soldiers to attack, but he stepped back.

'We'll come back another day,' he muttered. He clicked his fingers and his men followed him out of the square.

A sigh of relief rippled through the clearing. As soon as he was able, Caddoc disentangled himself from the grateful villagers and began his journey back to the camp.

'Thank you, Brunwulf's son,' the old man called after him.

Caddoc was unsure which was more uncomfortable: the lump that formed in his throat or the sudden stabbing of tears in his eyes.

'That was foolish,' Ulf remarked as they walked.

Caddoc fingered his dagger. 'I couldn't stand by and watch while they behaved in such a way.'

He had surprised himself with the impulse to aid the villagers, but on reflection he could see no other path he could have taken. Thwarting de Coudray's men had been satisfying; an unexpected of way of hurting the Pig while doing some good. For years he had dwelt on his own misfortune while others suffered, but now he realised that could change.

He would never be a warrior like his father and brothers, but he could still serve the people who would have been his. It would mean turning his back on everything and everyone he knew. He could not risk bringing danger on their heads. He realised he had made his decision.

When he reached the camp he found Gerrod and knelt in front of him.

'I've intruded on your hospitality long enough and my actions have caused unrest here. I beg your kindness to let me stay one more night, then I shall leave.'

Gerrod raised his eyebrows in surprise.

'I assume you have a reason?'

Caddoc explained the events that had taken place in Aldredley. 'I don't like to think of them unprotected. I may not be the fighter my father raised his sons to be, but I can help the people he left behind. I'll defend the people where I see help is needed. I won't risk bringing danger to you here.'

'And the Norman slut?' Osgood sneered at him from his mat by the fireside. 'You'll be closer to where she is. Do you think she'll reward you with a night in her bed?'

Caddoc seized him by the collar, dragging him upwards.

'I doubt anything I do will reach her ears and, even if it did, our paths are unlikely to cross again. You, however, will not speak of her in such terms if you wish to keep your tongue.'

He dropped the man and wiped his hand on his tunic. He caught Gerrod's eye and was startled but heartened to see a glint of approval in it. Ignoring Osgood, he began to gather the few belongings he possessed.

He played his *crwth* for them that night at Gerrod's request. He had not touched it since the night he had bedded Constance, but after two references to it in one day he did not want to refuse. He chose lively tunes for his companions to dance to and sing along with, and revelled in the pleasure of his audience. Elga, leaning against Gerrod, smiled for what might have been the first time since Wulf's death. When the notes of the final song had died away Caddoc lay down, staring into the flames.

He would miss this small group, but there was nothing for him here and the tower was sullied by memories of Constance. Better to leave. He would reach Aldredley by afternoon and ensure the villagers were safe, perhaps stay a day or two in case the tax collector returned. There would be other villages where Robert still wreaked destruction and Caddoc intended to do what he could there also to ease their lives. One day he might rise against Robert, but until then let his revenge be through other means.

He wrapped his *crwth* carefully in a spare tunic his Welsh uncle had given him that he had always considered too fine to be worn while living as he did. Holding the instrument to his chest like a lover, he pulled his cloak around him and slipped gradually into dreams of a different world. A world in which Constance lived at his side, where the warmth of her embrace and the laughter of their children woke him each morning rather than the gnawing aches of hunger, cold and grief.

Robert was shouting from the Great Hall. That in itself was nothing out of the ordinary, but his words drew Constance to the edge of the gallery where she was hanging bunches of sweet rosemary to dry. She had been lingering here outside Robert's private quarters, hoping for the opportunity to enter, feeling drawn to more desperate measures since the strongbox had revealed nothing. She began to tie the herbs to the railing, giving her the excuse to lean over and listen.

'And you left rather than cutting him down where he stood?' Robert bellowed.

A man stood in front of Robert, hands which bore fine rings twisting in anxiety. Constance recognised the official as Robert's tax collector.

'There were a number of men. He had a dagger. It seemed prudent to leave.'

'Coward! Tell me more of him. Was he one of the villagers?'

'No. He was a vagrant or wild man, with a tangle of hair like a savage and a beard full of knots. His accent was not from round these parts. He called himself Caradoc the Fierce or some such nonsense.'

Constance gasped. She clutched the banister, feeling light-headed. She would have known him from the description anyhow, but the name, even mistaken, was proof enough. Robert's head whipped round, his black eyes seeking her out. She lowered her head as tears sprang to her eyes and busied herself in her task. Why had he not gone back to the camp as she had assumed he would? Knowing where he was tugged her heart in that direction disconcertingly.

'You may leave,' Robert told the tax collector. He beckoned Constance to join him. She wiped a hand across her eyes, ensuring there was no sign of tears by the time she reached him. Evidently she had not succeeded because Robert scrutinised her closely.

'A Welsh name!' Robert remarked. 'In the village where you were discovered after gaining your liberty from a band of outlaws travelling to Wales. Perhaps these villagers know more than they have said about your abduction.'

'No! They are good people and know nothing of who abducted me. I don't recognise the man you describe,' Constance answered.

Robert smirked.

'I must discover what your new friends know about your abductor. I'm sure they are honest and loyal to me so will do everything they can to help me catch the villains who threatened you.' Robert clenched his fist, his eyes blazing cruelly. 'I'll have this Caradoc's head in a noose before the month is out. We want them brought to justice after all.'

Constance nodded in agreement. How could she do otherwise? Her eyes blurred.

'I beg your pardon. Sometimes the shock of my ordeal still catches me unawares.'

'I will have guests arriving in a three days' time,' Robert remarked. 'I expect you to be in full command of your emotions by then in order to meet your future husband.'

For the second time that afternoon the room spun around Constance.

'Husband?' she asked faintly.

'Yes.' Robert looked sternly at her. 'You met with his approval when he saw you on his last visit. He has an heir already so he did not even mind that buckled leg of yours or the fact that you've never produced a living child. He has agreed to the terms I put to him.'

Constance blanched at his casual dismissal of her failed pregnancies. The beating Robert had given her had been the cause of the first, and probably subsequent children she had lost. She wanted to run from the room, lose herself in sorrow and shut out the world around her.

'I told you I intend to enter a convent,' she said through clenched teeth.

'And I explained you will do as I command. We will draw up the deeds for Lord D'Avranches to formalise when he arrives.'

'Hugh is coming here?'

A small ray of hope began to warm Constance. Hugh would not allow her to be forced into something. If she found what he wanted.

She went to her chamber and sank on to the bed. Her attempts at finding out Robert's plans had failed miserably. Perhaps Hugh was mistaken and there was no planned revolt against William. She had nothing to report to him other than her defeat and an announcement of a marriage he had no obligation to help her evade.

The threat of being bound to any man once again made her stomach heave. She wanted no husband, but inside her grew a craving she had not expected. She could not escape the memory of Aelric's lips on hers, or the feel of his hands upon her body. His face filled her dreams, and he was in danger of losing his life. She must find some way of warning him his name had come to Robert's attention.

She rose from the bed and began pacing around the room. Perhaps it was not necessary. Aelric had come to the aid of the villagers and for that she loved him, but that love was surrounded by sadness. For him to do such a thing and to reveal his name was reckless. He must know Aldredley would be watched so he would not have done it if he had intended to return there.

It was Aelric she wished to tell of her marriage, him she wanted to call for aid to prevent it. She had never asked him to be her protector, had never imagined he would entertain such aims until he scornfully told her he would not take that role. Now it was beyond her hopes the fact of his absence was one blow to add to the many that assailed her and she gave into her sorrow, sobbing until her eyes ached as much as her heart.

Eventually her tears ran dry and she stared at the ceiling until the room began to grow dim. She shook herself; feeling strengthened and determined to take action. She would write to Hugh and warn him of Robert's plans for her marriage.

She began writing, but threw her pen down before she had completed three lines. She could not be sure that Robert would not read her letter. If only there was some way she could communicate without his understanding. A flash of enlightenment struck her and she gasped aloud. She rummaged through her box until she uncovered the poem and brooch she and Aelric had found in the secret compartment. She had believed the brooch to be what Rollo was guarding, but what if that was the diversion.

She read it again. It was poor in expression and contrived rhyme as Aelric had said, but perhaps that did not matter if the true meaning was not the poem itself.

She composed her letter, finishing the short note with the first four lines of the poem. It might be nothing, but Hugh could decide that for himself. She sealed the letter and tucked it into the tight sleeve of her under-tunic where it would be concealed by the folds of her outer dress. She hoped even Robert would draw short of searching her bodily.

She knew the route Hugh must take from Chester and where he must break his journey. Tomorrow she would take a horse to Aldredley, without Robert's knowledge if possible, and persuade

Guillaume to take the letter for her to leave at the hostel where Hugh was certain to stay. Easier in her mind, she managed to spend the rest of the evening in Robert's company, smiling inwardly at the secret she carried upon her.

Chapter Sixteen

The stench of smoke and grease first alerted Caddoc that something was amiss. It wafted on the wind from the direction of the village. He'd smelled it before and the scent sent him crashing back through the years to when the Bastard William had wreaked his revenge on the country after the failed uprisings. Fires did happen, but it was unusual at this time of year when the undergrowth was still soggy from the winter rains and snows. Sour acid pooled in his throat and belly. This fire was no accident.

He knew with sickening certainty what would await him when he reached Aldredley. The only question was how bad it would be and whether those who had carried it out would still remain. He drew his bow as he made the final part of the journey. The smoke grew thicker. Heavy and black, it filled his eyes and throat, causing tears to blind him. He pulled his neckerchief across his mouth and nose and broke into a run, already knowing he was too late.

The barn where he had slept two nights previous was alight and by the state of the remains it had been blazing for a good while. The straw had been dragged to the doorway and the logs he had chopped thrown on to the blaze. Torches had been put to the thatch in every cottage. He dropped his pack at the edge of the village clearing, already running to see what could be done.

The villagers had acted quickly and were running to and from the stream with whatever vessels they had salvaged, but there were too many fires to save everything and there was no method to their attempts. A small child struggled to drag a bucket that was far too heavy. Caddoc took the bucket gently from the girl who flinched as his hand touched hers.

'Let me help.'

He ran to the largest hut, which he knew to be the common gathering hall. If they could at least save that, it would give them shelter where nothing else remained.

'Save this first,' he shouted, hurling his water on to the flaming roof. The villagers obeyed without question. They returned again and again until the flames were extinguished, then turned their efforts to the closest huts. Hours might have passed, or days—Caddoc lost all sense of time. When nothing could be done he slumped to the ground alongside the exhausted people. Someone passed him a flask that had been saved. He tasted weak ale.

'When did this happen?' he asked. His throat was hoarse from the smoke and effort.

'This morning. They came just after light.'

The man who had passed him the ale spoke. It was the Frenchman who lived with the woman Edyt. He spat on the ground. 'They demanded money, but we had no more to give.'

'This is my fault,' Caddoc groaned. He buried his head in his hands, writhing with guilt. If he had not intervened, de Coudray's men would never have done this spiteful act of revenge.

'They would have come anyway. We are not the first this has happened to,' the Frenchman said.

He passed the flask once more and Caddoc drank with the man who should by rights be his enemy. The Frenchman was right. Anticipating harm or mending wrongs was not enough and never would be. Vow or not, the best way to help these people would be to travel to Hamestan and make his attempt on Robert's life.

Hoofbeats sounded. Had de Coudray's men returned to check their destruction was complete? Caddoc drew his dagger, anticipating a fight, relishing the prospect of sinking his blade into Norman flesh, but a familiar voice cried out in anguish.

'No! Edyt, where are you? What happened here?'

He jerked his head up to see Constance hurl herself from her horse. She pushed past Caddoc, limping as she ran and not even noticing him as she shouted her friend's name. When she spotted Edyt, who was working alongside the other women, pulling what they could salvage from the buildings, Constance flung herself upon her.

Caddoc didn't think he had made a sound, but perhaps his body betrayed his feelings because the Frenchman at his side offered him a hand.

'We should go to them. Our women.'

'She isn't mine,' Caddoc replied. His throat seized as he spoke the words. Oh, but he wanted her to be. So badly it tore him into shreds each time he pictured what could never have been. He took the Frenchman's hand and stood. Together they crossed to the women. Constance was sobbing, but Edyt was dry eyed and weary. Beyond her fortieth year, this destruction and malice was not new to her.

Caddoc spoke Constance's name. She froze, then straightened and turned to face him. Her face softened, her eyes flooding with some emotion he did not dare dream was love. It was the only good thing that had happened all day and Caddoc gazed openly on her, stowing the image away deep inside to treasure for whatever time remained to him.

'You shouldn't be here,' Constance cried. 'Robert knows your name now. Why didn't they take you today?'

'There was no one to take me. I arrived too late to prevent this,' he answered. That Constance had arrived only after the destruction and danger had ended was pure chance. If she had come here on his behalf and been hurt…

An inferno burst inside him and he yelled his next question.

'Did you know this was going to happen?'

He knew he was being unjust even as he took his anger out on Constance and that she was not the target he wanted to aim at.

Constance wrapped her arms tightly around herself. Protecting herself from him. He winced, wanting to comfort her so greatly the intensity of his need was alarming.

'Do you think I would have stood by without warning them?' Constance glared indignantly, then abruptly her face dissolved into tears. 'I knew he was angry, but how could he do such a thing? He's a monster!'

'Then let me…' Caddoc began.

'No!'

'Can you look at the destruction he has wrought and not crave his death?'

She looked at him scornfully. 'A convenient reason for you to justify killing.'

She might as well have called him a savage to his face, or spat at his feet. For all the tenderness they had shared, beneath the surface she clearly thought him nothing more than the lawless wild man.

'You insult me, my lady!' Caddoc growled, squaring his shoulders.

'Forgive me,' Constance said. She laid a trembling hand on his arm. 'But whatever your reasons and whatever provocation, you made a vow not to shed his blood.'

'And if I break that vow?' Her touch made the hairs rise on his bare skin, still sweat-slick from his exertion. Caddoc's hands shook, still furious that she had called his motives into question. He balled his fists and the muscles in his forearms knotted.

Constance removed her hand and drew herself up. 'Then you and I will never meet again.'

Caddoc lowered his head. Constance turned her back and looked at the Frenchman.

'Guillaume, I came to seek your help, but now I can't put such a burden on you. I know you're needed here.'

'For a while,' Guillaume agreed, 'but I think

my time here is over. Lord de Coudray is starting to demand anyone who fought under his banner return to him. I want no more part in wars. I shall return to France and Edyt will come with me.'

Edyt smiled up at her man, leaning her head against Guillaume's chest. Their obvious affection caused Caddoc's eyes to sting. What courage would it take to pull Constance into such a position? More than it would to hurl himself towards a burning building, Caddoc knew that.

Constance's eyes were bright with interest.

'He is gathering forces?' she asked.

'So it seems.'

Forgetting the quarrel they had begun, Constance and Caddoc exchanged a glance that sent his nerves tingling.

'What did you need my man to do?' Edyt asked.

Constance fished inside her cloak and wriggled a sealed parchment out of her sleeve.

'Hugh D'Avranches is coming to Hamestan. I need him to see this message before he arrives.' She spoke urgently.

'You have found what you hoped?' Caddoc interjected.

'Partly, possibly. But there is other news I must tell him.'

Her lips trembled and she looked into the distance, seeing something that troubled her deeply. Unexpectedly she seized hold of Caddoc's hand.

'I have no right to ask you and you have no reason to aid me, but would you take my message if Guillaume cannot?' she asked him hesitantly.

No reason other than the claim on his heart that she was unaware she had. His harsh words of their last meeting echoed in his ears. How could he have spoken so cruelly as to leave her thinking she was friendless?

'I'm sure Hugh would reward you if you helped uncover Robert's treachery.'

She must have interpreted his silent contemplation as reluctance, but she spoke so warmly of the nobleman that another throb of jealousy drove itself through Caddoc.

'Rewarded by one Norman for helping you betray another?'

'The best way to help your countrymen is to rid them of de Coudray once and for all.' Her voice dripped with frustration. 'By lawful means, not violence.'

'So you say,' he muttered.

Whatever his opinion, he could not leave Constance with no aid and he had to admit a curiosity to see the man Constance would put herself in danger to assist.

'Why would your noble friend even speak with a Saxon and an outlaw at that?' he asked.

Constance wrinkled her brow. She loosened a ring from her finger and held it out.

'Give Hugh this and tell him I sent you on my behalf. He will understand you have my trust.'

Caddoc closed his fist around the ring, wishing it were a token for himself.

'I will take your message, if it will ease your mind,' he said. An impulse struck him. 'But in return, when this is done with, I want to know two things. I want to know the cause of your hatred for de Coudray and why you still wish him to live.'

She bowed her head, remaining silent for a long time. Edyt gave Caddoc a look of immense suspicion. He met her eyes defiantly and moved a shade closer to Constance. Edyt sniffed, but her lips softened into slightly less of a disapproving line. She pulled Guillaume away to join the villagers who were still trying to inventory their salvaged belongings, leaving Constance and Caddoc alone.

'I agree to your terms,' Constance said with a heavy sigh.

She passed Caddoc the message. He turned it over in his hands, rubbing his thumb across the wax seal where her ring had pressed. He slipped it inside his tunic where it lay against his chest, wishing it was her hand and not the cold wax that he felt.

The anxiety vanished from Constance's face. 'Thank you,' she breathed.

'What will you do until he arrives?' Caddoc asked.

Constance glanced around her. 'I will do what I can to help these people. I shall offer them refuge in Hamestan if necessary.'

'Are you sure that is wise? Your brother-in-law will not thank you for your interference.'

She lifted her chin, her expression outraged. 'Should I think only of myself? I cannot leave them in such conditions. Besides, he wishes for my cooperation more than ever. He will allow me some concessions.'

'What makes you so sure?' he asked.

'Robert has talked of me marrying again.' Constance lowered her eyes. Her mouth twisted as if she had tasted something bitter. 'I do not think he would jeopardise my usefulness.'

'Marriage? And you consent to his plan?' The idea brought bile to Caddoc's throat.

'Of course not. I want no such thing,' Constance said angrily. The light in her eyes dimmed, searing Caddoc's heart. 'I told you before, all I want is to be allowed to retire from the world and live in peace and solitude.'

Caddoc tried to picture her living silently in a convent, working alongside the sisters. He failed. He had glimpsed too much of the fire in her to believe she would be satisfied with such a life of chastity and servitude.

'Is that really what you want?' he asked. His voice caught in his throat, coming out like a growl, fiercer than he had intended it to be. He put his arms on her shoulders and pulled her to him. She came without resistance until there was barely a hand's span between them.

'It is,' she answered.

Her words said one thing, but her lips parted and she tilted her head back. Caddoc slipped his arms around her body, feeling her bend against him, warm and pliable in his arms. He swallowed, eager at the prospect of tasting her sweet lips. Every part of him came alive with longing to give her reason to abandon the notion of a life of celibacy and self-denial. He could sense the need growing within her as much as he could feel it in himself. He slid his hand up beneath her cloak, spreading his fingers out across her spine to trace the line of her shoulderblades.

'Are you sure?' he asked.

'No. Yes! I have to.' Her voice was tortured. 'There is nowhere else I can turn to find sanctuary. I know Hugh will help me.'

A bucket of iced water drenched Caddoc's passion that Constance could talk of another man when she was in his arms. He dropped his arms to his side, feeling sullen until his unjust reaction pricked his conscience.

What other choice did she have but to rely on the Earl? Caddoc could offer his protection, but could hardly imagine her living rough as a fugitive. Less so now he was intending to spend his life wandering through Robert's lands even more of an outlaw than before.

'I should leave if you want me to find him.'

'Tell him what Robert did here.'

'I will.'

He walked to where he had laid his pack and hefted it over his shoulder.

'Are you going somewhere?' Constance asked in surprise, looking at the burden he carried.

'I don't intend to stay in the camp any longer,' he admitted. 'I will take your message first before I move on.'

Did he imagine the flash of misery in her eyes, or did he just wish so badly to see it? The corner of Constance's mouth twitched and she frowned, a crease appearing in her forehead. Either would be an enticing place to plant a kiss, but Caddoc forced his heart to harden. He walked from the clearing without looking back.

Constance raged as she rode back, each hoofbeat swelling the anger inside her. Almost as great as her shock at what Robert had done was her despair at realising Aelric was planning to leave. He'd held her with such alarming energy and given every impression that he cared something for her when they had been in the barn, so how could he intend to go without even saying farewell? Now she felt foolish for having believed something so unlikely.

She had planned to slip back into the house and hope Robert had not noticed her absence, but still seething inwardly she ignored Aelric's advice and sought him out as soon as she returned.

'What you did to that village was pure malice!'

'They don't respect me. They don't pay what they owe. Why should I be tolerant towards their insolence?' He rose from his chair. 'Have more care how you speak to me, girl!'

Constance stepped backwards.

'When Lord D'Avranches discovers what you have done he will be furious. They are his vassals…'

Robert snapped his fingers loudly in her face. His cheeks flushed scarlet.

'That for D'Avranches! He's weak. King William was a fool to ever grant him the title of Palatine Earl. I know half-a-dozen men who would rule better than he does.'

'You being one of them, I suppose,' Constance said.

'If I was in his place I would have crushed the borderlands by now, but I was passed over. To be granted such measly lands was an insult I will never forget.'

'Lord D'Avranches had to divide his land as

he saw fit and had many to reward,' Constance answered.

'You are overly fond of him,' Robert sneered. 'It is not becoming in a widow who will soon be a wife once more.'

He turned his back and stormed out of the room. Constance sank into the chair he had vacated, deep in thought. He had been ranting as he had done before when speaking of Hugh, but with a greater disregard for caution and Constance's scalp prickled. She had assumed any conspiracy or revolt would be against the King, but perhaps it was Hugh who was the intended victim.

Let Aelric reach him, she whispered fervently. And let Hugh have the sense not to dismiss the wild-looking, surly Saxon. She could not imagine the meeting between them, the two men she had risked herself to aid. Only when she imagined them side-by-side did she realise the stark contrast in the way she felt towards them.

She bore affection for Hugh as she might a brother, but the white-hot passion that seared her heart whenever Aelric came to mind eclipsed those feelings like a fire obscuring the glow of a candle. She could not help it, as much as she wished she could control the wild fantasies that filled her mind during every waking moment. Every touch of his hand on her face or body awakened an unquenchable need to be possessed by him. If he had kissed her today as she had been certain he intended to, or showed any sign that his need for vengeance had abated, she would have fallen into his arms and abandoned Hamestan to go with him without a second thought. She hugged herself despairingly. He no longer had the capacity for gentleness that had drawn her to him so many years ago, but she loved him all the same.

She would see him one more time as she had promised and would tell Aelric all he wanted to know. But only once Hugh had the information in his hands that he needed and she was beyond Robert's reach. Then she would retire to the convent as she had planned and live out her days, not in peace as she had once hoped, but instead with the torment of loving the man she could never have.

Hugh's eventual arrival was a relief to Constance. The intervening days had been a source of frustration. Men had arrived, some she recognised, others unfamiliar. They came bearing weapons they seemed reluctant to relinquish and huddled in groups, muttering among themselves. She passed among them uneasily, listening to conversations when she was able as she passed among them during the nights in the Great Hall. None of them showed her any regard out of the ordinary and her marriage was not spoken of. Perhaps the man in question had not arrived. It was too much to hope that he never would.

As they waited at the gate for Hugh's arrival Robert took hold of her arm, squeezing tightly.

'I don't trust you and I dislike the manner in which you conduct yourself. Any interference in my dealings and it will go ill for you.'

She stood behind Robert as her brother-in-law greeted his guest and directed the servants to show his retinue to their quarters. Hugh looked like he would pass by, but he stopped before her and lifted her from the curtsey she had dropped into.

'Lady Constance, it is good to see you again. It has been too long.'

'My lord,' she answered. She tried to keep the joy that she felt from showing too clearly on her face. When Hugh had taken her hand she had not failed to notice the ring that he wore on his smallest finger was the one she had sent with Aelric. She added in an undertone, 'My messenger reached you.'

'Your servant? Yes, he did.' Hugh narrowed his eyes, giving Constance a look she could not interpret. She wished she had been present for the encounter between the two men. 'He delivered your message and a few more thoughts of his own besides.'

'I am afraid I have little more to tell you. Every

time I draw near to a conversation the speakers end it but, please, be on your guard.'

'We will speak properly later,' Hugh muttered, leading her into the Great Hall. 'After we have dined tonight.'

Constance bowed her head, biting back her impatience. It would be safer to talk unobserved, but she longed to discover what Aelric had said and where he was now. Perhaps he would not return to Hamestan and the secret pain she carried would remain hers alone. Better that and never see him again than give him more reason to hate Robert than he already had.

The feast was a success. Even Robert could find no fault with what Constance had organised and the evening was an unexpectedly merry one. Tumblers had been hired and their antics drew wild laughter and applause. One of the guests called for a dance and Hugh raised his eyebrow at Constance.

'I do not dance,' she reminded him in a whisper, indicating her foot. She had paid little attention to her deformity for days, now it shamed her as it had done so many times in the past.

'Of course,' Hugh said. He raised his voice so all in the hall could hear. 'My Lord de Coudray, I have recently acquired the services of a new musician and brought him in attendance. If you would permit my liberty, I would like to provide entertainment.'

Robert waved a hand and settled back in his chair. More concerned with filling his belly, he had paid little attention to any of the proceedings. Hugh issued orders and a lone figure entered the hall. Constance felt a pressure on her foot. Hugh was nudging her beneath the table. She glanced at him questioningly and he flicked his eyes to the man in the centre of the room holding a stringed instrument in his arms.

The man wore a green tunic of good-quality wool, hemmed with brown. He had cut his hair until it barely skimmed his neck and his beard had been neatly trimmed. Constance's chest tightened. She gripped the stem of her goblet tightly. If she had not been able to picture every line on his face, every muscle in his body, she would not have recognised him, but there he stood, in the house of his enemy.

Aelric had returned.

Chapter Seventeen

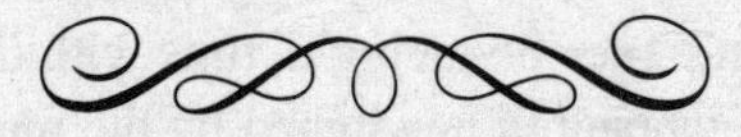

Constance shot a terrified look at Robert, but her brother-in-law barely gave the new arrival a second glance. Dressed finely with his close-cut beard he barely resembled the man she had seen only days before, much less the scrawny boy who had defied Robert.

'What are you waiting for? Play!' Robert instructed.

Aelric seated himself on a low stool, taking his time with an air of self-possession that was unfamiliar to Constance. An expectant hush fell over the room, the eyes of all on the lean figure. Alone in the centre of the hall he began his song. He drew the bow across the strings creating one long, drawn-out note. The sound was grating at first and harsher than the tone of a harp or lyre. People began to talk in low voices, but when Aelric's voice rose in song they fell silent one by one until only music filled the hall.

The melody came from him and not the strings, his voice harmonising, lifting above and dipping below the deeper sound of the instrument. The rhythm increased in speed, bow moving swifter and fingers racing across the neck in a riotous jig. The audience's hands began to clap and feet to stamp. From the corner of her eye Constance could see Hugh's knee bouncing in time with the song.

Aelric appeared bewitched by the music, unaware of the effect he was having. Constance smiled at the concentration on his face and the brightness of his eyes as he inclined his head over his instrument. His expression was intent, but there was a joy on his face she had rarely seen. She swallowed to rid her throat of the lump that had grown there.

The song came to an end and applause thundered around the room. Constance joined in as heartily as anyone. Aelric stood and bowed in all directions, his mouth a wide smile. His eyes came to rest on Constance and his lips softened. Her hands were still raised from clapping and she brought them together, placing them at her breast. Aelric pushed a stray lock of hair behind his good ear and smiled. The noise stilled and for Constance they might have been the only people in the room.

'Masterfully done,' Hugh said, beating his hands together.

'Shall I give you another, my lord?' Aelric asked.

Hugh waved a hand in assent and Aelric took his place once more. He rested his fingers on the strings, but remained silent for a moment. He plucked each string then began to bow slowly. The song was slower than the others, the melody melancholy and the language unfamiliar. Constance could not understand the words, but the intent behind them were clear, speaking of loss and unfathomable sadness. She lifted a hand to her cheek and was unsurprised that it came away moist.

When Aelric finished there was silence until Hugh clapped solidly.

'You have made the lady weep,' he remarked. 'I don't know whether I should commend your skill or have you flung in irons for your impudence!'

'Not that,' Constance murmured. Hugh was most likely jesting, but she did not want to think of Aelric placed in jeopardy because he carried out her request for aid.

Aelric's eyes fell on Constance, pools of ice that reached inside her until she feared her fast-beating heart was audible for all to hear. He walked before her and knelt, his eyes all the while holding hers steady.

'I would not intentionally cause distress to a lady, especially one so fair, but I cannot account for the effect of my song,' he answered.

'Perhaps something lighter to make her laugh,' Hugh suggested. 'Or a song of love to gladden her mood?'

Constance blinked back her tears. Hugh would never suppose how words of love from Aelric's tongue would tear her apart.

'Whatever pleases the player,' she said. 'But no more sadness.'

'I am yours to command, my lady,' Aelric said, bowing. He swaggered back to the centre of the room with a confident air.

He played song after song, jigs and reels until Constance yearned to be on the floor and dancing along with the others who had jumped from their seats. The serving girls who passed from table to table giggled as they watched Aelric play, daring each other to move closer to him, but thankfully Aelric appeared lost inside the world of his song.

'Why didn't you tell me you had brought him with you?' she demanded of Hugh.

'You were not expecting his return?' Hugh asked in surprise. 'He was very insistent that he travel back with me. That I discovered him to be such a skilled player was a happy piece of luck. He told me matters between you were unfinished and he was bound to return to receive his payment. Should I trust him? Do you?'

She thought for an age before answering.

'I think so, but he is his own man. I possess no hold over him.'

Hugh raised his brows disbelievingly in a way that caused Constance's innards to squirm.

She glanced over her shoulder nervously. There were too many people here for her liking. Most seemed captivated by Aelric's performance, but dread of being overheard made her shudder inwardly. She pushed her stool back and spoke quietly. 'I don't want to discuss this here. I'm tired and my head aches. I'm going to take some air outside. When you are free to discuss the contents of my message, please find me.'

She left the table and made her way around the edge of the room, slipping outside and down the stairs into the courtyard. Servants were milling back and forth and no one saw her leave. She could compose herself before returning to company. The dancing and merriment she could take no part in only served to confirm she was not meant for this life. Brockley and the convent called her.

She crossed into the shadows and leaned back against the door of one of the storerooms, staring up at the moon that shone full and bright. Her limbs might have been filled with iced water not blood from the way they trembled, but the sharp air was welcome. She was unaware of the precise time the sound of music ceased, but eventually there was calm, punctuated only by the usual sounds of the household preparing for bed. The servants who had accompanied Hugh and the other guests left the house and made their way to the quarters in the courtyard. If she did not go back inside now, she would be shut out until morning.

The door opened and closed quickly and a lone figure paused at the top of the stairs, looking about before quickly descending. Hugh must have finally found the opportunity to steal away. Constance walked around the edge of the courtyard and almost collided with the tall figure as he walked into the shadows beside the staircase. She squeaked in surprise, but a hand shot across her mouth, muffling the sound. Another took her hand, squeezing tightly. She pulled back in alarm.

'It's only me.'

Her limbs weakened once more. An assailant would have been welcome compared to the man who stood before her.

It was not Hugh who had joined her in the courtyard, but Aelric.

'What are you doing here?'

Aelric looked around, turning slowly as his eyes took in their surroundings. 'I wished to be alone. To remember.'

His voice was gruff and contained such depth of pain that Constance had to fight back the urge to wrap her arms round him in comfort. To be in this place again must be agonising to him. What strength it must have taken to return and what daring to stand in front of Robert and risk discovery.

'When I played, why did you weep?' Aelric asked.

Constance stepped towards him. The memory made tears spring to her eyes. Blinking sent them trickling down her cheeks and there were more that she had expected.

'Because I know your heart is not as dead as you would have me believe.'

Aelric dipped his head. His lips moved, but no sound emerged. When he lifted his face his brow was furrowed. He took her face between his hands and with a thumb wiped the tears gently away.

'I don't understand.'

They were closer now, without Constance being aware of either of them having moved. Heat rose from Aelric's body. The need to touch him was overpowering and she was certain he would not resist.

'No one could sing as you did unless there was true emotion within him. Not just hatred. There is more to you that that, deny it all you might. I saw it tonight and it gave me hope for you.'

'What hope do I have?' Aelric muttered. 'I am here in the house that should have been mine, performing at the table of the man I despise with all my being. If there is gentleness in my heart I cannot allow myself to acknowledge it. I told you, I live only for vengeance.'

'With *all* your heart?' Constance asked.

He said nothing, but the expression on his face was of such anguish that Constance wanted to draw him into her arms. She shivered with excitement that Aelric misinterpreted.

'It's cold. You should be in bed,' Aelric said.

'I am expecting Lord D'Avranches,' Constance replied. Aelric was still holding her hand. At Hugh's name his grip tightened briefly, then relaxed. She tried to ignore the warmth that spread along her arm from the hand that felt more sensitive than any other part of her body.

Aelric grimaced. 'Would you prefer his company to mine?'

He sounded annoyed and the sound of his jealousy sent a secret thrill through her.

'I have things to discuss with him.'

'You have things to discuss with me,' Aelric said darkly.

'Not now,' she entreated. 'We shouldn't be seen together,'

She tried to pull her hand free, but he looped it under his arm.

'We'll find somewhere quieter.'

He began to lead her into the shadows around the edge of the courtyard. She went unresistingly, unprepared to deliver the revelation he would demand, yet unwilling to leave his company. The door to the stable was ajar and they slipped inside. The horses shifted in their stalls, snickering and tossing their manes. Constance moved to her favourite gelding, rubbing his warm neck and velvety nose.

Aelric joined her. He leaned on the low stall door and folded his arms. His hair was still long enough that a lock fell across his eye. She wanted so much to smooth it back. She patted the palfrey again.

'Thank you for taking my message,' she said with forced lightness in her voice.

In the moonlight she saw Aelric's jaw tighten. His shorter beard revealed a strong, angular line and sharply defined cheekbones that lent his face a resolute air. Perhaps it was that, or the newly found confidence his playing seemed to have given him, but her urge to run her fingers along the contours made her fingers itch.

'Lord D'Avranches speaks affectionately of you,' Aelric replied, walking around the stable.

'We've been friends since I was barely more than a child. It was he who brought the news of my father's death to Jeanne and me.'

Aelric stopped abruptly. He folded his arms, leaning against the ladder that led to the hayloft.

'Just friends? The way he looks at you—'

He broke off, snapping his mouth shut. He was standing in the half-light, his eyes unreadable.

'He once asked me to be his mistress,' Constance said. Aelric winced and she cautiously reached a hand to his upper arm. It mattered greatly that this news affected him. 'I declined.'

'Why? A man that influential and rich who seems fond of you.'

'He is fond, perhaps, but I don't love him. All the wealth in the world is nothing without that.'

Aelric had never understood that. When she had first begged him to take her he had refused, not believing she could live as he did. She folded her arms and glared at him stubbornly. He cocked his head and fixed her with an intense stare.

'We have unfinished business.'

'I know. And I promised you I would explain everything, but not now,' Constance said. 'Give me tonight to remember the side I saw of you in the hall.'

Her stomach began to churn in dread at the thought of his reaction. She could not bear the prospect of the gentle man she had seen tonight vanishing once more behind the wall of hate. She reached a hand to his chest and felt the pounding of his heart. His hand shot up and he captured her wrist, pressing her tighter to him. She spread her fingers wider, acutely aware of the form and firmness of the muscles beneath his tunic.

'You must give me a compelling reason to delay when I have waited for so long,' Aelric said. His voice was thick with lust. 'Can you think of one?'

Constance nodded. The urges she saw written so plainly on his face were growing inside her, too. Last time they had been alone together he had kissed her. How much encouragement would it take for him to repeat the indiscretion?

'When you played you made me cry because I remembered how we cared for each other. I wanted so desperately to hold you one more time,' she admitted.

'We are alone. Hold me,' Aelric said, a hopeful smile flickering about his lips.

Before she could obey his command Aelric's arms were around her waist, removing all her uncertainty. She put her arms about his neck with a gentle sigh. One of Aelric's arms slid downwards, fingers spreading across the small of her back, the other slipping up to nestle between her shoulder blades. He bent and kissed her lips, not a brief brush as he had done in the cowshed, nor the ferocious, angry combat that had wounded her so deeply in the tower, but slowly and tenderly until her head spun. She tried to draw a breath, but her lips would not break free. They moved of their own volition against his, pushing back, shaping themselves to his movements in response. Her hands sought his face, fingers pushing into the tangle of hair at either side as she pulled him towards her.

'We cannot do this here,' he murmured, lips still on hers. 'We might be discovered.'

She did not need to ask what he spoke of. She knew well enough what would happen if they did not part. The delicious aching coursed through her, flooding her limbs and core and making her ache with a hunger that demanded to be sated. Soon it would not matter what she had done. She would be leaving the world behind her and Aelric with it.

'Up there,' she gasped, pointing to the hayloft.

They climbed the ladder and threw themselves down on to the straw, lying side by side, facing each other.

'You want this?' Aelric growled.

They were almost re-enacting her disastrous seduction in the tower, but it would not be like it had been. This time there was no reluctance, no coercion on either side, just a sense of need that was so great it was physically painful.

'I do.' Her heart was thundering. 'My husband used me for his own pleasure and I had no choice but to submit to what he demanded. When I seduced you before it was to try to buy my freedom. Tonight I want to know what it is to share myself for love.'

Aelric pulled her towards him and she went

willingly, pushing herself against him. His breath was hot on her neck, his hands travelling methodically across her body above her heavy gown, his legs working their way between hers.

With fingers that were as thick and ungainly as tree branches, Constance reached to Aelric's waist and unbuckled his belt. She slipped her hands beneath his tunic. His stomach was taut, the skin smooth. With a fingernail she traced the fine line of soft hairs that stippled his torso. He groaned at her touch, clenching handfuls of her skirts and dragging them upwards, rolling his body on top of hers until she could feel how ready he was, but as she began to skim her fingers from his belly around to his back he stiffened.

She must lie still, of course. He had demanded it in the tower, just as Piteur had. She began to pull away, to lie motionless and ready herself for him to take her, but this time he seized her hands and brought them back to his chest, pressing them against his bare flesh where they brushed against the fine hairs.

'No. Not this time. Stay with me. Just not there,' he breathed.

The last time they had done this he had said the same and those two simple words, *not there*, flashed like lightning in Constance's understanding. She would never have dared to question Piteur's instructions, but Aelric held no terror for her.

'You don't want me to touch you?' she challenged.

He leaned up on one elbow. In the moonlight his face was a mask of disgust.

'Have you forgotten what he did to me? How he mutilated me? I would revolt you.'

'Do you think I care about that? I am twisted and crippled so that some would not touch me for fear it would taint them and others saw me as little more than an animal.'

She wriggled from underneath him and sat up.

'I know what he did. In case you have forgotten I was the one who cleaned the blood from your back. Show me.'

He said nothing, but lifted his tunic. Constance tugged it over his head and threw it aside. She turned Aelric around and knelt behind him.

Even by moonlight it was clear the flesh was puckered and twisted where the flayed skin had healed over. Lumps and weals scarred the length and breadth of his back. It was ugly and she fought down the urge to recoil, knowing if she did she would lose him forever. Greater than her revulsion was the fury that Robert had caused this and sadness that Aelric believed it made him any less desirable. With one fingertip she traced the longest scar running diagonally from his shoulder to his waist, then leaned close and pressed her lips to it.

He eased himself around to face her, still

kneeling. His eyes were too bright to be dry. His mouth was curved into a wide smile of disbelief. He reached for her hand and kissed her palm, then her wrist before continuing up her arm in small, delicious increments. When he reached her shoulder he hooked his thumb into the collar of her gown and pulled it aside, moving his mouth downwards onto the mound of her breast, his tongue darting rapidly across her skin.

Fire spread through Constance. Outwards from her neck across her face, cheeks, throat and chest. Inwards like chains of molten metal wrapping her limbs, belly, heart and further down to clutch at her centre and bind her to his body.

The sensation was exquisite, the hairs of his beard prickling against her delicate flesh as his lips travelled further down. She gave a long, high gasp that seemed to drive him wild because he bunched his fingers deep into her hair, tilting her head back and flickering his tongue against her jaw, tracing a line from ear to collarbone and beyond, teeth grazing. She pulled at the ribbon holding her bodice fastened and helped Aelric slip her gown and shifts off until she was naked. She shivered as the chilly night air caressed her body.

'Are you cold?' Aelric asked. His eyes gleamed with longing as he shrugged himself free of his remaining clothes. 'I had better warm you through in that case.'

He reached out a hand and ran his fingernails lightly from between her breasts, across her navel, down to the downy hair between her legs. That such a light touch could stir such intense sensations inside her was incredible. She shivered again, but from longing, not cold. He wrapped his arms tightly around her, bare chest pushing up against her breasts. He began to kiss and caress her, exploring her body with such thoroughness that she was left gasping and breathless, and before long the cold no longer bothered her in the least.

Chapter Eighteen

It was Caddoc who slept, but Aelric who awoke, returning to consciousness in a tangle of naked limbs, covered in straw and the discarded clothes from the night before. He vowed he would no longer go by another man's name.

Constance's face was buried in the crook of his arm, her legs drawn up around his thighs and one arm slung across his chest. Her long dark hair fell across her upper half, giving her some degree of modesty should she have wished for it. She looked small and fragile. Last night he had half worried she would break in his arms if he had used her too roughly.

She hadn't, though, and the passion that had been absent when they had coupled with such anger in the tower had been shackled by no restraint this time. Twice they had made love last night and both times she had met him with the full force of her appetite that both hardened and melted him to think of it.

He would stop time itself to remain here with her. He had almost asked her to go with him, right after he had cried out in a crucial moment that he loved her. She had given no sign of hearing and he was not sure if this saddened or relieved him. Perhaps she had not heard, or perhaps she had ignored his words.

She began to stir and, not quite awake, twisted away from him, her spine curving against his side. Aelric rolled on to his side and tucked himself around her, enveloping her protectively, chest to her back. He sensed the exact moment she awoke, her limbs tensing and her breathing becoming even. He held her tighter, savouring the moment in case he found her changed. She craned her head around and bestowed on him a smile so sweet his stomach turned over with longing. A piece of straw was stuck to her cheek and he plucked it free.

'One day we'll find a bed to do this,' he joked, but his voice was flat as he weighed up the chance of ever repeating what they had done.

Constance rolled back towards him, stretching her limbs with a sensuality that set him on fire with desire. As she turned her hair fell away from her shoulders and what Aelric saw then caused his blood to run cold. He had failed to notice in the darkness and amid his enthusiasm that her shoulders and back were marked by a series of thin white lines. He had seen such marks before, bore them himself and was certain to his core that the person who had inflicted them was responsible for these, too. He rubbed a trembling finger across her shoulder.

'Your back,' he murmured. 'How did this happen?'

Constance closed her eyes, her mouth twisting.

'When I returned to the house after freeing you Robert discovered me readying to leave. He beat me, but I refused to tell him what he wanted to know.'

A touch of pride crept into her voice and broke Aelric's heart in two. His throat seized until he had to force the breath through the space that remained and he dropped his head into his hands.

'For me? Why did you do it?'

She gazed at him frankly. 'Because I loved you.'

Loved. The tense of her word spun in his head. Then she had loved him, but not any more? There had been no reason for her to do what they had done last night. She was under no obligation and had no need to bargain with him, yet she had done it anyway.

'I spent years resenting you for not coming,' Aelric confessed, guilt cresting over him at the bitterness that he had felt for so long. 'Why didn't you tell me before now?'

'We hardly met again under the right circumstances!' Her fingers found his. 'I didn't want you to find out this way.' She stopped speaking at the expression on his face and gripped his hand tightly. 'I could not come because I was barely conscious for days. I would have crawled across flints to reach you if I had been able.'

'If I had known what he did I would have turned back and come for you,' Aelric declared. The muscles in his belly clenched as he imagined her enduring such agony.

'You would have died,' she replied simply. It was the truth, but it did not lessen his self-reproach in any way.

'You should have told him where I was.'

She smiled sadly and shook her head, absolving him. 'It would have made no difference. I passed out, but still he carried on.'

'So that is why you hate him,' Aelric muttered in a tone that sent chills through her. 'You were right, you have just cause.'

Constance sat up and pulled Aelric's tunic around her like a cloak. Her face changed, becoming bleaker and her eyes darkened as she looked into the past. 'There is more I haven't told you. I bled when Robert beat me. A lot, and not just from the wounds on my back. When I reached the convent at Brockley I was still bleeding. The sisters told me I had been with child.'

She looked at him with an expression of immeasurable grief.

'Our child.'

The room spun. A low roaring sound filled Aelric's ears. He shook his head, his fingers digging into his palms until his knuckles went white. Constance began sobbing, drawing her knees up and making herself small. Aelric drew her close, wrapping his arms tightly around her, far too late to comfort her for the torture she had endured. He held her as she wept. His own tears fell freely on to her bowed head as together they shared the grief that she had carried alone for far too long.

'What do we do now?' Constance asked.

Aelric was unsure whether she was referring to the immediate future or what they would do once the matter of de Coudray was dealt with. He was not sure he could answer either question.

Once her tears had spent Constance had recovered her self-possession remarkably quickly. Faster than Aelric, if he was honest, but she had had years to reconcile herself to what had happened while the devastation her news had wreaked on him was a fresh wound. To look at her no one would guess she had been weeping in his arms a short while ago, much less that she had been crying out for a different reason the night before. Years of marriage to the brute she had described must have trained her to bury her feelings deeply and quickly. Now she busied herself dressing, running her fingers through her hair to remove the tangles and straw that served as evidence to where she had spent the night.

Indecision tore him. From every corner of the house the ghosts of his family stared down at him, their silent voices demanding vengeance. If he satisfied his honour he would lose her forever, but if he did not at least make the attempt how could he continue to live with himself? What could he offer her anyway? Life as the wife of a wild man was not for her. One night sleeping in straw was different to years of hardship.

He longed to touch her again, to roll her back on to the straw and begin the delicious prelude to lovemaking once more, but her revelations had changed the tone of their encounter into something too sombre. Last night every embrace and kiss had been driven by an all-consuming need for gratification. As he had held her now it was a different sensation, a sharing of grief between two people who clung to each other for comfort. As much as he wished to begin another bout of lovemaking, the day was beginning and the time for that had passed.

Constance bent her head forward and eased her

dress up to her shoulders. Her hair was wound into a long braid and Aelric ran his hands over it, slipping it forward over her shoulder, delighting in the intimacy. He kissed the nape of her neck; savouring the sharp intake of breath such a small gesture drew from her. The fine scars that rose above the neckline of her shift caught his eye.

She had endured the torture de Coudray had inflicted on her to protect him and the knowledge tore him into shreds. He bunched his fists, imagining it was the Pig's neck he was squeezing. If he had not staked the last of his honour on his vow he would have walked from the stable and plunged his dagger into Robert's heart without a second thought.

He rubbed his thumb gently across the scars, only slightly raised and not as unsightly as the ones he bore but they wreaked a worse pain on him than being flogged had done. Constance reached her hand to his shoulder, running cool fingers across the twisted skin of his own back. Tears shone in her eyes. Already knowing what the answer would be, Aelric tried one last time to beg release from his oath.

'And despite all this you will not let me end him.'

'Not in bloodshed,' Constance insisted. She lifted her head and the expression in her eyes was more terrible than any Aelric had seen on the faces of condemned men or those about to pass judgement on them.

'I am a woman. I have no swords or arrows so I have to use the means I can. I want every man in the country to see him for a traitor, but I need him alive for that to happen.'

Now he saw the truth. The reason she denied him what he wanted was because she refused to admit she wanted it herself. He gave a bitter laugh.

'If I had met your brother-in-law on the field or had bested him in battle, you would not condemn me.'

'No,' Constance said, tilting her head to one side to look at him seriously. 'Because wars are fought in blood. We're beyond that now.' She tossed her head back, sending the thick braid swinging. 'My father died in battle. He was eager to join William and fight. He wanted honour for his name and riches for his family. All he won was a grave.'

'Is that what you worry will happen to me?' Aelric asked quietly. 'I'm no longer the boy you remember. I spent years learning how to stay alive. I'm a good fighter.'

Constance reached a hand to his chest, running her fingers lightly across the firm muscles to confirm his words. His skin burst into flame where she touched him and he felt once more the all-consuming need he had given in to the night before.

'I'm terrified you would still lose to him,' Constance admitted. 'Not in a fair fight, but he's never without his bodyguard. I've lost too many people to bear your death, too.'

'But if I did seize my chance?' Aelric asked keenly. The blood began to race through him. He sat forward, but stopped as she covered her face with her hands. He reached for her wrists and drew them away, forcing her to look at him.

'I am tired of living as I do, with a heart heavy from knowing I failed to avenge my family. Now I know what you suffered to save me my burden is greater still.'

'Becoming a killer would make you happy?'

'It would ease the ache I feel. It would make me the man my father never saw me become.'

'But it would not bring him back, nor any of the other lives lost at his hands.' She gazed down at herself, possibly mourning the child she had lost. Later Aelric would grieve for the unsuspected infant, but that must be put away for now.

'It may prevent any future lives being lost,' he argued.

Acid filled his guts as a realisation struck him. Three times now he had bedded Constance since they had met again. Three opportunities to create life that he had not even considered or taken even the most basic steps to prevent. The idea knocked his breath from him.

'If you were to die it would break my heart,' Constance whispered. Her words sang in his ears, an admission he had longed to hear. He put a hand gently under her chin and lifted her head, but instead of softness her eyes were steel. 'You come to life whenever you speak of your revenge and I dread that if you won it would turn you into him. Someone who revels in the killing.'

'That will never happen,' Aelric swore, hearing the falsehood in his voice and hoping she did not. He would relish de Coudray's death and he understood that, despite all Constance's affirmations to the contrary, so would she. She wanted Robert dead even if she would barely admit it to herself. She suffered agonies of reproach and guilt knowing she craved it. He would not ask her again to release him from his oath. The responsibility—and repercussions—for doing so would be his alone to bear.

He wrapped his arms around her and drew her head on to his chest and turned his attention to her unanswered question. The part he could face answering. He would not dwell on what would happen if he managed to succeed in his intention to kill de Coudray.

'You asked what we do. We go see your friend

the Earl,' he answered. 'You discuss your message and put the matter into his hands.'

'You're content to do that?' Her voice was warm, her eyes bright and full of hope as she lifted her face to his. 'You promise to take no further part?'

'None,' he lied once again.

'Thank you,' she whispered. There was a catch in her voice. 'I've been too long surrounded by men who enjoy inflicting pain.'

Her words destroyed him. He found himself wishing her husband were alive so that he could kill him, too.

Not able to look at her, he pulled his tunic over his head, then helped her to her feet. They climbed down the ladder cautiously. The stables were still deserted though the courtyard was busy. It would be easy for them to slip out separately and mingle with the servants moving about. As they waited for an opportune moment Constance slipped her arms around Aelric's neck. Her fingers were light against his skin, waking his senses once more. He kissed her slowly, relishing the sensation of her lips and how her body instinctively cleaved to his.

'What we did… I'm glad,' she breathed. 'At least now I know what it could be like with someone I cared for. I'll remember it always.'

She stood on her tiptoes and planted a light kiss on his cheek before slipping through the door.

Aelric watched her go, her words causing him to fall into a pit of foreboding. There had been a finality to what she had said. Had she guessed he was unlikely to see her again or was the intention not to repeat the act because she had plans of her own? Surely she would not continue with her intention to take holy orders after what they had done together. He left the stables and returned to his own quarters, lost in worry.

'Your message told me little.' D'Avranches sighed. 'The poem is intriguing. It was so mediocre it must serve another purpose. Verse is not unheard of as a method of passing messages and no man would successfully woo a lady with such a poor song.'

Constance blushed and exchanged a glance with Aelric. D'Avranches could not possibly know what had passed between them the previous night, but they were still highly conscious of each other's presence in the way new lovers were.

They had made their way back into the house separately before coming together to join the Earl as soon as they were able. Neither had spoken of what Constance had revealed, but the tears they had wept still felt white hot on Aelric's cheeks despite having long dried. She had bathed and changed her gown. He wore the same tunic. He had few garments to pick between and the scent of her was still on him, which he was reluctant to relinquish for as long as possible.

'I need further evidence and I need it soon,' D'Avranches said. 'A cipher, or another example of a code. Three of the men here have been named suspected conspirators and I would act before I leave Hamestan in two days' time.'

'I'll keep looking,' Constance insisted. She sighed irritably. 'I need to find a way into Robert's room. It is the only place I have failed to search and the answer must be there.'

'A good idea,' D'Avranches said, at the same time as Aelric cried out,

'No!'

He glared at the Earl, not caring that the man could have him crushed for such insolence. He stepped closer to Constance, doing his best to ignore his senses stirring the nearer he came to her.

'Lady Constance cannot put herself in such danger. Let me do any searching that needs to be done.'

'You would be at more risk than I would,' Constance protested. Her face softened and she laid a hand on his arm. 'If Robert found you, he would cut you down without pausing for breath. I might excuse my being there as carrying out my duties in the house. He is unlikely to harm me when he intends to announce my betrothal.'

'Do you really believe that?' Aelric growled,

slipping a hand to her shoulder. Jealousy threatened to consume him at the thought of Constance betrothed to another man.

'Lady Constance is correct,' D'Avranches said. 'You would risk endangering your life more than she would, which would serve no purpose. I want you alive in case I have need of your strength.'

'I have told you both I want no killing!' Constance exclaimed.

'Of course not,' D'Avranches soothed. 'If it was as simple as assassinating him I could have done it without having to bargain with you for help. But he may resist arrest and I want to know I have good men at my side.'

She looked suspicious, but D'Avranches gave her a look of such innocence she could make no accusation.

'Very well. But you agree to let me play my part without restraint. I choose freely to do this. It is my right and nothing you can say will stop me.'

Aelric drew her to one side, aware now how her skin fluttered at his touch and how his body responded in kind.

'After what you told me this morning I would not presume to stop you, but please, do not put yourself in danger.'

She paled at his intensity, desire flashing in her eyes that was quickly extinguished by annoyance. 'I gave you my body. I did not give you the right to dictate my life,' she muttered.

He put a hand to her cheek and bent in close to whisper words for her alone.

'When I gave you *my* body I did not realise I was signing away my right to be concerned,' he said firmly. 'There are enough deaths at his hand for me to grieve over without yours. If I choose to protect you, I will. With or without your consent.'

Her eyes widened, but her lip trembled. Abruptly she gathered her skirts and, without bidding her companions farewell, swept from the room with all the dignity of a departing queen. The two men exchanged glances and Aelric saw the affection in D'Avranches's eyes that he felt himself. He bit back his irritation. If this man truly cared for Constance as he professed to, how could he put her at risk? And what bargain did he mean?

'I thought Lady Constance had merely sent a messenger, but I see you are more than that,' D'Avranches mused. 'You care for her.'

Aelric dipped his head in acknowledgement, privately thinking what an understatement the word was.

'I would die for her if I have to,' he said.

D'Avranches smiled briefly. 'You may yet be called to if we do not reveal what de Coudray is planning to do,' he said.

'I won't let him harm Constance. If it means losing her love, or my life, I would willingly end de Coudray's life.'

'Any woman would be fortunate to have such a champion as you,' D'Avranches remarked.

'What bargain did you make with Constance?' Aelric asked boldly.

Hugh's shrewd eyes narrowed. 'I will prevent her being forced into any marriage she does not want, if she helps uncover what I need.'

Aelric's scalp prickled. He understood the reason for Constance's determination that Robert could not die. His conviction in law was the key to her security.

'You could help her anyway.'

'I could. I may still, but this way I get the proof I need.' Hugh's voice was hard and Aelric was reminded that for all the man's easy charm, he would not have achieved his position without making difficult choices.

Hugh turned the poem over in his hands.

'This *is* significant. Constance was right, but I need to know why. Whether it is a code or the cipher and what it says. It will mean something to someone other than de Coudray.'

The Earl's fat hands grasped the parchment. Aelric stared at the words, wishing he knew the origin of the song. He scratched his beard thoughtfully. A song.

'There may be a way,' he said slowly.

D'Avranches raised an eyebrow. He poured two goblets of wine and passed one to Aelric. They drank together as Aelric outlined his idea.

'You're a clever man,' the Earl said. 'I need men like you. When we are done here you and I should talk more.'

Aelric's guts clenched. Devious behaviour aside, he liked this burly Norman, but the life of a servant, even for a man as D'Avranches, would be hard to stomach. Constance had talked of rewards, but he dared not hope for such a thing. What else could Aelric offer her? She had turned down D'Avranches, saying wealth was not enough, but if Aelric asked her to leave with him, to live as he did, would she follow?

'My plan might not work,' he cautioned. 'It's risky and may come to nothing.'

D'Avranches shrugged. 'Then we're in no worse position than we are now and Lady Constance can continue her own investigation.'

Aelric clenched his fists. 'I would rather she was not involved. We are putting her at risk for our own ends.'

'Lady Constance has reasons to hate her brother-in-law. I do not know what they are, but I would not deny her the right to her vengeance. You have your reasons, too, I gather?' D'Avranches asked. 'Constance believes she can trust you. Tell me why she can.'

'My name is Aelric. This was my family's home.' He briefly recounted his history. He did not expect the execution of a handful of Saxon rebels to trouble the Earl and it would not matter now if his identity were known.

'De Coudray was always known for his cruelty. Myself I would not have chosen to reward such a man, but in battle William did what he had to. I believe even he regrets the way he dealt with the North, something I doubt has ever troubled de Coudray. We have an interesting situation. You wish him dead, I want him alive and dealt with officially and Lady Constance wants…'

'She does not know what she wants,' Aelric snapped. 'Or rather, she denies what she needs. I promised Constance I would not shed de Coudray's blood in order to gain my freedom. It has been a heavier burden than I anticipated.'

'Will you break that oath if necessary?' D'Avranches asked. 'Would you break it if it were to save Constance?'

'Without hesitation,' Aelric answered. Constance hating him and cutting herself off from him forever was unbearable, but he would choose that a thousand times over Constance hurt or dead.

'I want him unmasked first. There has been too

much intrigue. The people of this country need to know we bring laws and stability,' D'Avranches said. 'If it is treason he has planned, he will be dealt with fittingly and will meet his end. Will that satisfy you, Saxon?'

Could he accept this compromise? Robert's death, but not necessarily at his hands, while he was innocent in Constance's eyes?

He gave a slight nod.

'Carry a weapon tonight,' D'Avranches warned grimly.

Chapter Nineteen

Constance lingered outside the small chamber where they had met for as long as she dared. She hoped for Aelric to emerge before long, but he remained shut away with Hugh for longer than she expected.

Cursing her rashness for storming out, she twisted her long braid between her hands anxiously; not knowing what she would even say when Aelric came out. A word stirred in her mind and she pushed it down deep. It was not one that she imagined crossed Aelric's mind and was one that could only bring pain to admit to herself and humiliation to confess to him.

The best thing she could do was to busy herself trying to find out what she needed to. She crept down the narrow passageway back into the Great Hall. While she was standing alone, hesitating over what to do, Robert's booming voice echoed through the hall. Constance pressed herself against the wall into the gloom, concealing herself behind one of the thick hanging tapestries as he stomped down the staircase from his chamber in the gallery. He was dressed in his hunting cloak, as were the three men who stood in the Great Hall waiting for his arrival.

Constance smiled. If he was to be out all day it would make searching much easier.

'Where is Lord D'Avranches?' Robert barked.

'He indicated for certain he would join us?' asked a bald man.

The men moved into a huddle. If Constance had not been close she would not have heard their words. She could not leave without drawing their attention.

'He's slippery as goose grease. He would commit to nothing,' said another, his back to Constance. 'Perhaps he can be persuaded by the mention of the fat buck he will get to eat.'

'Do you think he suspects?' asked the bald man.

'No. He would not have accepted my invitation if he did.' Robert sounded certain. 'He'd just rather stay and gorge at my expense than exert himself.'

'You just hoped he would come so you don't have to marry de Coudray's stump-legged sister,' laughed another, elbowing the side of the man with his back to Constance.

'If her legs part as easily as other women's do I'll wed and bed her quite happily,' the prospective groom laughed, loud enough for his voice to carry throughout the hall. 'I just think it would be better if matters could be completed today.'

Tears of disgust burned in Constance's eyelids. She pushed herself further back behind the tapestry. Beneath her revulsion Constance's mind began working furiously. Why did it matter if Hugh went hunting and what could be accomplished more easily if he did?

'You! Singer! Come here!'

Robert's sudden shout made Constance jump. Aelric was walking across the Great Hall. He bowed his head humbly as he walked to Robert.

'My lord?' he asked.

'Is your master intending to ride out with us?'

'I cannot answer for my master's intentions, but he has settled down with papers and a flask of wine,' Aelric answered. His voice had taken on the melodious accent he had used the night before. He sounded as deferential as any servant in the presence of his superior, but Constance noticed his knuckles were white from clenching his fists.

'There's your answer,' the bald man said. 'We're wasting good hunting time here. Let's go.'

Robert nodded. Without a backward glance at

Aelric he led his companions out of the building. Constance let out a sigh of relief. Aelric's head jerked up and his eyes flew to her, pinning her to the spot. He beckoned her out.

'You play a dangerous game, spying so blatantly.'

'I wasn't spying. At least, not intentionally. I hid when he came so I didn't have to speak to him.'

Aelric's shoulders were high with tension. How great must the effort have been to speak civilly with the man he hated? The powerful muscles that she could picture in exhaustive detail beneath his tunic would be iron hard. She ran a finger across his hand until his fist unclenched enough for her to slip hers into it. Even this contact drove her mind to such impure desires she began to blush.

'Did you hear what they were discussing?' she asked.

'I heard what he said about you,' Aelric growled. His hand tightened around hers to the point of discomfort. She wriggled it free gently.

'It is nothing that has not been said before. No one wants a deformed wife.'

'Do you know the man?'

'No. I don't recognise him and I didn't know his name.'

'Why are you waiting here?' Aelric asked.

'I was waiting for you,' she admitted. The warmth of his smile was like the sun after winter.

'To tell me you do not need my protection?' he asked drily.

'We should never have quarrelled in Hugh's presence. What if he suspected there was something more to our association than mistress and servant?'

A faint smile flickered across his mouth, his lips enticingly kissable. 'Is there more?'

She hesitated before answering. What more could there be? She stared at her feet miserably.

Aelric's throat tightened. 'Lord D'Avranches told me of your bargain and why you want to keep de Coudray alive. I will hold him to his promise even if you find no evidence.'

She squeezed his hand tighter. 'You would help me reach the convent?'

'If that is what you wish.' Aelric dropped his gaze, then raised it suddenly, his blue eyes full of pain. 'Do you regret what we did?'

'Never!' she said.

She reached her hand out once more and was gladdened to feel him clutching for hers. She lifted her head, blatantly attempting to incite him to kiss her. He seemed happy to oblige because he stepped closer until their legs brushed. He ran his hands lightly from her wrists to shoulders, sending shivers through her. His eyes darted over her shoulders and without the slightest change of his expression he gripped tightly and jerked her so she stumbled against him.

'The lady is feeling faint,' he called, his voice filling with alarm. Constance noticed absently that his accent had become more lilting, taking on the Welsh tone.

'Someone aid her, please.'

'What are you doing?' she exclaimed.

It was only then she heard the murmurs behind her. In her passion she had forgotten to take note of their surroundings and the servants who were going about their work now their master had left.

He clutched her arm. 'Do you want to provide another explanation?' he muttered through gritted teeth. She shook her head and sagged against him, sighing gently in an exaggerated manner and lifting a hand to her forehead.

His cries had brought servants running over. Women crowded round Constance, but Aelric would not relinquish his hold. The servants looked at each other in confusion at this recent interloper ordering them about and holding the lady of the house in such an intimate manner.

'She needs somewhere to lie down. Find me a chamber where she can rest in comfort,' Aelric instructed. He snapped his fingers at the closest woman. 'Where does your lord sleep? He will not be using his chambers at this time of day?'

A flustered-looking woman pointed to the

upper gallery room. 'He will not allow that,' she protested.

'I insist,' Aelric said firmly.

'What are you doing?' Constance muttered beneath her breath.

'Giving you access without suspicion,' he replied.

He bent slightly and scooped her into his arms. If she had not truly been feeling faint until that moment, the instant his hands were upon her body she almost swooned in truth. Her pulse began to speed and waves of overpowering lust crashed over her. The feverish sensations she felt must surely have been apparent on her face, or perhaps it was the force of Aelric's determination, because the servant made no further protest. Aelric followed the maid up the staircase and into Robert's private quarters.

The room was in near darkness and stiflingly hot even in the daytime.

'Bring her some wine,' Aelric instructed and the servant scurried out.

Aelric crossed to the bed—much grander than the thin straw pallet Constance slept on—and laid her down with the care a groom might show to his bride. His hands lingered on her for longer than necessary, sliding along from underneath her buttocks down the back of her thighs. Their heads were close. The scent of wine was on his breath and she wondered what he had been discussing with Hugh to merit sharing a drink together. Would the taste of wine still be on his lips? She licked hers and tilted her head back, rising up to meet him.

Aelric detached her hands from around his neck with a knowing grin. She had not been aware that she had forgotten to let go of him.

'I said we'd find a bed one day. I did not expect it to be so soon, or belonging to this particular owner,' he said.

'Don't jest!' Constance hissed. There would never be a bed for them. She would be leaving before long. Oh, but the temptation of taking him in her arms again and indulging in such pleasures made her shiver with delicious, violent tremors.

'Don't fear. I value your head too much to see it parted from your body,' Aelric said lightly. He stood and brushed his tunic down. 'This is all I can do to assist you, though I feel like I'm leaving you in a bear's pit. Rest first. Drink the wine when it comes, then use the time you have here to discover what you may.'

As he turned to go Constance called his name. He turned back, his lean frame silhouetted in the doorway.

'What about your head?' she asked. 'Don't you care about that remaining on your body?'

He dipped a slight bow and left without answering. His lack of answer was tantamount to a denial and sent fear coursing through her. His eyes had been dead when she had asked her question, but there had been a reckless confidence in his actions she had not seen before. His conniving determination to see her admitted to Robert's private chambers, what they had done the night before, his being in Hamestan at all, were all a change from the truculent, reclusive man she had first encountered.

Still, he had accomplished with ease what she had not dared to do and she must make the most of the opportunity he had won her. She sipped the wine as Aelric had ordered and, once the servant had departed, slipped from the bed. Keeping alert, she began to examine the papers that littered Robert's table. She had started this venture for Hugh, but she would finish it for Aelric.

Methodically she unfolded each sheet, skimming the contents. The black, wax seal on the ninth parchment caught her eye. It was the same pattern as the brooch that had accompanied the poem. With shaking hands she opened it. The familiar lines of poetry leapt off the page. She almost cried out in excitement before caution snatched her breath away. The two sheets were identical in every respect other than on this version certain words had faint indentations underneath, as if scored by a fingernail. Her flesh tingled. She had been correct, there was a message hidden in the poem. The words indicated made no sense, but she recited them until she had them committed to memory. She returned to her own room where she underlined them on the original copy, exhilarated by the thought she was one step closer to solving the mystery and achieving the revenge she craved.

By the time Robert returned from the hunt she was weaving by the fireplace with her maids in attendance. Even this picture of domestic peace seemingly raised his temper and she was relieved when he dismissed her to prepare for the evening's meal.

As her maid rebraided her hair and fixed a fine veil to it Constance turned the enamelled brooch over in her hands. Now she knew it to be a seal it was obvious. She believed she had seen similar on the cloak of one of Robert's guests, but had been unable to get close enough to him to confirm her suspicions. On an impulse she fixed it to her shoulder, pulling the edge of the veil forward to conceal it from view. She tucked the poem into her sleeve and walked to Hugh's quarters.

He welcomed her with a goblet of wine. The taste was richer than Robert usually served and the wax-topped flask unfamiliar.

'I travel with my own unless I am drinking in company,' Hugh explained.

'Do you think you are in danger?'

Hugh laughed. 'I survive by assuming I am.'

Constance thought of what she had overheard passing between Robert and his friends that morning. Would hunting have been dangerous, too? Perhaps an accident might have taken place deep in the thick forest. She was beginning to see the shape of what she had been searching for. Constance explained what she had overheard and Hugh looked grave but unsurprised. When she showed him the poem his face cracked into a smile.

'Well done.'

'The words make no sense,' Constance cautioned.

'The words don't, but particular letters will,' Hugh said with more confidence than she felt. 'It will take time to decipher, but it shows Robert is in communication with at least one of the men I know for definite is involved in instigating dissatisfaction.'

'Does it give you what you need?'

'Enough that with luck and a little bluffing, I should be able to ensnare him tonight.'

Constance bit her lip.

'Then my side of our bargain is fulfilled. Now you must keep yours.'

'You still wish to take holy orders?' Hugh asked.

Constance examined her goblet rather than meet Hugh's eyes. It was not what she wanted, but the desires that consumed her heart seemed so unobtainable. Aelric had promised to help her reach the safety of the convent. Why would he do that if he had any hopes of something more?

'You promised to help me retreat when I asked. I am asking now.'

Hugh took her hand. 'I asked you before if you would become my mistress. You refused, but I would still make that offer if it would give you the security you need.'

He intended no insult. The mistress of the Earl of Chester would live in comfort and safety, but would be a mistress nevertheless.

'If I wanted a man—' Constance said. She broke off, closing her eyes and seeing Aelric's face rising and falling above her as they made love. Flames kissed her throat and breast, a powerful throb between her legs made her nearly moan aloud. The things she had permitted—no, urged—him to do and the ways they had used each other's bodies should have mortified her, but she felt no shame. It was as well he had shown self-control when they had been alone in Robert's chamber because the ideas that had run through her mind were indecently sensual.

All the wealth and security Hugh could give

her could not match the ecstasy she had experienced in his arms. 'If I wanted a man, I would not want to be a mistress. I thank you for the honour you do me, but my answer is still no. When you leave Hamestan so do I, if not sooner.'

She walked from the room.

She might have been imagining it, but to Constance the air was filled with tense expectation throughout the meal. Hugh sat placidly beside his host, but ate uncharacteristically little. The guests appeared weary after their day's hunting. When Constance sought out Aelric sitting at the far end of the hall his eyes darted from side to side before he raised an eyebrow questioningly. She gave the smallest smile, hardly daring to meet his eyes in case she revealed everything she had discovered and felt in a single look.

The evening was half-done and Constance had begun to believe her fears were unfounded when, with an unpleasant grin at her, Robert put down his knife and stood. He walked to midway down the table and gestured for a man to rise. His neatly trimmed hair was what Constance recognised first from the morning's meeting. From the front he was as unremarkable as any man in the hall.

Robert raised a hand to silence the room.

'I wish to formally announce the joining of my house through marriage with that of my good friend, Guy de Brançoise. My dear sister Constance is to become betrothed to Sir Guy.'

Constance's heart thumped in her stomach. She didn't know the face, but she recognised the name. It had been Guy de Brançoise's servant that Rollo the bodyguard had met on their journey. Now she understood why Robert had demanded her return: she was the coin by which he would secure the loyalty of the other baron. Her body felt leaden and she could not move, but her eyes sought Hugh's in an attempt to communicate her realisation. He nodded gravely and stood.

'I think such news as this calls for a celebration. Let us have some music. Where is my bard?'

She spotted Aelric. He was staring at her intently, his lips a tight line. If the announcement of her marriage affected him he did not show it.

He picked up his instrument and walked to the centre of the room with the same composure as he had demonstrated the previous evening. There were murmurs of approval from all round. Aelric's playing had met with an excellent reception.

'What would you play for us tonight?' Hugh asked.

Aelric met his eyes. Only because she was watching so intently did Constance spot the way they slid towards Robert, sitting at Hugh's other side. They filled with hatred, then he blinked and the emotion vanished.

'A song not of my own composing, but one which I hope will meet with your approval,' Aelric said. He bowed deeply to Robert. 'It may be familiar to some, of course.'

He waited for silence as he settled on to the low stool, running his fingers across the strings to loosen them. Drawing the bow back slowly, he began to play.

Chapter Twenty

As before there was nothing but the bones of a tune until Aelric's voice started. The melody was unfamiliar, but when she recognised the words a chill settled over Constance. She started forward, but Hugh's warning hand on her wrist restrained her.

Disbelieving, she sat and listened as Aelric sang the words to the poem.

She was not the only one startled at what she heard. Before the verses were halfway through a whispering began around the Great Hall, quietly at first, but rising in volume to become a tumult of voices. When she heard the sound of a sword being drawn she leapt to her feet, pushing her chair back.

Beside her, Hugh was stony-faced.

Robert was scarlet. 'Enough! No more music.'

Aelric stopped playing.

'Does this song displease you, Lord de Coudray?' he asked.

'How did you learn this song?' Robert hissed.

'That's D'Avranches's man,' one man growled, cutting in sharply.

'This is no accident,' another muttered. 'He knows.'

'Shut your mouths, you imbeciles,' Robert bellowed. The colour drained from his face, leaving only the creases beneath his chins remaining red.

'It is a song I have recently become acquainted with,' Hugh said darkly.

'Shall I tell you which words speak the most to me, my lord?' Aelric asked, his voice ringing clear.

Constance gazed in wonder. Hugh could not have deciphered the code in time, but between him and Aelric, they were contriving to give the impression all Robert's secrets were laid bare. And it appeared to be working. The mood had turned deadly. Constance bunched her fists, feeling her hands clammy. She looked towards Aelric, who was still standing alone, his instrument in his hands. His head was raised and he looked watchful, his body tensed and ready to move. He caught her eye, a momentary glance, but his head moved slightly and a smile flickered on his lips. It was only a small gesture but, filled with confidence and reassurance, it was enough to calm her.

'You can prove nothing,' Robert said to Hugh.

'Your denial condemns you. The words of these

men condemn you all,' Hugh said. 'The words on this page condemn you further. All of you.'

'You've led us into a trap,' shouted de Brançoise.

'You have only suspicions.' Robert smirked, folding his arms with a complacency that was intolerable to see.

Constance pushed herself from her seat on shaking legs. She walked slowly towards Robert, aware of all eyes on her.

'My escort died to protect that poem. He spoke with a man at the house of William de Warenne. Your servant,' she said, turning her attention to Sir Guy, who shot her a look of hatred. 'Your servant gave him something. Rollo concealed it in my strongbox, then left me to my fate at the hands of the wild men. He cared more for this than my safety.'

Robert looked at her for the first time, his eyes filled with loathing. She hoped hers gave him back the full force of her hatred.

'I only have your word for that. You've told me yourself you know nothing of what took place.'

She reached beneath her veil, unpinned the brooch that had accompanied the poem and tossed it on the table with a contemptuous sneer. She slipped the poem from her sleeve and held it before Robert's eyes. He moved to snatch it from her hand before pulling back too late to disguise his interest.

'This was meant for you. If only you had not removed my jewels I would never have wondered why Rollo was so keen to defend an empty box.'

'I was witness to it.' Aelric's voice rang out above the noise. 'I will swear in the Hundred Courts, or any you choose, that what Lady Constance said took place.'

Robert rounded on him.

'Who *are* you? Why does D'Avranches's bard dare speak in such a way and how could you have been present?'

Aelric stepped forward. As he walked to Robert his was the only movement in the room. He placed his instrument carefully on the table. For a brief instant his eyes met Constance's and he nodded his head almost imperceptibly. The colour came to his cheek, but as he took another step towards the man he hated above all, his face was serene. He raised hands that were perfectly steady and brushed his hair behind both ears, holding it back and displaying the missing lobe and scarred neck.

'I am Brunwulf's son. I am here in the house of my forebears to witness your fall.'

'The Saxon whelp,' Robert said in surprise. 'I supposed you long dead. You failed then and you'll fail now.'

'I'm not alone now and it isn't your life I want, but your dishonour.' The colour began to rise to

Aelric's throat. 'There are men by the thousand in England who have every reason to hate your King, but you have everything you could want. Greedy and power-mad traitor!'

'My King?' Robert sounded genuinely surprised.

Hugh walked around the table. Aelric moved to allow him closer to Robert, positioning himself closer to Constance in the process. She edged towards him, easing herself along the table until they were standing beside each other. Surreptitiously he reached for her hand hidden in the folds of her skirt and gave it a tight squeeze before releasing it.

'The plot was not against William,' Hugh said. 'After the earls failed in Shropshire no one would be foolish enough to rise against him again. It is *my* land and title Robert covets, with these men to assist him depose me as Earl and set himself in my stead.'

Guilt was written clear on Robert's face, his lips drawn back in a snarl.

Behind Hugh a man began to draw his sword. Before the blade was halfway from the scabbard Aelric's voice rang out in warning.

'My lord, guard yourself!'

Hugh drew his sword as Aelric pulled the dagger from his belt.

'Leave here,' Aelric instructed Constance, pushing her gently in the lower back with his free hand.

'No. I'm staying until this is over. I have the right to witness this, too.'

He did not argue and his eyes lit with approval.

'Sheath your weapons or you die!' Hugh warned. 'Submit and I will show mercy.' He whistled and the half-dozen guards in his escort rose from their seats and drew their weapons. The three conspirators sat back down, placing their weapons on the table.

'No one will stand with me?' Robert asked in astonishment. He drew the sword at his side.

The men averted their eyes and Constance understood what Robert did not. They had no intrinsic loyalty to him. It was only what he had promised that drew them to his side.

'Will you submit now, de Coudray?' Aelric asked through gritted teeth. 'Your men have deserted you. Kneel before Lord D'Avranches and beg him for forgiveness.'

'You call this man "lord", Saxon boy!' Robert laughed. 'Is that how you survived? I thought you an outlaw, but you're a lapdog? Will you be the one to strike me down on your master's whistle?'

Robert's end had come. He would have to die or submit, but even now he was baiting Aelric and, from the way Aelric's eyebrows were knotting together and his jaw was set, Constance saw it was working. He gave a snarl and slid into a fighting stance, his face contorting with anger. The dagger in his hand tilted until the tip was pointing at Robert. It would never match Robert's longsword. To engage him in a fight would sign his death warrant.

Constance gave a small moan and stared at him, filling her eyes with as much love and pleading as she could muster not to take this final, unalterable step. She had no way of knowing if he had understood what she asked, but Aelric took a deep breath and his expression became serene once more.

'I am no man's dog. Lord D'Avranches will deal with you. I won't be the one to strike you down, though I wish to with all my heart and soul. It is enough to be here to witness your disgrace. You took everything from me. You killed my father, my brothers, my kinsmen.' He swallowed and raised eyes full of hell. *'You murdered my child.'*

The anguish in his voice sent chills running the length of Constance's body.

'You had no child, boy,' Robert sneered. 'On whom did you breed one?'

Aelric's eyes flickered to Constance, who looked back, stricken. Her mouth began to tremble. For her transgression to be revealed in so public a way was unbearable. Robert followed

Aelric's gaze and as understanding began to dawn on his face he drew his lips back in a snarl.

'Slut! No wonder you defied me and betrayed your people to save him. I should have left you destitute when your father died rather than bringing you into my home. If I had known, I would have cut the bastard from your belly!'

Constance gave a shriek of fury, hurling herself at Robert.

'You had no need to, when you beat it out instead!'

Quicker than she was, Robert reached an arm out and landed a blow on her cheek. Lights burst behind her eyes and she sagged down. As she reeled his hand came about her throat, dragging her to her feet. The pain brought tears to her eyes. Through blurred vision she saw Aelric tense. The weapon in his hand quivered. His hand had never been less than steady in anything she had seen him do.

'Throw it down,' Robert instructed.

'Let Constance go before you make things worse for yourself,' Aelric warned. 'Your time here is done, de Coudray.'

'Constance?' Robert asked. 'Is she more to you than just a warm sheath to sink your blade into? Shall I take her from you, too?'

Constance stood very still as Robert's words sank in. He would hurt her. Kill her if necessary to spite Aelric one last time. Her heart thumped in her chest and ears, pounding with a painful intensity. She willed herself not to faint.

'I will kill her!' Robert snarled. 'I have no reason not to. I'll do it with pleasure now I know the bitch has been working against me.'

Aelric took one step forward. Robert gripped tighter around Constance's throat, until the cry she gave came out as a weak gasp. He began edging backwards until he was in the centre of the Great Hall, dragging Constance with him. She clawed at his fingers, but they were shackles of iron around her throat.

'Stop!' Aelric shouted. He held his dagger out at arm's length over the table and dropped it. It fell on to a serving dish with a clatter that reverberated around the silent room. He raised his hands to show they were empty.

'Constance, forgive me,' Aelric said. 'I love you.'

He turned his back and took a step away from the table. He had abandoned her. Constance whimpered in disbelief, but no sound emerged. What took place next happened so quickly that it remained forever jumbled in Constance's memory, never to be untangled.

Did Robert's fingers begin to squeeze the life from her before Aelric's feet moved, or was Aelric already running across the room when her brother-in-law uttered his final laugh of triumph? What she was certain of was that as the black spots of pain in her lungs grew too unbearable something whipped past her ear and an animalistic gurgle issued from Robert's lips.

The pressure eased, air filling her lungs in one great rush, and Aelric was there, pulling her to his chest. Behind them Robert crumpled to the ground.

She looked round to see Robert's hands clutching weakly at the dagger that protruded from his throat. The dagger with a red stone that Aelric had taken from her in the forest. Still holding her, Aelric bent and pulled the dagger free with a twist. Robert gave a sucking, gasping, wheeze as with nothing to hold it back his blood spewed out.

Constance gave a cry of disgust and found herself gripped tightly against Aelric's firm chest, his arms locked around her, his head bent over hers.

'Don't look. It's over,' he said softly. 'Forgive me for what I did. I love you. I love you. I love you.'

He was repeating it as a priest might give a benediction and she didn't understand why, because she loved him, too, and the tears that fell from his eyes, wetting her hair, made no sense. She opened her mouth to explain, but no words came out, only a hoarse aching rattle. Her head spun and she felt herself passing out, but she did not care. She was in his arms and Robert was dead and she was too tired to fight the darkness that closed over her like a shroud.

She revived quickly and came to her senses, reclining on a fur-covered settle in front of the fire. Someone lifted a goblet to her lips. Rich, dark ale filled her mouth, but swallowing it down hurt more than she had expected. Robert had very nearly succeeded in his intention.

She opened her eyes, expecting to see Aelric, but it was a servant who had administered the draught. Constance pushed herself to her elbows and searched around the room. Aelric was standing in a huddle at the other end of the hall, deep in conversation with Hugh and his guards. She opened her mouth to call to him, but drawing breath hurt too much. He might as well have been in Wales for all the good seeing him did.

Women clustered around her, men surrounded him. Panic shot through her, seeing him surrounded by the Norman knights. He would have to answer to Hugh now his identity had been revealed. After all, Aelric was an outlaw and Caddoc was guilty of too many petty crimes to list. Hugh clapped him on the back and she reflected that perhaps Hugh had already been aware of his identity. After all, they had trusted each other enough to devise their ingenious plot together.

Aelric glanced over and his eyes widened. He

spoke to Hugh, then strode down the length of the hall to where Constance lay. He held his hand out for the goblet and took it from the maidservant. The girl glanced between them as she passed it over, her eyes settling on Constance's belly with clear meaning. Flames of humiliation burned Constance. She turned her head towards the fire.

Aelric knelt by her side and brushed a hair back from her cheek where it had stuck in the track of her tears.

'You won't speak to me?'

She kept her eyes averted. His breath was warm on her cheek. If she turned, she knew what the expression on his face would be like and that his lips would be close and kissable, but to give in to those cravings would be to confirm Robert's branding of her as a wanton.

'You publically shamed me,' she croaked. 'How could you share what I told you? I've carried that secret for seven years and you blurt it out in front of everyone.'

'I'm sorry, I did not intend for that to happen.'

His voice was heavy. He reached for her hand. She did not resist as he took it, but she held it tightly, drawing strength from him before she twisted her head round to face him. They stared at each other in the firelight. She wondered if she looked as dishevelled as he did.

Robert's blood had soaked into Aelric's sleeve.

It was smeared across his cheek, drying to a crust where he had used that arm to wipe the hair from his face. The sight revolted her, threatening to make her stomach empty itself. He looked as fearsome as he had the first time she had encountered him: a wild man, dangerous and unpredictable. Outside the law and so unavailable it made her want to weep.

'I can't talk to you now,' she whispered. 'I need to be by myself.'

Grief flashed over his face, but Aelric nodded in understanding. She pulled her hand free and staggered from the room. In her chamber she dragged her travelling chest to the centre of the room. Sobbing quietly but earnestly, she began to hurl everything into it, not caring about the mess, only wanting the task to be ended so she could leave Hamestan forever.

Aelric watched her leave. What else could he have done?

The look of abhorrence on her face before she fled would stay with him always, branded on his heart. He did not blame her. He had broken his vow and done it with full and deadly intent. His long years of practising throwing his dagger had repaid him and the blow that had slaughtered the Pig had been delivered with the full force of his hatred behind it.

He finished Constance's abandoned ale and watched from a distance as D'Avranches completed matters and the three conspirators were taken under guard. He had no part to play in that. His role here had ended when de Coudray had died.

D'Avranches joined him.

'Where is Lady Constance?'

He answered in a thick voice, describing her departure, opening wounds afresh.

'Was it true what you said about the child?' D'Avranches asked.

The look in his face must have confirmed what the Norman asked. D'Avranches sighed heavily.

'So many years she kept that burden to herself. How she must have suffered.'

'Her marriage was not good. I know she suffered much more than she will admit,' Aelric muttered. Snatches of conversation, revelations she had made assailed him. He smiled for the first time in what had been an extremely long day. 'She will not have to marry now.'

'She intends to enter holy orders,' D'Avranches remarked. He folded his arms. 'Do you intend to let her?'

Aelric bit his thumb. Visions of the camp with its paltry accommodation flashed through his mind. When he had first run and agreed to take her he had known nothing of the hardship it would entail. He wouldn't ask Constance to live travelling the country, scraping a living day by day without friends or kin.

'I haven't the means to keep a wife.'

D'Avranches nodded. 'So be it. I have matters to deal with, but come to me tomorrow morning.'

Aelric bowed his head and when he looked up D'Avranches had gone. He rolled on to the settle where Constance had lain and stretched out before the fire, too exhausted and defeated to move.

The following morning, after sluicing himself down in a trough of cold water, he presented himself to Lord D'Avranches in the Great Hall. There had been no sign of Constance.

After a few cursory exchanges on how Aelric had slept, the Earl stood and walked round the table to stand before Aelric.

'Tell me, how do you feel about the events of yesterday?'

Aelric had thought of nothing else as long as he had lain awake and his answer came quickly.

'I've dreamed of vengeance for so long and now I have it I feel…hollow. Robert's death will not bring back the other dead. It won't rebuild the homes he has destroyed or replant the fields.'

'No, but with him gone that will be easier.' D'Avranches pursed his lips. 'I neglected this part of my estate too long. I need to attend to that.'

'To make it better for your people,' Aelric said bitterly.

Hugh raised an eyebrow, chiding him gently. 'For everyone. You could play a part in that.'

'How?'

'We are here to stay. I would have peace if I could and I need men of honour to help me achieve that. Work with me. Live alongside us and help rebuild England.'

'Serve you, you mean?' Aelric asked.

D'Avranches tilted his head in acknowledgement.

'You said you would die for Constance,' he said. 'I'm offering you the chance to live for her. It will be harder and require more courage on your part. I cannot give you your family back, but I can give you a future.' He held Aelric's gaze. 'I can give you Hamestan.'

'That is in your power?'

'I am Palatine Earl. I have powers that other men of my rank do not have. I would give you your house back. Not to rule independently, you must understand, but as my vassal.'

Aelric looked past D'Avranches into the flames. The great fireplace had not been there in his day, nor the gallery or outbuildings. Hamestan had changed, but so had he. He understood that D'Avranches was offering him more than a building; he was offering him a future, one that he might share with Constance, if he had not lost her completely.

As he thought of her he knew there was only one answer he could make.

The day was bright. Too-clear skies for a heart so sore. Constance left the house for what she intended to be the last time. Hugh's manservant carried her chest over his shoulder. It was not heavy. She would not need much for the life she would be leading. Her eyes blurred as she crossed the courtyard and as she walked towards the stable a figure stepped out and blocked her way.

'Do I not even merit a goodbye?' Aelric asked. 'Have I wronged you so greatly?'

'You were leaving without saying goodbye to me before,' she answered petulantly.

She looked into his eyes and was taken aback by the sheer intensity of the love that she saw gazing back at her.

'You haven't wronged me,' she whispered. At the moment Aelric's dagger had struck she had wished Robert dead as much as he did. She could not condemn him for what he had done when she had truly craved her brother-in-law's death.

'I wronged you by holding you to such a vow. It is I who should be begging your forgiveness.'

'But instead you are slipping away to the convent? I won't let you.'

He folded his arms, barring her access to the stables. As she remembered what they had done there two nights ago desire began to rise within her, but she shook her head in misery.

'Robert is dead. There was no trial. Hugh is not obliged to keep his side of the bargain and I will not be made to marry again.'

'Not even to a man who loves you?' Aelric asked.

Constance's lip trembled. 'You said a wild man living in the woods had no means to keep a wife.'

'Maybe not, but a shire-reeve with land granted by the Palatine Earl of Chester himself can do so ably.'

She bit her lip before she started crying. Could he be speaking the truth?

'You're prepared to swear loyalty to Hugh? To William?' she asked incredulously.

'My loyalty is to you,' Aelric said. He seized hold of her hands and held them tightly against his breast. 'You're not meant for the cloister, to spend your days in sackcloth in a dreary cell.'

'What am I meant for?' she asked. His touch was setting her senses aflame.

'Life and light. Days in the sun.'

'Days in the sun, you say?' Constance said, a smile beginning to bloom on her lips. She raised her face and looked at him frankly. 'And what of my nights? Where should I spend those?'

He wove his arms around her waist.

'The nights you'll spend with me. In my bed.'

He kissed her on the forehead, then drew back and held her gaze intently.

'In my arms.'

His lips moved to her cheek. He pressed his forehead against hers, hands either side of her head so that his fingers could bury themselves in her thick mass of hair.

'In my heart.'

Constance leaned her head against his chest, feeling the powerful beat of the organ he described.

'I was afraid you would revel in the killing, but you didn't, did you?'

Briefly Aelric's eyes became distant.

'I imagined I would feel triumphant that he was dead, but I just felt relief that you were safe. I was prepared to let him live, but not at the expense of losing you.'

Throughout her life she had been used. Robert, Piteur, even Hugh had determined her path and made use of her for his own ends. Here was the man who had never done that. Who had risked his own life and freedom so that she might not be in danger.

'Can you let go of the past now Robert is dead?' Constance asked.

Aelric smiled. The angry light had vanished from his eyes, hopefully never to return.

'I can. And you? You'll never have to endure what you once did. The past is dead.' He bent his head to kiss her gently. 'It's time we started living for the future. Together.'

'Together,' Constance agreed, lifting her face to his.

Aelric wrapped his arms around her tightly, enveloping Constance completely in his embrace, and the sensation that assailed her was greater than any need to satisfy her ache of desire. As their lips met, Constance understood that in that simple gesture he claimed her in a way far greater than when he had held her with more passion.

She loved him and knew without question that he loved her as no man ever had.

* * * * *

MILLS & BOON®
HISTORICAL

MILLS & BOON®

EXCLUSIVE EXTRACT

Wealthy gentleman Benjamin Lovell has his eyes on the prize of the season. First, though, he must contend with her fiercely protective sister, Lady Amelia Summoner!

Read on for a sneak preview of
THE WEDDING GAME
by Christine Merrill

'I merely think that you are ordinary. My sister will require the extraordinary.'

The last word touched him like a finger drawn down his spine. His mind argued that she was right. There was nothing the least bit exceptional about him. If she learned the truth, she would think him common as muck and far beneath her notice. But then, he remembered just how far a man could rise with diligence and the help of a beautiful woman. He leaned in to her, offering his most seductive smile. 'Then I shall simply have to be extraordinary for you.'

For Arabella.

That was what he had meant to say. He was supposed to be winning the princess, not flirting with the gate-keeper. But he had looked into those eyes again and had lost his way.

She showed no sign of noticing his mistake. Or had her cheeks gone pink? It was not much of a blush, just the barest hint of colour to imply that she might wish him to be as wonderful as he claimed.

In turn, he felt a growing need to impress her, to see the glow kindle into warm approval. Would her eyes soften when she smiled, or would they sparkle? And what would they do if he kissed her?

He blinked. It did not matter. His words had been a simple mistake and such thoughts were an even bigger one. They had not been discussing her at all. And now her dog was tugging on his trousers again, as if to remind him that he should not, even for an instant, forget the prize he had fixed his sights on from the first.

She shook her head, as if she, too, needed to remember the object of the conversation. 'If you must try to be extraordinary, Mr Lovell, then you have failed already. You either are, or you aren't.'

Don't miss
THE WEDDING GAME
by Christine Merrill

Available January 2017
www.millsandboon.co.uk

P1216_2